THE GHOST OF MUNICH

THE GHOST OF MUNICH

Georges-Marc Benamou

Translated from the French by Shaun Whiteside

Quercus

First published in Great Britain in 2008 by

Quercus
21 Bloomsbury Square
London
WC1A 2NS

A CIP catalogue record for this book is available
from the British Library

ISBN (HB) 978 1 84724 289 1
ISBN (TPB) 978 1 84724 290 7

10 9 8 7 6 5 4 3 2 1

Typeset in Sabon by Palimpsest Book Production Limited,
Grangemouth, Stirlingshire

Printed and bound in Great Britain by
Clays Ltd, St Ives Plc.

To my mother.

To the memory of General Eugène Faucher.

CHARACTERS

ADOLF HITLER, German Führer and Reich Chancellor.

ÉDOUARD DALADIER, President of the French Council.

SIR NEVILLE CHAMBERLAIN, British Prime Minister.

BENITO MUSSOLINI, Duce and President of the Italian Council.

ALEXIS LÉGER, Secretary General of the Quai d'Orsay, alias the poet Saint-John Perse.

SIR HORACE WILSON, personal adviser to Chamberlain.

COUNT GALEAZZO CIANO, Italian Minister of Foreign Affairs, Mussolini's son-in-law.

JOACHIM VON RIBBENTROP, German Minister of Foreign Affairs.

PAUL SCHMIDT, interpreter.

HUBERT MASAŘÍK, Czech diplomat.

VOJTĚK MASTNÝ, Czech Ambassador to Germany.

FIELD MARSHAL HERMANN GÖRING, second in command of the Reich, commander of the Luftwaffe.

SIR NEVILE HENDERSON, British Ambassador to Germany.

FRANK ASHTON-GWATKIN, British diplomat.

ANDRÉ FRANÇOIS-PONCET, French Ambassador to Germany.

CHARLES ROCHAT, French diplomat, close colleague of Alexis Léger.

MARCEL CLAPIER, head of Édouard Daladier's cabinet.

CAPTAIN PAUL STEHLIN, Assistant Air Attaché to the Berlin embassy.

Also mentioned:
EDVARD BENEŠ, President of the Czechoslovak Republic.
GENERAL EUGÈNE FAUCHER, head of the French military mission to Prague.

PART ONE

THE APPARITION OF THE GHOST

I was disappointed as I arrived.

It was, indeed, an island where the President-who-everyone-thought-was-dead had taken refuge. But it was tiny, much smaller than I had imagined, barely an alluvial spit, tucked away in a bend of the Rhone, vast and unsettling in the background.

From outside, the house didn't look like much.

I'd made a mistake; a man like that couldn't live in a place like this: a wretched fisherman's shack, a Daudet landscape, dilapidated green shutters, a scrappy little patch of garden, a giant mosquito screen protecting the front door and, on the doorstep, a clutch of wooden figurines, 'little Savoyards', flat caps on their heads, the bright colours bleached by the sun.

I didn't have to knock at the door. He was waiting for me.

I gave a start as I saw him under the arbour by the shack, sitting on a bench, leaning on a cane. He welcomed me wearily, as if he had been waiting there for too long.

'So . . . Here you are . . .'

At the age of eighty-four, the President had none of the look of those paunchy, decorated dignitaries you sometimes see, self-satisfied and preserved alive in the gold of the Republic. The sturdy physique seen in the mythical pictures of the Popular Front – around the time when he was railing against the wealthiest '200 families' in France and posing on the cover of *Time* magazine like an anti-Mussolini in his Sunday best – hadn't changed. It was a body without a neck, the same corpulence, the same broad shoulders, the same immovable peasant mass. Against the summer light I had no trouble recognising the famous form from before the war. In his glory days, the French had loved his impatient, tetchy and threatening, air; 'taciturn', they called it. He was their boss. Like the Maginot Line, Daladier put their minds at rest.

But as I drew nearer, I found the old President surprisingly unkempt. His razor had missed a few hairs of his beard. His hair was slightly too long for a man of his standing. His white shirt, like the shirts of workmen before the war, opened on to a chest which had clearly been powerful once, but was now hairless, gaunt and bony. There was his boxer's face which had, thirty years before, been as legendary as his fits of rage. But there too the strong nose, the square jaw, the angles, once so clear – everything well defined in that face had blurred. The familiar features had almost vanished; the nose, the cheekbones, the chin had been erased, as though the face had undergone some kind of trauma. His arms were like anvils, but the flesh was saggy.

And then there were those eyes. They had turned vague, glassy, moist. It was as if they were lost inside him. It was a dead expression, through which something twitched from time to time, something electric, at the mention of some notable figure, the title of the newspaper I worked for, the name of that friend we shared, a duchess in Bonnieux in the nearby Lubéron. At such moments the old man would straighten up with a suitable degree of solemnity and consideration. His face opened up with a benevolent smile and he nodded with his chin as though experiencing a memory dear to his heart. His eyes brightened. It was only a reflex, a survival of the old cunning of a politician who must on no account be caught out. He was there for a moment, his interest fleetingly aroused, and then he sank back in on himself, and seemed to embark once more on some gloomy reverie. Meeting his eyes, one saw nothing. A fixed, empty space. The famous blue, ironic gaze of the President had been wiped away by the years, perhaps by that mistral of northern Provence that is said to 'kill uncomplicated joy'.

He rose and stared at me for a long time with an uneasy, mistrustful eye.

It was early in the summer of 1968. I was, in those days, a young journalist, a girl in a hurry, and I thought I had what is called a scoop. I had decided to leave my peers at the *New York Times* with the raked-over ground like the Vietnam War or the inquiry into the assassination of Bobby Kennedy, who had just been shot in Los Angeles. I had persuaded my editor-in-chief to devote a series of articles to the famous Munich Agreements of September 1938, whose thirtieth anniversary was about to be celebrated. I had been arrogantly vague as I sold him the idea. I had contacts, thanks to a grandmother born in the old Austro-Hungarian Empire. I would have eye-witnesses, of course, and revelations about 'the day when the Second World War really began'. The expression must have pleased him.

In fact I'd been bluffing – except about my grandmother. All I had retained of my European origins was my first name, Milena. I had yet to find those famous witnesses.

I very quickly realised I was on a hiding to nothing.

There was no credible account of the meeting in Munich, at the Führerbau, on 29th September 1938, the photographs of which had travelled all the way around the world. Not a single first-hand witness willing to tell the tale, not the most elementary verbatim report on that meeting, no full and believable version of that decisive day in the impressive archives of the Nuremberg trial. Nothing but the atmospheric tales told by the special envoys of the day; the (contested) archives in Wilhelmstrasse, and the (doctored) ones in the Quai d'Orsay.

Munich was like a black hole. It was like something by Agatha Christie. Of the nine who took part in that 'accord of shame', as it was known, hardly anyone had survived. Certainly no Germans: Hitler dead in his bunker; Ribbentrop, his Minister of Foreign Affairs, hanged on 16th October 1946. Not a single Italian witness: Mussolini, liquidated with his mistress Clara Petacci, on 28th April 1945; Ciano, his son-in-law and Minister of Foreign Affairs executed in January 1944 by the fascist Republic of Salò. Not really any Englishmen: the British Prime Minister Arthur Neville Chamberlain had died of a heart attack during the Blitz in November 1940.

There was only one major Munich player left, and he was far from loquacious. None of the American – or European – press had got near him. He was the President of the French Council, Édouard Daladier.

And then there was Alexis Léger, the influential Secretary General of the Quai d'Orsay, the French Minister of Foreign Affairs. As I began my investigation, I had told myself that Léger was the right man. Alexis Léger had in fact received, a few years previously, the Nobel Prize for Literature for his poetic work, published under the name of Saint-John Perse. Surely a writer couldn't refuse. I had bombarded him with nicely-turned letters sent to his publisher in Paris; and to his house on the Giens Peninsula. The illustrious author sent me a reply, via an aged secretary, that he had nothing to say about this 'event so long ago', and was too busy working on the Pléiade edition of his complete works.

I had even less hope with Daladier. He refused, our Paris correspondent told me, requests for interviews, journalists, historians, and even shunned the company of the world. 'Daladier! What's the point?' My Parisian colleague had added that my notion of reportage struck him as incongruous: 'Why take an interest in him? He's a dead man. And in France everybody thinks he *is* dead.' Édouard Daladier had never given an account of the Agreement, and I was under no illusions when I wrote to President Daladier, at the insistence of one of my old friends, Martha Gellhorn, who also said she would put in a word for me.

Martha, Ernest Hemingway's third wife, was my elder and my journalistic mentor. She had been reporting from Czechoslovakia for the popular newspaper *Collier's Weekly* at the time of the Munich Agreements, and had often told me of her anguish over the loss of the little Central European democracy. She had been one of the few foreign observers present, along with the founder of *Le Monde*, Hubert Beuve-Méry, who was then writing for *Temps*. 'We were alone in Prague,' she sighed as she told her stories. 'While the world's journalists – starting with dear Hemingway! – swore only by the romantic war in Spain.' In Czechoslovakia, Martha had been more than a reporter; she had been a kind of heroine. She had organised rescue networks for the Czechs, Sudeten democrats, Jews endangered by Hitler's annexation. It was then that she had saved my grandmother.

Such a long time later, I still don't know how dear Martha – who left this world nearly ten years ago – got by; nor what she had said in her letter; nor whether, as she did with finicky administrations, she had signed her mail 'Mrs Ernest Hemingway' – which she hadn't been for ages. In fact, what she had said to me was: 'Daladier ... Édouard Daladier? Don't worry.'

She was fond of me, she liked me; she must have seen herself in the young woman I was in those days. So it was that one morning when I had given up hope – and was preparing to admit my failure to my editor-in-chief – I received a letter from France, signed Monsieur Édouard Daladier.

> Madame
>
> For several years I have been obliged to refuse many writers' requests, and the questionnaires that they sent me from various countries, notably from Great Britain and the United States. The flood of them would have ended up drowning me. I am making an exception to this today because of your personality and that of the woman who sends you to me . . .

I had imagined this meeting with the President from every angle, in every conceivable way. I had worked over the question of Munich, I had absorbed the Memoirs of President Masaryk, the founder of Czechoslovakia, of Beneš, his successor, of Churchill and De Gaulle. I had read William Shirer's *Collapse of the Third Republic,* and of course Martha's novel, *A Stricken Field.* I had prepared for the encounter. I knew the price of this interview – and I never stopped thanking dear Martha in my cables, but I hadn't expected a situation like this.

The man before me was in no condition to testify.

At our first interview I asked him a question about his state of mind the day before the Munich Conference.

His reply took him far away, too far. He got lost in his memories. A name escaped him. He struggled in vain. He travelled back down the century, mumbling, sorting through all his ministers, dragging from the limbo of the Third Republic the Christian name of the wife of his Air Minister in 1938. He went on searching and searching, wondered out loud where he could have put that name that he couldn't find. He stayed for a long time in the fog of his memories; and when he came back towards me, he grabbed my arm and asked me *what I really wanted of him . . .*

When I answered something about History, Truth and all those grandiloquent concepts, fear flickered across his face: 'What's the point? Whatever I say, I'm condemned in advance . . .'

Then he fell silent, his chin resting on his cane.

I couldn't help thinking that he had climbed into the ring with Hitler on that notorious day in September 1938, and had never recovered. He was the last survivor of the Four, the one who had escaped the curse of Munich. The other three had been swept away. No one had survived the curse. None but him. He was like those people of whom Shakespeare speaks in *Julius Caesar*, who 'die before their deaths'.

He held out an old newspaper, stuffed it into my hand and said: 'I said everything I have to say in here. I have thought very hard. I will not give you this interview.'

I was furious, it's true, and I didn't attempt to hide it.

He looked startled, he was intimidated by my rage.

So, I would have no interview, no revelations. I had crossed the oceans, travelled for 20 hours, to find a man lost in the back-end of Provence. I had made a commitment to my editor, I had announced my scoop to all and sundry. I had given up everything, and even cancelled my summer holiday in Palm Beach for him. And this was all I was getting. A polite phrase, thanks and goodbye.

He vaguely tried to mock me with a ludicrous attempt at witticism:

'And when the weather's so lovely! Munich! Munich! A funny sort of day to come and talk to me about Munich!'

Since I had nothing to lose, I brusquely interrupted him.

'So are you going to go on lying till the end of time, Mr President?'

He snubbed me with the abrupt gesture of a sleepwalker who's just been woken up.

'Don't push the point, mademoiselle. I have nothing to add.'

He wanted to defend himself, but could only repeat: 'Whatever I say, I am condemned in advance.'

Having run out of arguments, he stopped. He eyed me suspiciously before continuing, suddenly unctuous, his voice ponderous and meek: 'But since you have had a long journey and since I hold your friend Martha in . . . in esteem, I will make you a suggestion.'

He led me into a little barn adjacent to his shack. It was pretty rough and ready, and seemed to fulfil a number of functions: spare room, garage, shed, and also library. Facing the window there was a kind of schoolmaster's study. Two walls were lined with books, and on the others carefully labelled boxes were arranged in rows according to three colours.

The old man opened the curtains, with a wide and nimble gesture that astonished me. He waved his hand at the dusty air, and solemnly announced to me:

'Here are my archives.'

He was proud and mysterious. His arm described a circle. I tried to follow the old man's explanations, but found myself unable to concentrate. I was in Ali Baba's cave. I was surrounded by unsuspected treasures. There must have been more material here than an interview, even one destined for the Pulitzer Prize, could possibly have needed. Thousands of pages, a good hundred files, sure to reveal historical secrets unseen for 30 years.

I was shaken by such an unexpected turn of events. To avoid betraying my confusion, I decided to fix my gaze on something: the old man's finger as it wiped the dust from those labels and coloured boxes, those stacks of dossiers stuffed to the brim, those rows of files whose labels had been carefully filled with impeccable handwriting in purple ink.

'After my death, I plan to leave everything to a university foundation. In here you will find my notes, those of my colleagues, the reports by the diplomats and the military officers, both ours and those of the other nations.'

The old President paused, breathless, before going on in a detached voice: 'And since these old things seem to interest you, you can make yourself at home here for as long as you like.'

Then the old man left me alone.

I was staggered by the proposal. Clearly things weren't going as I had imagined. There would be no interview, but he was suggesting a curious pact. I could consult everything, I could rummage, dig, peruse those treasures – but without ever being able to question him. So I would have access to everything except his memories, his feelings, his doubts, the *feel* of the event that only eye-witnesses can help you reconstruct. He would stay there, a few feet away, within speaking range, but silent. I tried to remain calm. To gather my wits together and try to control a situation that was suddenly beyond me, I stupidly began counting the cardboard boxes in the archive.

It was very tempting.

I had everything to gain, because he wasn't – or that was what I thought then – in a fit state to testify.

I walked towards the wall of boxes and tried to assign a logic to the coloured labels which were all that brightened the room.

Red: between the wars.

Blue: the run-up to the war.

Yellow: the war.

Green: France's preparation for war and the responsibilities of defeat.

*   *   *

So I set about exploring the great wall of boxes.

I took a room in the town, not far from the island. I came and worked at the President's house each morning. Contact between us was minimal – good morning, goodnight – and sometimes he brought me a cup of tea. One day I found a bunch of daffodils in a vase on the desk.

Three weeks passed like that, and the pact of silence remained unbroken. Until that evening.

I had spent the whole day working on the 'Yellow Book', the Quai d'Orsay's official version of what was modestly known at the time as the 'Sudeten crisis'. Night had fallen. I was exhausted, and had fallen asleep in the little shed when I was woken by a noise, a shout, or perhaps, as happened frequently on the island, the creak of a tree-trunk trapped against the riverbank. It took me a little while to work out where I was. I'd missed the ferry back! Slumped on the little desk by the window I heard the Rhone raging and boiling louder than ever. I was helpless, lost and ashamed in that little place where I shouldn't have been at that hour. It wasn't part of our agreement.

He was sleeping there, in the house, only a few yards away. What if he heard me? What if he surprised me there in his house, at dead of night, violating his privacy? And even if he didn't discover I was there until early morning, what would his reaction be then? When I briskly said my daily 'good morning', to which he barely responded, busy as he was with his gardening, I wouldn't be able to hide anything from him. Tired and dishevelled, in stale clothes.

I prayed to be elsewhere. He was so mysterious, always quick to anger, so unpredictable. I wanted to cry. All of a sudden I missed New York. I felt exiled in that terrifying night.

At that moment everything looked bleak. I was stuck in

an impasse. My research had become futile, pointless. For almost a month I had shut myself away in that room. My life had changed: I had put America and even my editor to one side, I had gone through the contents of those fifty-seven boxes with a fine tooth comb, but I hadn't made any headway. The more I thought I was learning about the events of that day, about the 'mechanisms of cowardice' that led France to abandon its closest ally, the democratic Czechoslovakia of Edvard Beneš, the further I moved from the subject. I was getting lost. With each passing day I was becoming more and more stranded. Too many facts, too many unknowns, too much doctoring and silence in all the versions – German, French, English and Czech, and Daladier's own – as preserved in those archives. I was claiming to catch hold of history; but I was the one who was trapped. Files that chattered but didn't speak. Knowledge that had crushed me in the end. The enigma of Munich had reached a state of deadlock.

I tidied my hair, tried to smooth away the indignities of the night, then picked up a file that I had already read and annotated, and from which I had gained nothing. But I couldn't concentrate. My writing had become automatic and senseless. I clung to it to keep from thinking of this absurd situation. The rumble of the Rhone drowned out everything else. When it became a roar I froze with terror.

To trick my anxiety, I came up with a diversion.

I thought of the drawers of the old desk that I was working on. I had noticed that they were always locked, and wondered what might be in them. In that room that I had consumed so greedily, it was the only area that remained unexplored. The President had hidden nothing from me. In spite of his silence, he had opened up his house to me, this shed, his archives, his Munich files. He had given me access to everything. Except to his memories, and those four little drawers.

In that troubled night my curiosity overcame my scruples. I decided to apply an old trick I had learned at school. A paper-clip. I opened it out, I looked for the trigger mechanism, I wiggled it in the lock: it gave immediately. Very carefully I opened the forbidden drawer. From it I drew – with such a shiver of excitement! – a very large book. A family album, a luxury edition, leather-bound, gilt-edged, its leather inlaid with the initials E.D. The kind of pretentious tome that was supposed, before the war, to grant good families a bourgeois eternity.

I flicked through the heavy bound pages quickly, too quickly. I was in the wrong: I had invaded someone's privacy. But I thought I had a mission, I was in search of a trail, a confession or admission that might have been slipped – who knows – between those pages.

The photograph of the father in his Carpentras bakery; the photograph of the proud history graduate, a grammar school teacher in Nîmes in 1909, with his first class; the picture of the young mayor of Carpentras in 1911 – he's 28; his first photograph as a deputy – he's 35 now; and the one of him as a minister – not yet 40. The photograph of his wedding to Madeleine in 1919, the birth of Jean in 1922, of Pierre in 1925 in the big apartment on the Champs-Élysées, a present from his father-in-law. In a few pictures, the prodigious career of Carpentras's local boy made good. Until that full-page, black-cornered photograph of Madeleine Daladier, the wife who died in 1932. His ascent continues in spite of everything. In 1933, President of the Council . . . Young President Daladier is solid, young and proud. His frock coat can't quite conceal his peasant appearance. He isn't posing, he looks gloomy, embarrassed by the lens.

For the French, he had ended up as a potential leader. In 1938, he was the 'recourse' between a bankrupt Popular Front and the stupidest right wing in the world.

He was the man of the future; that was the tone of the press at the time, weary of Poincaré and other worthies of the pre-war period. He was the most solid figure in this assembly of old men, the most honest man in his generation of profiteers. He was perhaps less cunning and less rich than Laval, but he was much closer to the people. Didn't people refer to him as a 'modern Robespierre'? In this fearful Republic, he was more vigilant than anyone else in his response to German rearmament. He represented the ideal synthesis that France then needed. In 1938 he was the grand master, and he would remain so for years.

Lifetime president, 'republican dictator', the French elites thought as one. Daladier was their man.

The President would have been that if . . .

If history had not decided otherwise.

If Munich, the derailment of September 1938, had not happened.

The album ended with the photograph of his great return: head of government in 1938, the year of Munich.

And then nothing.

Blank pages, as if life had stopped there.

My imagination roamed. I decided to pursue my exploration.

The second drawer yielded easily.

And there I came upon a real mess: hundreds of typed pages of India paper, at least as many other notes on index cards, written in his tiny hand, folded Bristol boards filled with notes, invitations covered with dates.

In the third drawer, the same thing: more typed pages, other scraps, hundreds of them, scribbled on the reverse of his governmental headed paper; more scraps, more Bristol boards. In all, thousands of pages of what appeared to be a manuscript.

I started reading.

It was basically a sort of book, a muddle; not really an outline as such, more a complete shambles. Hundreds of chapters, short or long, many of them bearing the same name. A multitude of chronologies of the 'Sudeten Crisis' – one scholarly one breaking down all the facts across six tables; others written on the corner of a menu or the invitation to a private view. Some long passages were repeated, outlining the history of the kingdom of Bohemia. Probably essays leading nowhere. I discovered a recent correspondence with a Czech exile in Los Angeles concerning Beneš – a minutely detailed indictment of the former Czechoslovak president, it seemed to me.

The former President had never stopped repeating to me, 'I have nothing to add about Munich . . . I have nothing to add.'

He waxed loquacious on the subject.

So many archives, particulars, exchanges of letters, so many minute investigations into the tiniest details of the Sudeten crisis, the slightest gestures of President Beneš, or even of his own ministers!

I tried to work out the order of this disconcerting object. Now it was a meticulous account, as serious as a university dissertation, as tedious as a history manual; now it was loose notes, clues, hobby-horses such as the author's insistence, pursued over ten chapters, on holding Beneš responsible for the French defection. Or regrets, like that German military plot against Hitler, coinciding with Munich, in the event of an invasion of Czechoslovakia. That belated revelation, which probably emerged after the war, seemed to obsess him as well.

These weren't 'memoirs'. It wasn't a first-person narrative, or even an account of the fateful day; it was a sum, the gigantic muddle of an impossible thesis. One of those books that old men never finish, clinging to them so that they can go on living; storing up everything, as if this were the attic of their lives, more and more notes and memories, promises, aborted chapters and more and more ambitious summaries. It was a disjointed monster which, since just after the war – judging by the dates of the scribbled-on invitations – fed upon the minutest details, devoured all available archives, stocked up on all kinds of information, even the most useless, fed from them and could in truth make no further progress.

It was a plea, his memorial.

My hope returned. I had found the key. I had the confession of the century. When suddenly, during the night, I heard the words ring out behind me:

'You're a tough one, Mademoiselle!'

The voice petrified me.

I didn't turn round. I didn't dare to move. I was holding the bundle of forbidden pages in my hands. I was frozen, trembling, terrified as I sat before these open drawers that he couldn't help but see. I was guilty, guilty of everything, of violating those sodding drawers, of opening his family album, of descending, in the course of that night, to the greatest depths of his privacy. Of looting memories.

He said again, in a voice that was less gloomy now, ironic and almost amused: 'Yes, a tough one . . .'

He was wearing his dressing-gown. He walked towards me. I kept my head bowed. He abruptly closed the contentious drawers and, to my great surprise, took an interest in what I was reading. He fell upon the open album, and that Robert Capa photograph taken in 1936, two years before Munich. He began to study it at length. He turned it over to check the date, returned to the photograph, looked surprised, smiled faintly and then whispered to me:

'In those days they called me "the bull of the Vaucluse".'

He had forgotten the violated tabernacle, the confusion on his desk, the hundreds of loose pages. There was no storm, no rage. He hadn't chased me away, not yet. For now he lingered over that photograph. He seemed to like it, perhaps this was my chance. This picture of him, forgotten, healthy, flattering, seemed to have altered the course of his anger. He contemplated it, studied its details. He remembered the young man he had been, he remembered him with astonishment and tenderness, emotions that he didn't hide. He was rediscovering himself.

He repeated: '"The Bull of the Vaucluse"! Do you think I look like a bull?'

He had regained his grandfatherly voice. He sighed bitterly and contemplated the photograph again, before continuing in a voice that was angry once more:

'And what do they call me now?'

I was stupid enough to reply that I didn't know.

He went on in a kind of groan:

'They don't call me anything any more, mademoiselle! Everyone thinks I'm dead, apart from a few obsessives like you. Old Daladier dead! Spirited away after the war in a conjuring trick by the Communists and De Gaulle ... Thrown into a common grave of history. No one any the wiser. Daladier dead, but without a trial, unlike Pétain or Laval. Without a death sentence. That would have been too complicated. So I'm a clandestine corpse, a man cursed and condemned to wander among the living. One of the damned. According to them I was in league with the devil. But don't believe them, young lady. We were all in league with the devil.'

He spat. He spoke in a sing-song voice. He exhausted himself, apparently giving voice to too ancient a rage.

'Munich ... Munich ... Munich. The shame of Munich. Daladier's dishonour. They said "Daladier" the way people say "Munich". As if they were barking: Munich – Daladier. They have become synonyms, twin names. Worse, Siamese names! You can go on living without a twin, but a Siamese twin you carry on your back, which is his too, you're fed by the same tubes as he is; you live and die with him. You can't get rid of him until you die; that's how I've been dying, gradually, for thirty years, with Munich on my back.'

He started tottering unsteadily on his feet. His words were becoming increasingly disconnected. He raved, his eyes half-closed:

'Poor ancestors, poor old Daladier, by what Devil's detour did that good line of northern Provençals, pure, hard-working peasants, come to be afflicted – like so many others – by that curse? Cursed all around the world, for centuries, and all because of a few hours spent in the office of Chancellor Hitler.

'Thirteen hours!

'Thirteen hours which, in a man's life, bear more weight than all the rest. More than a good war, more than the hell of the trenches. In everyone's eyes those hours count more than the many months I spent shivering, stinking, seeing the others die, especially Cheminade, living in mud like a rat. Thirteen hours that wipe out a whole life. Thirty years in the service of others, Carpentras, the Vaucluse, all my ministers, all my Council Presidencies, and even the prisons of Bourrassol and Buchenwald where Pétain and Hitler locked me up . . .

'My fate, all for those thirteen hours . . .

'Young lady, they know nothing. They have never been locked up with him for thirteen hours. They can't understand. I was alone. I was so alone. My fate for those thirteen hours.'

When he ran out of breath, he slumped into an armchair before feverishly continuing: 'My fate for those thirteen hours.'

A flash of horror crossed his face, and then he lost consciousness.

The President came to inside the house. The doctor who had helped me transport him seemed familiar with Daladier and his dizzy spells. The President had questioned him, his voice broken and his eye uneasy. Was it his 'trench headache' again? Like before? The doctor had reassured him, without denying it. Before leaving, he asked me to give him news of the patient the following day. I didn't dare tell him I was only passing through.

The doctor had just left. Lying on a little sofa, wrapped up in three blankets, shivering in spite of the August heat, the President wanted to return to – as he put it – our conversation.

'Mademoiselle, it is important that you know that I did what I could that day in Munich. But I was so alone. France was so alone. I thought that ... I decided ... I shall tell you ... You may do with it what you will.'

PART TWO

1

PLACE DE L'OPÉRA

At the Place de l'Opéra he asked the driver to stop at the crowded corner where it meets the Boulevard des Italiens. The news had just appeared on the rolling illuminated screens at the top of the buildings. Before going to record his message on the radio, the President wanted to see French people coming out of offices or factories, on foot or on bicycle, the salesgirls from the big stores or bank clerks, it didn't matter, just French people, real ones; not the ones invented by the ministries and the newspapers. When the car had double parked he crouched down, like a stage spy, in the depths of his seat, holding a newspaper up in front of him, and started watching the crowd.

The crowd was in a hurry. It gathered. It became excited. It read the information ten times over; and each time, during the brief pause between two messages, 'La Marseillaise' was played. During the message the crowd was like a single enormous body, a single neck craning towards the miraculous news. Then it exploded. Workers' caps flew into the air. The cars honked out their joy, drivers left their taxis standing. Lovers kissed and waltzed around. Old grandads with gasmasks, who had come from the Champs-Élysées where they'd been billeted, began a strange dance, a kind of bourrée. On a fashion-house balcony dressmakers whirled in a furious round dance, while others tried to make a red, white and blue flag out of ribbons. Big families, setting off to take refuge in the countryside to escape the air raids that had been predicted, had set their bags and bundles down on the ground. Should they go home, or continue on towards the Gare Saint-Lazare? Students started their rag processions, which wound and jostled and grew until they spilled into the road. One young fellow bumped into the car of the President, who immediately lifted the newspaper over his face.

The people adored one another as if it was 14th July; no, hang on – thought the President – as if it was 11th November 1918. Had it not been for the civil defence sandbags, the uniforms of the draftees among the crowd, and the signs pointing to the air-raid shelters it would have seemed like Paris was celebrating.

Standing slightly apart, two men in bowler hats, probably senior officials in the nearby Council of State, read and reread the incredible news before hugging one another. On the Boulevard des Italiens a madwoman, tousled and thin, her age impossible to guess, had gone down on her knees. She was praying. She was in a trance. Other women joined her. They seemed to be communing, and when they saw a war veteran passing in his wheelchair, they called him over. They started crying, 'Never again,' as they cornered him, as if he was a relic. The hairy old man, who wanted to be left alone, broke away from them, waving his cane. That didn't stop the first woman in the group from rounding up other zealots who imitated her, on their knees, elbows on the civil defence sandbags.

It was then that he understood.

After the recent announcement of the Munich meeting, he hadn't wanted to listen to them. He hadn't listened to any of them; neither the hardliners nor the soft. Not Mandel, or Reynaud, or Massigli, of the Quai d'Orsay, who all talked like that eccentric Churchill – France had to 'choose between war and dishonour'. Neither had he listened to the Marquise,

nor Madame de Portes, nor Bonnet, his Minister of Foreign
Affairs, nor his loyal Clapier, when they had maintained that
on the contrary, the French would see nothing but smoke
and mirrors. As so often, he had been suspicious. The fact
was that the President still had his peasant head, *testa dura*,
and he was proud of it. Even when his colleagues in the
Ministry, the oldest and the least calculating among them,
the ones who had known the horror of 1914, had exploded
with joy, even then he had seen it only as the effect of pressure that had been building for months throughout the
Sudeten crisis. He had wondered why they were all talking
about a 'miracle'. Upon learning of the meeting arranged
for the following day, he himself had recoiled. The horror
of finding himself hurled into this affair.

Then he had tried to imagine what the meeting would be
like: the course of the conference, the behaviour of the participants, the crisis management solutions, France's margins
of manoeuvre. He hadn't succeeded. For the first time in his
career, the President had faced a test that he dreaded, one
whose very reality he refused to acknowledge.

But he was no rookie; he had attended other stormy
summits; he had resolved international crises, three times
President of the Council of Ministers, nine times War
Minister! And like a schoolboy he had started counting on
his fingers the numbers of heads of state, heads of government, important monarchs that he had met in fifteen years
of power. He listed more than ten, and tough ones, too!
That had calmed him down.

And yet it was true. Something was happening.

France was mobilised, 750,000 reservists had been called
up, the Maginot Line was ready. A million Czechs were
prepared for war, and almost as many Germans. The count-
down to war had been interrupted, a few minutes before
the expiry of the ultimatum set by Hitler. Czechoslovakia

had not been invaded. Perhaps tomorrow Europe would not go down in flames, as Spain, so near a neighbour, was already doing.

The President could see the relief on everyone's faces. The 'miracle', as they said. Concretely, and not in the abstract or cynical way of someone like Alexis Léger, that Guadeloupean brought up in the Gironde, or Léon Blum, too cerebral, or Geneviève Tabouis, too happy to be insulted by Hitler in his speeches. They were all cut off from the people. Not so the President.

He was fascinated by that jubilation. It was like being at the theatre, watching those French people in their trance. He wanted to forget the meetings, and the government, and the Party, and the arguments, and especially the battle between the 'hard' and the 'soft', the ones who wanted war and the ones who wanted to avoid it at all costs. He wanted to forget everything, including what was planned for tonight, the inauguration that bored him, the speech that he would have to deliver on the radio, the nervous deputies waiting humbly for his arrival, the crisis that had to be defused between the Minister of Foreign Affairs and his colleague, Léger. The President refused to think of all that. He merely watched. Besides, he didn't even want to think about tomorrow's meeting.

He couldn't break away from that strange, archaic, convulsive scene of the French learning that war had not been avoided, but adjourned. The sound of the people barely reached him. It was deadened by the padding of the limousine. The hubbub of the street became almost burlesque. The nasal voice of a news vendor stirred the President from his contemplation: 'Daladier to visit Hitler tomorrow Exclusive, Daladier to visit Hitler tomorrow . . .'

He gave a start.

'Exclusive. Daladier to visit Hitler tomorrow.'

The news vendor pressed the edition to the window of his car.

It was a shock. It was only then that he grasped the reality of his meeting.

Tomorrow, Hitler. Face to face with Hitler ...

After a moment he remembered that his driver was there, sent him off to get the late-afternoon special additions, not to find out what *Paris Soir* or *Le Temps* had to say, or to gauge the temperature of public opinion – he knew that already – but to be alone for a moment. The driver did as he was asked and got out. But as the news vendor handed him the papers, he turned to face the car.

He saw the President. And recognised him.

The paper-seller couldn't believe his eyes. He stared at him and walked over to the glass as if peering into a fish tank. No, he wasn't mistaken.

Then he tried to attract the attention of an onlooker, who ignored him. He ranted at a pair of girls, who thought he was a lunatic. In desperation, the poor man began bouncing up and down like a spring, shouting:

'Daladier ... Daladier. He's there! Special edition ... Daladier, there he is ...'

The President crouched lower in his seat. Too late.

The crowd collected by the back window, the windscreen, to his left, to his right. The car was encircled. It rocked back and forth, it vibrated to the ringing cheers. Dozens of hands stretched out and tried to touch him. Behind the glass, pleading women's lips, almost mute, implored him: 'Please, bring us peace.' An old woman, the dishevelled woman of a few moments before, pressed her toothless hag's face against the door. The President gave a start.

The scene was terrifying. He was caught in a trap. He was surrounded by those contorted faces, by the distant echo of cries of joy, or war, he no longer knew which. He could make out cries of 'Never again.' Old soldiers, including one unfortunate chap without a nose or a lower jaw, gave him a military salute. Some students pushed them aside to show themselves off to him. They mocked Hitler. They had come to encourage him. They brandished a placard on which they promised to 'burn the *boche* at the stake', and chanted '*Vive Daladier*'.

A 14th-of-July banger went off, followed by a burst of them. The volley of explosions seemed endless. Each one reminded him of the sound of the 'bee'; in his old military jargon, the sound of bullets from the German machine-guns splitting the air and buzzing like the insect, before exploding a skull or an arm or a bit of gut in the trench. He couldn't stand the noise; he heard it as a coming attack. His body, trickling with sweat, began to stiffen. His teeth clenched like a vice. It wasn't his heart. The doctors had checked. They had examined him in turn and had all – or almost all – diagnosed 'overwork', the 'burden of state', as they put it. He had been advised to cut down on his eating. Only one military doctor had seen something else. It was the sequel to the war; he had talked about 'shell-shock', a strange sickness of the trenches also known in Napoleon's time as 'wind of shot syndrome'. The President had said to himself that this doctor was a quack. The attacks had begun a long time after the war, in about 1932 or 1933; and he had come out of the war relatively unscathed, unlike his friend Cheminade, dear Jean who had died in his place in 1917, during the battle for Mont Cornillet.

The President couldn't breathe.

He ordered the driver: 'Get us away from here.'

2

HÔTEL DE BRIENNE

He liked the Hôtel de Brienne. Having returned from his Paris escapade, he noticed once again how protected he felt by what, after so many revolutionary and architectural upheavals, the Rue Saint-Dominique had become. The headquarters of the Republic. The Minister of War. The lair of the great Clemenceau. The former residence of Maria Letizia Bonaparte. He liked the Hôtel de Brienne, with the cosy affection that he had felt for the boarding school of the Lycée Ampère in Lyons. He liked the Republic, and he liked its temples; that was how he was. The Rue Saint-Dominique was, like the public primary school of his childhood, a sanctuary, a place without rich or poor where everything became possible, even for the nobody from Carpentras that he had been. A cocoon protecting him from the swarming, nasty world. A kind of lay monastery.

He felt quite at home there, but not in the proprietorial way of the political right, not that. More as a servant of the state arriving in a place and returning there with constantly renewed astonishment. First in 1925, when he was appointed Minister of Colonies. Minister of War at less than 40, a remarkable promotion. He had returned to it often. As President of the Council, he had insisted on also remaining Minister of War. Like Clemenceau. And like him he had insisted on remaining in the austere Hôtel de Brienne rather than moving to the Hôtel Matignon, whose gardens aroused the jealousy even of the President of the Republic.

But tonight nothing felt the same. The President returned overwhelmed by what he had seen. And well informed about the mood of the French. Better informed than he was by all the wire-tap files that he normally so enjoyed, more than by that strange study that he had been shown – a 'survey', some newfangled American invention which claimed that the French were divided on the question of the war, between 'hard' and 'soft'; and better informed than by the reports of the chaotic security police, or the summaries from the *préfets* about 'French attitudes towards the war' that were dumped on him night and day.

He had seen.

The microphone and the transmission devices were installed in his office; but before making his announcement to the French about his meeting with Hitler, the President insisted on one point; one final point.

He didn't want to make the same mistake as President Sarraut. In 1936, during Hitler's remilitarisation of the Rhineland in violation of the Versailles Treaty, Sarraut had threatened: 'We are not willing to have Strasbourg put under fire from the German cannon.' He had gesticulated, before having to make a pitiful retreat after General Gamelin had explained to him that 'the French army was in no state to move'. The President had responded similarly, six months earlier, to Hitler's annexation of Austria. This time, it was Chautemps who had resigned. France had gone absent for the duration of a ministerial crisis.

But Daladier would not prostrate himself before Hitler, not like Sarraut.

Daladier would keep to France's obligations. Daladier would remember the 1924 pact between France and Czechoslovakia, which committed both countries to military solidarity.

He would remember that it was the French Slavists Louis

Léger and Ernest Denis who had, at the start of the century, come up with the idea of Czechoslovakia, that Federal, Francophile and Rousseauist nation. He would remember the genesis of the friendly Republic in Paris in 1916, with Masaryk's creation of the National Czechoslovak Council; the integration of the fine Czech Legion with the French Army in 1918; the birth of the fellow State in 1919; the country's political constitution modelled down to its tiniest details upon that of the Third Republic; and also the creation of the Czechoslovak army by French generals.

How could he forget all that? The Czechs in Paris had put themselves to a lot of trouble ...

Daladier wouldn't forget, as he went to see Hitler, everything that united France and Czechoslovakia. Daladier would forget nothing.

Nonetheless, the President reckoned that, taking into account this last-chance invitation, the speech that he had prepared the previous day no longer applied.

He had spoken of 'general mobilisation', of 'going to war', of Czechoslovakia as a country 'crucified for the salvation of the peace', a 'peace that would be the ransom of our dishonour' ... A powerful speech, but it could be dangerous, even useless, the President said to himself. He crossed out any emphases that seemed too bellicose, shortened the whole speech, hesitated, and finally got rid of the 'general and immediate mobilisation' that he had intended to announce. Take care, above all, not to insult the future – there would still be time after the Conference.

Once he had rewritten everything, using simple and well-chosen words, the President delivered his message in a slow and serious voice that he knew sounded good on the radio:

'Before I leave, I wish to give the people of France my thanks for their courage and dignity. I should particularly like to thank the Frenchmen who have been called to follow the flag for the composure and resolution that they have demonstrated once again. My task is a harsh one. Since the start of our present difficulties I have not ceased for a single day to work with all my strength to safeguard the peace and the vital interests of France. Tomorrow I shall continue this effort, with the thought that I am in complete accord with the whole nation.'

After the recording, the President tried to contact the British Prime Minister, Neville Chamberlain. This was indispensable. Everything had happened so quickly that he had not had time either to accept or to refuse to go. So quickly that he still didn't know if the Allies were going to defend, in Munich, the Franco-British plan of 19th September, which was very painful for the Czechs, but which they had finally and inevitably accepted. Or whether they might go to work tomorrow on the basis of the Bad Godesberg memorandum signed by Hitler, the one which anticipated, so to speak, the dismantling of that poor Czechoslovakia.

Munich, he had been told, was the last chance before total war. He was going. That was that.

His Majesty's Prime Minister was incommunicado, his adviser on duty informed him.

Then he asked someone to find Corbin, the French Ambassador to Great Britain. Shortly afterwards he received a call from London: the British Prime Minister was incommunicado even to Corbin.

The time had come.

He thought of asking Bonnet, his Minister of Foreign Affairs, to find him the Englishman. He quickly gave up on the idea. No, not Bonnet. He wouldn't lower himself to ask him that service; nor to show him his confusion in the face of the British government's silence. And besides, he didn't trust Bonnet. He suspected him of not playing fairly: his excessive proximity to British appeasement; his links with Ciano, the circle around Mussolini and all the Italophiles in Paris; his 'far-right' tendency, thinking only of succeeding Daladier, allying himself this time with the real political right; not to mention the arrogance of a Parisian who dines with whoever it takes, receives whoever it takes, and greases the palms of the press from his own funds. He himself, Daladier, was pretty good at politics. He knew how to get on with the biggest party in France; but the obsessive manoeuvres of the Bonnets – because the formidable Odette Bonnet also had to be taken into account – repelled him. No, not Bonnet, a bad idea. Bonnet would risk confusing him. The day before his visit to Hitler, that was the last thing he needed!

Then the President resolved to call Alexis Léger. Ah, Léger, the Secretary General at the Quai d'Orsay, the true boss, in fact, was quite different from Bonnet! A class above!

He found Léger. You always found Léger on the phone. Inevitably, his mother or his sister – who lived with him on the Rue Camoëns – would guide one either towards his office, the home of his current mistress, or the town-house of his girlfriend, the Duchesse de Flers.

Léger called him back straight away. He couldn't track down Chamberlain either.

As he waited for the call from London, Daladier set about organising his briefcase for the following day – an old school-teacher's habit. He decided, given the importance of the meeting, to do it ceremoniously, standing up at first the better to imagine the huge amount of documents. The whole Republic seemed to have been mobilised over the issue. There were several stacks of files entitled 'Sudeten Crisis'. The notes of his Matignon cabinet. The documents from the Quai d'Orsay. The reports from the War Ministry, of course, from the General Staff, from the Deuxième Bureau (the external military intelligence agency). Exchanges of telegrams with *those poor Czechs*, including the desperate ones from President Beneš. Correspondence with the British. A memo on the – rather poor – state of France's relations with Italy since the country's condemnation at the League of Nations over Abyssinia. A series of maps of Czechoslovakia and the surrounding region, a memory of the time when France still lived in the illusion of the 'Petite Entente', supposed to contain Germany, along with her Romanian, Czechoslovak and Yugoslavian allies. And a series of contradictory military reports. He flicked through the lot.

Daladier then returned to the account of a crucial meeting that he had held with his armed forces a few days previously, when he had thought war was inevitable.

The three heads of the armed forces were in his office. There was Admiral Darlan for the navy, General Vuillemin for the air force and, of course, General Gamelin representing the army, their superior – in theory – as head of the National Defence General Staff.

'Gentlemen,' Daladier had said, 'I have summoned you here at a very grave moment. The decisions of the government and the fate of France depend on what you tell me.'

The President had leaned forward. With a confidential air, he had whispered in his husky voice: 'If France sees herself forced to declare war on Germany, can she count on her army?'

Gamelin had thought for a long time. An eternity for the President, who felt suddenly anxious.

He had finally replied in a soft voice, like a model pupil: 'The army is ready, sir!'

Daladier could have kissed him.

Then it was Admiral Darlan's turn. Straight away the seaman replied stoutly, 'The fleet is ready. If we have the

British fleet by our side, France will have nothing to fear on the sea.'

Finally, Vuillemin set out the position of the air force. He took no prisoners: 'If war breaks out tomorrow, we won't have a single plane left in a fortnight. We will have to have the planes in our possession piloted by reserve officers, for we will never see those machines again. We will have to save our good pilots till we have suitable planes. In May we ordered aeroplanes from America; the first will be delivered in October, and the last in the spring of 1939. Until that happens, our pilots might as well go for a walk ... They have nothing to do.'

General Vuillemin narrated, itemised, insisted, replied: 'You know, gentlemen, that I visited General Göring three weeks ago,' he gave a strange, almost sadistic little laugh, and paused for effect. 'And when I was over there I was shown all sorts of things, but by no means everything.'

Daladier remembered that last observation of Vuillemin's. He hadn't been able to shake it off for several days. He repeated to himself once again what he knew only too well.

The army, all right.

The navy, all right, although ...

But the air force, how are we to wage war without the air force? How are we to manage when Prague is pushing closer to conflict every day, and at every hour of the day; and while Beneš is writing, pestering, making Blum intervene, plotting even in the heart of Paris?

Lest he be disturbed in his patriotic determination, the President tried to forget Vuillemin. He conscientiously returned to the task of tidying and memorising.

He underlined here, he annotated there with the calligraphy of a town clerk. He devoured and absorbed, just as he firmly advised his young colleagues to do. His plan had been to sum up the essence of those kilos of documents on little card files, as he always did. Sometimes he skipped a few hundred sheets, but he did so with a bad conscience. He was interested in everything: the latest British telegrams – surprisingly more severe the past two days; the declaration by the Soviet Minister of Foreign Affairs, Litvinov, an advocate of firm treatment, and isolated in his country; the final position of France's Romanian ally, which had reservations – according to the Quai d'Orsay – about the Red Army flying over its territory on its way to support Czechoslovakia.

He spent an hour on this exercise before abandoning it.

He repeated it over and over to himself. He didn't need any of that to confront Hitler.

He pushed it all aside, and from the stacks of files he extracted only the 'Gamelin note', along with the map of the Czech fortifications. The fortifications were the thing that had to be kept, and defended. Without her fortifications, Czechoslovakia would lose her borders. The heavy fortifications of Zamberk-Fridaldov-Opawa to the north, and the light fortifications of Znojmo-Breclaw had even been underlined in red – high priority – on the note from the Deuxième Bureau. It was also feared that the seizure of such territories by the Germans would be dangerous to France, plans of Czech fortifications having been largely inspired by the Maginot Line.

The Czech fortifications were the sinews of war, or perhaps of peace, of that he was sure. Of the thousands of pages that his colleagues had drawn up, the 'Gamelin note' was the only one that struck him as really useful. Besides, he trusted Gamelin, whom he had appointed National Defence Chief of Staff some months previously. Gamelin was his man. A serious soldier, not a loose cannon; a republican soldier in a world of fascists; and, most importantly, the disciple of the great Joffre.

Once more the President railed against Sarraut and his predecessors, who should have stood up to Hitler in 1935 when he reintroduced conscription in violation of the Versailles Treaty; in 1936 when he invaded the Rhineland; early in 1938 when he undertook the Anschluss. If they had done, they wouldn't be where they were today. He stuffed the 'Gamelin note' into his old briefcase, put a copy in his jacket – you never know; he added two more files, one about the private life of the Führer, passed on to him by the secret services; weighed it all with a weariness mixed with a certain satisfaction. He was not a fantasist, not like that damned Chamberlain who was nowhere to be found.

It had struck ten, and still no word of the Englishman.

The President cancelled his evening duties: two late meetings and that dinner of old Vaucluse radicals that always bored him stiff. But he was anxious to apologise to the Marquise who was entertaining that evening. He was sorry. He wasn't feeling sociable, but he promised Madame de Crussol – in a soft voice – that he would be in touch soon. He hung up with a heavy heart, and decided to wait, in the deserted ministry, for Chamberlain's call.

Later, he phoned home to his house in the 16th Arrondissement. His sister was still waiting for him to come to dinner; she regretted the fast life he was living, and worried about the war and this trip to Munich. What he wanted most was news of the children, how was Jean? And Pierre, still as quiet? He wanted to talk to his two sons, particularly Jean, but it wasn't easy on the phone. By way of excuse, he had told his sister that it wouldn't be easy to set off from the 16th Arrondissement the following day to go all the way east, to Le Bourget, with his colleagues and his stacks of files.

In actual fact, he didn't want to go home. He didn't want to spend the night in Rue Anatole de la Forge, in that little flat, too dark, too well-polished. That evening he wouldn't have been able to bear Marie, with all her suggestions, her sighs, her indispensable-big-sister ways – and it was true, he reflected, that she had been indispensable since Madeleine's death. But more than anything, more even than Marie's intrusions, what he dreaded was his two boys. Their questions, their devoted admiration, their wonderful bluster against nasty old Hitler, whom Papa was going to crush with his fist. He wanted to avoid those sessions, Jean's face, so mournful since his mother's death. Jean, his Jean, so puzzling and such a nice chap, a bit tight-lipped like himself: a true Daladier. At his school he had even, despite the hostility of his philosophy teacher – one Jean-Paul Sartre – set up a section of the Patriotic Youth of the Empire in order, as he put it, to fight Hitler in his own way.

The other evening Jean had announced to him, with a resolute swagger: 'I'm going to wage war against Hitler too, Papa.' The boy's phrase had chilled him. He had understood not only that his son Jean would soon be an adult but, more importantly, would soon be sent to his death. Since that conversation, the image of Jean dying in a trench had risen up to pursue him. It came and went, it played tricks on his consciousness. It smuggled itself in without warning. Like a 'trench headache', it could strike in the middle of an official inauguration, during the dictation of his correspondence, during a council of ministers devoted to rearmament, a dinner with the Marquise, at any time. It was a ghost that invited itself in unexpectedly; like an internal cinema, an uncontrollable nightmare.

The scene was always the same. It was disturbing, and there was a certain déjà-vu about it. It was like the death-throes of Jean Cheminade in 1917, during the terrible battle for Mont Cornillet. Cheminade, his friend, a working man from northern France, a big-hearted Catholic, had died right next to him – in his place, he had said to himself over and over again for 30 years.

At such times he relived that moment, and was gripped with panic . . . Jean's face merged with Cheminade's. He saw once again the dead man's mask, calm, eyes open. His head had settled in the middle of the crater formed by the shell, which was scattered with scraps of flesh, his comrade's broken body. The President had never spoken to anyone about it; it was always that image, so terrifying it made you want to scream, that burst into his mind. He tried to chase it away, but it took him by surprise, like a whiff of anxiety. In the moments when it left him alone, he told himself that it was the face of war.

At 10.30 he requested for another call to be put through to London. This time the President was furious, in one of his famous rages. He ranted at the incompetents on the Quai d'Orsay, shook his adviser, roared at the sleepy secretary. They couldn't have looked properly . . . They must have called the wrong number . . . They mustn't have dared to disturb him . . . And still the President tried to reassure himself: the Englishman must have been caught up in one of those official dinners that you can never escape before eleven o'clock . . . That was it, they'd be sure to find him this evening. They would find him. Of course they would! With his undertaker's appearance, the Englishman wasn't the type to while the night away with a dancer, or even with a marquise, he chuckled to himself.

But while he might have been able to find explanations, the British nonchalance on the eve of such a summit was beginning to worry him.

What could he do? Just wait.

It was too early to go to the Marquise's flat on Avenue Henri-Martin; she would still be entertaining.

He had no desire – not this evening, of all times! – to rub shoulders with the socialites who attended her salon, one of the most famous in all Paris. He certainly didn't want to find himself enduring the arguments of all the 'hardliners' in Paris: Pertinax, Kerillis, Cot, Campinchi or Mandel, who would explain to him all over again that France would be supporting Hitler if she didn't support the Czechs. Or indeed to meet representatives of the 'soft' stance who, like Barthélemy, Fabre-Luce or Berl, would demonstrate to him, obsessively and knowledgeably, that the 1924 pact with Czechoslovakia actually had no legal force. He had heard enough about that since May, with Bonnet and his henchmen, and even that afternoon with the clutch of far-right deputies based at Rue Saint-Dominique. They all repeated the same thing: 'Die for the Czechs? But my electors – and yours, Mr President – don't even know where it is, this Czechoslovakia of yours.'

And the President particularly didn't want to risk chancing upon Reynaud, besotted with his Madame de Portes. They would be all too happy to inflict their 'good advice' upon him, to disturb and confuse him. On no account did he want to have to listen to that jealous man, that scheming woman, who were both capable of anything. To allow himself to be influenced would be to slip up in front of Hitler ... And – he had no illusions on the matter – Reynaud and the Duchesse de Portes were waiting for him to do just that so they could pounce upon the presidency of the Council. They had dreamed of it for so many years. Certainly not!

He had had enough of their advice and their opinions, their theories and summaries; enough of their maps, small format, large-scale, in black and white or tri-coloured; enough of the various notes they struck, alarmist one day, triumphalist the next; enough of their proposals for the 'correction of the Czech borders', more or less generous according to Hitler's tone.

He knew enough about that for the following day.

Eleven o'clock. Still no Chamberlain.

He stretched out on the Empire sofa, near the radio which was set up there for special occasions. The last time had been a fortnight before, on 12th September, Hitler's famous speech at the Sportpalast in Berlin. The whole world was waiting to know. They had had speakers installed in the office. The whole cabinet had gathered together, on the sofa, in the armchairs, sitting on every available surface around the radio. He had stared at them. The old members of his cabinet, the more sober ones, the men who had known 1914. And the younger ones, more excitable, who thought that in this crisis they were seeing war for the first time. They were all so serious. They waited in silence; you could sense that they were anxious, feverish, impatient. What was the German going to say? What was he going to do? Would he give the signal for war, after the failure of Chamberlain's second trip and its trail of humiliations for the Allies? Or would it be the signal for peace? Which way would the wind blow? What would he come up with this time? A temporary translator had been urgently requisitioned from a corridor in the Quai d'Orsay. The poor chap had done a good job, but he had been so shy. Sometimes the contrast was comical, between the blushing young functionary and the roars of Chancellor Hitler, who made the radio vibrate till it distorted. Especially when, his rage following on from his tears, he evoked his 'persecuted fellow-Germans', and bellowed the name of 'Beneš'.

At the end of Hitler's speech no one said a word. They were all flabbergasted. Except for a diplomat from Bonnet's cabinet who started holding forth after a long minute of silence. The man knew his way around the salons; he had worked out that he would charm those present – and certainly Daladier – by repeating to anyone willing to listen that 'the Führer was certainly violent in form, but moderate at root . . . In the end it's all very good for France, because the Führer recognises the French position on Alsace and Lorraine.'

But Bonnet's man, and even Alsace and Lorraine, were of little importance right now. The President had been knocked senseless by that furious voice, that speech as long as an endless nightmare, those threats, that din, the guttural rumbles evoking Beneš and the Sudetenland. He had concentrated so hard on the speech that he was exhausted by the ordeal. He could no longer think; and at any rate, reasoning would have been in vain. He was in a state of shock. The Medieval fanaticism of the sermon had alarmed him. He had already witnessed speeches by Hitler, in Pathé newsreels and elsewhere. He had had them screened at the Ministry. There was nothing he didn't know about the circus, the arm brandished in the air, the adoring crowds, the voice that cooed and then crashed, the great solemn masses of the Party. He had even attentively followed the propaganda operation of the Berlin Olympic Games in 1936. But he had never listened to the man like that. It had made his head vibrate. Since then he had never quite been able to shake off that lingering buzz.

'A barbarian,' the President gave a start as he remembered that day. Alone in the dark office, he lay on the sofa, repeating out loud: 'A barbarian. He took Austria six months ago and we did nothing. But he won't take Czechoslovakia. Not our ally. A barbarian. I won't have it. Daladier isn't a man to be walked all over . . .'

* * *

The Hôtel de Brienne suddenly made him feel anxious; its creaking parquets, those unsettlingly high ceilings, the heavy foliage stirring in the garden, that tapestry showing Vauban building fortifications which, by electric light, assumed a menacing appearance. He was one of the most powerful men on the planet, the head of the greatest army in the world (apart from the air force, according to that peculiar chap Vuillemin), the uncontested head of the French Empire, the head of the Radical Party; but tonight he was a wretch gone to earth in this office.

Not knowing what to do or where to spend the night, or what the next day would bring, his body sagged slightly. He felt sorry for himself.

He began to doze as he waited. As he waited for he knew not what: Chamberlain's call, time for the Marquise's guests to leave, or for this night to pass. He went to sleep with the roars of Hitler in his ears, he heard once again that voice that came from somewhere far away, not from the belly, not from the throat, but from the German forests; that faint music, those almost inaudible words, that extended magic spell: until in a word or a cry the thunder exploded, accompanied by the worshipful rage of the German people.

He woke in a daze. He was drenched in sweat. His detachable collar was too tight, his suit a prison. It took him a moment to work out where he was. He thought it was already morning, no one had come to get him, he was late.

Nearly midnight. Within reach of his hand, on a silver dish, he found two messages from Prague.

An usher must have brought them while he was asleep. President Beneš, urgent. And again, President Beneš, urgent. And still nothing from Chamberlain!

He didn't open the letters from the Czechoslovak President. He knew the pleas, the advice, the exhortations and probably the tears that they contained. He knew them all too well.

Sleep had calmed him a little. He sat up on his sofa, and decided to imagine events from a new angle.

An idea came to him:

'What if I didn't go to Munich!'

He tried to think, then continued, this time out loud:

'What if I didn't go? After all . . .'

He seemed perked up by his bright idea.

'Hitler summons us, he whistles to us, and we're supposed to go crawling on our bellies to him? Is that how France is to be treated?'

He smiled. He had found the flaw.

'After all, I haven't given my agreement. The news arrived at three o'clock. No one asked my opinion. I've been presented with a *fait accompli* and now I'm supposed to go along with it. No, really, I haven't given my agreement.'

He clung stubbornly to the idea.

'Let Chamberlain go to Munich on his own. He must have developed a taste for Germany. He's no longer afraid of anything, after those two humiliating meetings with Hitler. First he visits Mr Hitler at his holiday home – that beats everything! And then he goes running off to Bad Godesberg to make himself look ridiculous in the eyes of the world. Then he leaves me without any information for days. And now he wants it all to start over again with Munich? Well he can do it without me!'

His mind was growing heated. He paused for a moment; and to calm himself down he stared at a detail he had never noticed before in the tapestry showing Vauban and the fortifications. Then he set off once again towards his new resolution. One step at a time.

'After all, I don't even know where I'm going. No provisions have been made for the protocol. You never know with these dictator chaps . . . No agenda has been fixed for the conference. And we don't even know whether the Czechs will agree to come, or whether they've been invited in the first place. And besides, I have no sense of what the British are up to. In the six months that we've been talking about Czechoslovakia, they've come and they've gone. They'll be "soft" three times in a row, "hard" the next. Today, there's no way of knowing what Chamberlain is thinking. I thought he was "soft", and now here he is, if the *Times* is anything to go by, turning into a warmonger. No, definitely, not Munich!

'He still hasn't called. And it would mean going to Munich without conditions, without preparation, without knowing.

'No, they won't do that to me . . .'

The President repeated that phrase several times. He got to his feet and said it again as he paced up and down in the gloom of his enormous office. This time he had completely removed his detachable collar; he had thrown off his suit jacket and unbuttoned his shirt. He had become the open-shirted peasant once again.

'After all, France doesn't go running like a dog behind the English! Even if England has been the alpha and omega of our diplomacy since 1904, the Entente Cordiale, as those fine souls at the Quai d'Orsay never tire of repeating, nevertheless, we're not going to sacrifice everything to the Entente Cordiale. We must keep our word to our Czech allies. They won't make me do that. No, they won't make me do that.'

He froze, his face illuminated with fresh ambition.

He imagined that by saying 'no' to Hitler like that, he would create a new front. And that in the face of that, Germany would retreat.

So he began to count France's 'possible allies'. The ones who would understand, the ones who would join him, the ones who might be prepared – who knows – to fight.

'The Czechs, obviously! With their armoured divisions – a high quality fighting force thanks to their French army training – with their eight hundred thousand mobilised men, with their fortifications, particularly in Moravia, which are almost a match for our Maginot Line, and which in any case supplant the Siegfried Line which is barely under construction, they could withstand the shock for ... let's say three months.

'And then who?'

One finger remained in the air.

'The Russians? They had a pact with Czechoslovakia as well. Their Minister of Foreign Affairs, Litvinov, advocated firmness, but is he still part of the Kremlin court? Wasn't it too late? Calling them to our rescue after keeping them out of everything? In any case, allying ourselves with the Russians would be a deadly business. It would please the Communists, even part of the right, Reynaud, Kerillis and Mandel, but it's risky, too risky ...

'The Americans? Roosevelt was one of the ones who first came up with the idea of a conference in Munich. He claims to have understood the threat from Hitler. But what will he do when it comes to the crunch? America is cautious, selfish, isolationist, as they say. And besides, she will always prefer Britain over France.

'The Hungarians? Certainly not, they're jealous of the Czechs, of their economic triumph, of our friendship. They're nostalgic for the Hapsburg Empire. They will ally themselves with Hitler.

'And what about our friends in the Petite Entente, the Poles? They hate the Czechs and dream only of taking over their western border.

'The Romanians? Not to be trusted. They always say they love us passionately but, as they also say, they're in love with Paris, not with France.'

He lowered his hand. He saw himself as Don Quixote, setting off on a crusade without allies. Ridiculous, gesticulatory, powerless . . .

'So who are we to ally ourselves with? The Emperor of Ethiopia?' The joke cheered him up slightly.

All of a sudden he had a worrying thought. He got to his feet, on point like a hunting dog. He exclaimed in a strangled voice, 'Yes . . . But then . . . If I don't go . . .'

And he saw the scene, Munich, the conference, without him.

He saw Hitler, Mussolini and Chamberlain in his black jacket. He saw all three of them, around a table. For the first time really, and in a very terrifying way, the President finally imagined the meeting in Munich. The scene was there, right in front of his eyes. The vision of it was alarming. In his agitation, the President surprised himself by crying out, 'But they'll eat him alive!'

An image appeared in his mind, even more terrible than a painting by Goya. The two ogres and that poor Englishman, all locked away in a suffocating room. They were leaning over big maps criss-crossed with blood red. Bending over the beast, the poor Czech beast. He saw old Chamberlain, hoodwinked by the two dictators. He saw that friendly country as a horizontal mass being cut up into slices, the best portion being served to the Germans. The two dictators were at work, like butchers. Czechoslovakia would not be defended by Chamberlain. They would carve up the friendly country. They would carve the best bits for themselves, they would swap the offal between them: the Moravian corridor against a little bit of Ruthenia. They would throw the rest to the Poles, the Romanians and other Hungarians who would each claim their share.

The President saw with horror the one thing he wanted to avoid: the carving up of Czechoslovakia.

His nightmare.

The application, pure and simple, of Hitler's final plan, the one he had made at Bad Godesberg. The worst possible solution!

He was suffocating, pacing the room like a lost soul.

'Not that . . . Chamberlain would let the whole thing slip through his fingers . . .'

He tried to calm himself, and got his breath back; 'No! The Bull of the Vaucluse will not desert the arena. Not this time.'

He felt in the inside pocket of his jacket, and was re-assured to find that the 'Gamelin note' was still there. It was something like his talisman, he thought stupidly, or rather his vade mecum.

'And the fortifications, whatever you do don't forget the Czech fortifications.'

3

THE CZECH BROTHER

'Well, mademoiselle, you have done a remarkable job there. Your account is fairly accurate. That's more or less what happened. The evening before the conference, I was alone, terribly alone, more alone than ever before. There is one detail that you are quite right about, the fortifications, the Gamelin note. It was useful to me, it kept me from falling either on the side of the warmongers or the pro-Hitler lobby. Thanks to that note I was able, let's say, to limit the damage. And then there are two things that I would have added to that picture. The war in Spain that had been raging for two years. You can't imagine the impact it had had on us. It was right on our doorstep. And then there's one strange detail that I remember, too. That day, on the way back from the ministry, I found in my post a dedicated copy of Colonel De Gaulle's book, *France and Her Army*, which had just been published.'

'So is there something you're forgetting to tell me about?'

'What do you mean? I've told you everything, I've handed myself to you on a plate, you've penetrated me to the bone.'

'No, there's one thing you've forgotten. That evening in your signature book there was a text. An official warning addressed to General Faucher, the head of the French military mission, based in Prague. Punished for refusing to abandon his Czech brother . . .'

'Have you seen Faucher?' he asked, worried and suspicious again.

'No. He's been dead for five years. Martha Gellhorn talked to me about it a lot. Together they organised the evacuation of the democrats and the Jews from the Sudetenland, the day after Munich. They took, she told me, crazy risks. She often told me that Faucher was French heroism personified, and for an American woman you can imagine what that means. I've also read Churchill, who talks about him in almost Biblical terms:

There was in Prague at this moment a General of the French Army named Faucher. He had been in Czechoslovakia with the French military mission since 1919, and had been its chief since 1926. He now requested the French Government to relieve him of his duties, and placed himself at the disposal of the Czechoslovak Army.

'I do have a memory of General Faucher. I think he made life difficult for the General Staff because he sided systematically with the Czechoslovak Republic. He had been friends with Masaryk and Beneš. But I don't remember signing so serious a sanction.'

'Here it is. But first here is what Faucher wrote to Gamelin and to you when he was presenting his resignation, and seeking to enrol as a private soldier in the Czech army:

There were in Czechoslovakia deep, old and touching feelings of love and admiration for France. I know the country well enough to assert this, based on something other than statements or expressions attributable to mere politeness. These feelings are making way for hatred and contempt; we have betrayed, with the aggravating circumstance that we have tried to camouflage the betrayal. "You may one day find yourselves facing Skoda cannon and Czechoslovak soldiers," an old friend said to me. Already they have stopped saluting French officers, and to avoid any incidents, the mission staff only ever go out in plain clothes.

> Coded telegram
> That reached General FAUCHER
> On 28th September, 1938
> At 6.30 pm
> Head French Military Mission. PRAHA.
> OF WAR PARIS.
> No. 2447 2/ EMA-SAE, 28th September, 1938 – 12 io
> I acknowledge receipt of your letter no. 3196/cab. If the Czechoslovaks thought in this way, we would only have to abandon them to their fate. But I do not believe it, and I am sure that they will realise the efforts that France is making to save them.
>
> I hereby give you the official warning of the Head of the General Staff and invite you to continue to do your duty as a French General.
>
> WAR MINISTER

Having read the telegram, the old man raised his head. An expression of astonishment was frozen on his face. He had happened upon an old acquaintance.

'Monsieur Daladier, you have sullied this man because he was right before anyone else! Because he wanted France to keep her word and stand by the signed treaty. And you could bring yourself to sign that, on that evening?'

'That evening? Are you sure? It must have been Gamelin who schemed that one up. He must have given it to me to sign; I must have signed without seeing it. I can't remember. I had other things to think about that evening.'

'Thinking about President Beneš, for example? All that time he was trying to get in touch with you. In vain!'

'But we'd said everything there was to say. Beneš and I

agreed, Hitler's *Diktat* would not be applied but, in return, Czechoslovakia would make an effort over the Sudetenland. It had all been agreed already!'

'No, Monsieur Daladier. On the eve of the conference, President Beneš was still hoping. He was waiting at Prague Castle, the seat of the presidency of the Republic. He still hoped that France would keep to its commitments; a call from you; at least a sign before the conference from which he had, in fact, been excluded. Until 25th September, he had thought that France would keep her commitment. In spite of the British manoeuvring, he repeatedly assured everyone of his faith in France. He said it again to Beuve-Méry before he returned to France; and to Faucher, too. But Beuve-Méry hadn't left him with a lot of hope about France's solidarity. Beneš hadn't wanted to hear; he was even insulted. But that night, he began to think that Beuve-Méry might be right.'

'So Beuve-Méry knew before I did what I would be doing in Munich, and even if there would be a Munich!'

'Well, yes, Monsieur Daladier. That's the peculiar thing about these tragedies. There are always some men who see better, sooner, than the others. Martha Gellhorn, Faucher, Beuve-Méry ... a strange trio ... But let's get back to that night.

'Beneš was waiting at the castle, like you, a wretched king. He had summoned together the heads of the Czechoslovak army. His cabinet had alerted him. His generals were distraught, ready for war, ready for anything, although without being seditious – because in the Czechoslovak Republic people weren't. President Beneš had been keen to receive them in his library at the castle, the famous library of the founder of the Czechoslovak Republic, Masaryk. At that terrible moment he needed to sense the presence of the giant who had preceded him.

'The generals had come from every corner of the country.

General Krejci, the chief of staff, had left Moravia and his mobilised troops. He was accompanied by three provincial commanders, General Vojcechovsky, General Prachala and General Luza. The four men were introduced to Beneš at the same time as the new prime minister, General Syrovy.

'And then the generals pleaded.

'They were ready for war. They were ready, with or without France.

'General Krejci, the chief of staff, spoke first: "Mr President, we must fight whatever the cost. And when we do perhaps the western powers will follow us ..."

'Then came the turn of the three provincial commanders.

'They spoke in chorus: "Mr President, the people are completely united. The army is strong and resolute ... And it has decided to fight to the last drop of blood."

There were tears in the generals' eyes.

'After listening to them, Beneš rose to his feet. He invoked the history of Bohemia and the ancient battles against the Teutonic tribes, Václav, patron saint of the old kingdom, the golden age under Ottokar II, and President Masaryk.

'He was stiff. He was grey with exhaustion – he hadn't slept for nights. He really wanted to shout at his generals but instead, heart aching, he declared: "They have abandoned us ... They have abandoned us. It would be a disastrous, an unforgivable error to allow the nation to be slaughtered ..."

'The generals understood. Their president was resigned. He would accept the verdict of the Munich meeting the following day. He would follow the instructions of London and Paris. The little group dispersed and it is said that, in the hall and the corridors of the castle, terrible words of rage and despair were heard that night.

'At that moment, Beneš also thought – like you, President Daladier! – that he was the loneliest man in the world. And he really was.

'The little president remained alone, in his deserted castle. He tried to contact you. He also looked for Chamberlain. He wanted assurance that a Czech delegation would be present in Munich. He couldn't get through to either of you.

'In the course of that long night, the wails of the people of Prague and the cries of rage of a furious crowd rose up to the President's castle, a roar of menace. It is said, Mr President Daladier, that on that night, Na Príkope Street – National Street – Masaryk Quay, all over the city, being French was far from pleasant. Not that there was any violence – acts of violence were rare, there was a little demonstration outside the offices of Air France, with people shouting, "French cowards!" But when anyone inside the crowd spoke French, they were subjected to a curious interrogation. The people didn't understand. Bertrand de Jouvenel, a reporter in Prague, relates that the Czechs' questions were baffled rather than violent: "Why did you do that? You're so strong. Does it mean you're afraid of Germany? We aren't!"

'President Beneš made one last attempt to get through to you at your ministry, Mr President. He couldn't reach you. He must have been wondering if his generals weren't basically right: if Czechoslovakia defended herself, the French and then the English would be obliged to follow.

'But you, Mr President, didn't answer.'

4

LE BOURGET, OUTWARD BOUND

Le Bourget airport finally appeared.

He wasn't displeased when the chattering of his Air Minister, Guy La Chambre, and the sententious observations of General Vuillemin about the French air force and the Luftwaffe, the relative merits of the new Heinkel 112 fighter and ours, the Dewoitine 510, began to subside. They were boring him to death with their comments and their last-minute recommendations. They were keeping him from thinking of the day ahead, from letting his mind wander over the morning mist of the plain of St Denis, and emerge from that restless night.

A nightmare had left him with a bitter, vague and dangerous taste in his mouth. As his chaperones droned on, he tried to reassemble the scattered pieces. There was a stadium, and in that stadium a kind of ring . . . he was a boxer . . . He was being pushed into the ring . . . A huge Asian gong sounded . . . The gong had made him vibrate . . . He was blinded by the columns of light that lit the vast hall . . . And there was someone in front of him, probably his adversary, but he couldn't see him . . . He made out a face . . . The huge crowd around him fell silent for a moment . . . He made out a face; it wasn't Hitler's, as he might have thought, but his own . . . The crowd had begun to shout. Weirdly, it was the barking of dogs that spilled from the speakers in the four corners of the stadium.

Without succumbing to that new fad called 'psychoanalysis', often praised to him by his friend the American ambassador, William Bullitt, a close friend of the celebrated Dr Freud, the President imagined that his dream must have some connection with the present situation, but he couldn't provide a clear interpretation of it. He tried to plunge back into his night in search of other elements of the puzzle, to understand why the enemy, at first without a face, had taken his; and why a sports hall, a ring and barking. He had barely had time to start unpicking his dream when Vuillemin had begun talking about his visit to the 'Hermann Goring' aeroplane factories again. It still made him quiver with military ecstasy.

The Air Minister – recently married to one Cora Madou, a singer who also had an interest in politics – interrupted the general's flow. He emphatically wanted the President to visit him at his 'new home' as soon as they were back from Munich. The President, lost in his thoughts, didn't reply. The minister was insistent. Daladier honoured him, quite at random, with one of his usual grunts. That morning more than ever he wanted to remain silent. He had never been talkative. He had been 'taciturn', that word that had been very quickly attached to him at primary school; he had been lumbered with it ever since. He had thought at first that it was an illness. He was 'taciturn' the way other people were tubercular. He had got used to it.

As the limousine drove in to Le Bourget aerodrome, the solemn tension of the early morning called to mind another morning thirty years ago. He had got up before the rest of his family and dressed himself up like an usher. He was going to leave Carpentras. He would get his university degree, and then study for a teaching diploma in Lyon; then they would see. He was leaving under the eye of three generations of working people, all lined up on the front doorstep. He was their hope.

Today, it was the dignitaries of the Republic who, affection aside, watched him with a similarly imploring gaze. All the major ministers were there: Bonnet in the front row, so keen to cut a fine figure because he had been excluded from the Munich conference; the Prefect of Police of the city of Paris; the director of Air France; all the foreign diplomats in Paris, the German ambassador to the fore, warmly shaking his hand, a confusion of journalists with flashes and micro-phones and even, he noticed, ordinary workers from Le Bourget, greasy mechanics and packers with cigarette-stubs in their mouths. Together they formed a kind of solemn, emotional hedge. He thought of his father, who had died long ago. That morning of 29th September 1938, he would have liked to feel his arms around him.

5

LETTER TO IDA

When Sir Arthur Neville Chamberlain's plane took off from Heston airport, the British Prime Minister thought of his sister. He hadn't given her any news of himself since the previous day. Sir Neville had one passion in life: his sister Ida. He wrote to her every day, about anything at all. When he came home in the evening, after all, he couldn't confide in a servant, even the most sensitive of servants, the small disappointments and great plans of his life. There was Ida, and then there was his wife. She came second to Ida, who was his favourite woman of all, his confidante, the one with whom he shared his life, albeit at a distance. She was his double, his soulmate. Now, to make his thoughts as clear as he liked them to be, he needed to write to her again, to talk to her.

Like him, she understood everything, so well, so quickly. The passing years had done nothing to change that; they had even reinforced the bonds between them. At the age of 69, he still needed her. She shared his vision of civilisation, and even of business; she was a Chamberlain. Although a woman, she was part of a dynasty of meritorious commoners that counted no fewer than three ministers and a dozen Birmingham councillors. Ida believed in Arthur Neville's destiny. She had always believed in it, even when, quite advanced in years, during the Great War, he had decided to go into politics. She believed in him more than she had in their half-brother Austen, who had died the previous year and, long before Arthur Neville, had had a fine political career, a career, moreover, consecrated by the Order of the Garter, so seldom awarded to a commoner.

She had an unrivalled understanding – most unusual in a woman, he thought – of the greatness of empire, the good-ness of the Crown which allowed its meritorious commoners to aspire – like the Chamberlains – to the highest office, and the theories of Mr Keynes. And, most of all, she was convinced, as a fervent Unitarian, that Providence had singled out her brother to be the 'Messenger of Peace'; for it fell to a Chamberlain to accomplish this sacred mission.

My dear Ida,

It has taken me sixty-nine years to get to it. I must confess that I am developing a liking for aeroplanes. Our fleet of British Airways planes is a marvel of comfort and progress. The flight attendants are delicate, refined, attentive, at any rate more than the domestic staff at Bamburgh Castle – on my last fishing weekend there I found that they really left a great deal to be desired. The Lockheed 10 Electra is an ultra-modern aircraft; the first in the world to be pressurised. It means that one no longer suffers from that horrible ringing in the ears that Austen so fervently warned me about, as you probably remember.

In a word, travelling by plane is truly marvellous. You should try it some time. For my part, I shall do it again without hesitation, and even with a degree of pleasure. The first time, when I went to see Chancellor Hitler, a month ago, I had no choice. The peace had to be saved, without delay; I went to Germany without apprehension, telling myself that the Lord would protect me in that sacred mission. This morning, I no longer felt the slightest fear as I climbed aboard the plane.

Except the fear, my dear Ida, that the day might go badly.

As you know very well, I have done everything in my power to mark out the road to peace. I have been an impenitent pilgrim for it since May, when the poor Sudeten Germans were in revolt; but now I dread Chancellor Hitler. He is so unpredictable. Nothing is ever enough for him. So I am dreading that the same thing will happen in Munich as happened in Bad Godesberg on the occasion of my second visit. The Sudetenland was no longer enough. It was the whole of Czechoslovakia that he wanted! Hence the untenable situation in which I have found myself since that *diktat*. I shall say it to you as I said it to him: Chancellor Hitler is not reasonable. Hitler could have everything he desires – which I am prepared to grant him, as are the French, I am quite sure – if he behaved differently. For Hitler's Germany has a stabilising role in the region. In his own day our father, as you are well aware, dreamed of this 'Anglo-Teutonic union' . . . But there is always a risk where Hitler is concerned. His position can suddenly become so extreme that it becomes – even for me, and I am not, as you know, hostile to him in principle – actually indefensible.

But in the end, let's take heart! I'm counting on some allies today. On Mussolini who, I know, may turn out to be a very useful intermediary; on Göring who, according to his friend Nevile Henderson, has no desire to make war, and perhaps also on this good man Daladier who doesn't want to go there all alone. I am also counting, my dear Ida, on the 'tender moderation' that the Lord has taught us. And I will stand firm regardless of the opinions of that drunkard Churchill, our cousin Austen who is so cool with us, or the dandies grouped around Anthony Eden. Because they are not the ones who will go to war, if it is declared! I will stand firm, Ida, even if I know that Hitler is amoral, perhaps dangerous, most probably a homosexual, I am told, for I will be able to stop him in his desire for destruction. Today I am going to prove to all of them that it is possible to negotiate with Hitler.

I am doing it without great joy, as you know. I am doing it because world peace is at stake.

And because, as so often in history, the interest of the British Crown is intermingled with that of universal peace. And besides, why break today with that doctrine which has brought us happiness and prosperity since the 18th century? Shall we, for a faraway country of which we know nothing, send our boys to their deaths, destroy our fleet, lose India, our interests in Europe and also our positions in Africa and Arabia? It would be suicide!

And I am not alone in thinking that way.

In the course of a dinner at Lord Runciman's a few days ago, I once again had the great pleasure of meeting the new United States ambassador, Joe Kennedy. Very pleasant, very good manners for an American, a man of conviction, too, who doesn't always see eye to eye with Roosevelt, his President. Well, you see, my dear Ida, Kennedy, Runciman and I have all agreed about the Sudetenland, and this necessary sacrifice to our democratic pride. For two reasons:

Because the peace of the world is at stake.

And also – there is no point hiding the fact – because Chancellor Hitler can be of great use to us against our true enemy, Bolshevism. At least you can talk to Hitler – and I am even convinced that neither the industrialists of the Ruhr, nor the officers of the Reichswehr have any cause for complaint. With Stalin that's impossible. He is a predatory bear with but a single dream: to fall upon us, to devour us and our colonies, to destroy our civilisation. Bolshevism is true barbarity. It will respect nothing: not family, or property, or freedom, or the Crown. So that evening we took on board the slogan that had been hurled at us as an insult in the intellectual papers: 'Better Hitler than Stalin'.

To which Lord Runciman, a decidedly poetical character, has given a witty twist: 'Better Hitler than Blum'.

Kennedy and I both roared with laughter.

But thinking about it, what Runciman said is not entirely wrong. We must be wary of Bolshevism and its derivatives. Western socialists – often, it should be pointed out, of Jewish origin like Mr Blum – are attempting to establish questionable regimes in Western Europe.

It is also against them, those Communists in disguise, that Mr Hitler may be valuable to us in Western Europe. On condition that we leave him a free hand in the East. I am not shocked by this, as it was also the doctrine of our ancestors.

Your affectionate Neville.

6

MONSIEUR LÉGER IS OF THE PARTY

The roar of the Air France twin-engine plane, the *Poitou*, dragged him from the torpor into which his dream had plunged him. He turned round in his seat and considered, almost affectionately, his colleagues behind him. There was Clapier, the head of his Cabinet, his companion in misfortune; Alexis Léger; and Charles Rochat, a close colleague of Léger's, the man responsible for 'Europe' at the Quai d'Orsay. As he observed them in turn, studious, concentrated or lost in dreams, he congratulated himself, once again, for not having brought Bonnet, his Minister of Foreign Affairs. Without Bonnet he would be free to move as he wished; they would waste less time bowing and scraping to the British, whispering with his great friends the Italians, or simply in the drawing up of an agreement that the twisted mind of the head of French diplomacy could only complicate.

Léger was the one he had wanted at his side.

Alexis Léger was competent and precise. Indispensable. He had been in one way or another the Minister of Foreign Affairs more or less since the time of the great Aristide Briand, 'the apostle of peace'. Since 1925, in fact. After China, where he had been a mere embassy attaché, Léger had taken Briand's fancy. On the boat on the way back from a conference in Washington, the journalists, after a press conference, had laid siege to President Briand. They harangued him with personal questions, calling upon him to write his memoirs. Briand was in the evening of his life, but had no plans to write anything at all. Léger, who knew him barely at all, listened in a corner, and got him out of his fix in an unusual way. He dared to reply in Briand's place: 'A book is the death of a tree.' Just a simple phrase, and it was love between the legendary old man and the young diplomat. He immediately appointed him head of his Cabinet; they imagined the European peace together; and together they came up with precise, utopian dreams about the construction of this new Europe. The President didn't like Briand, too naïve, too high-flown, too incautious, but he was fascinated by this anecdote told to him by Bonnet, who had it from Emmanuel Berl.

Léger almost dropped out of the trip at the last minute. He had vanished all night, after telling the President that he refused to go to Munich without 'written instructions from his minister' – the minister in question notoriously maintaining a 'soft' stance, while Léger was considered to represent the 'hard' line. Sensibly enough, he wanted to give Léger only simple verbal instructions. Léger, for his part, demanded a written note from his minister, to 'cover himself', according to the prudent practice of the Quai d'Orsay. The President had had to intervene, making promises to one and demands on the other, and flattering them both.

Bonnet had come to Le Bourget, but he had delayed passing on the famous 'written instructions' to Léger. The whole delegation was already aboard the plane, the engines were running and he was still reluctant. Only Bonnet and Léger remained on the tarmac. Léger planted himself in front of his minister. Staring him coldly in the eyes, he demanded his instructions once more: 'Are going to give them to me or not? If you don't give them to me I'm not going.'

Daladier had poked his head out of the cabin. He was getting worried about the situation and the possibility of their being late. Bonnet finally drew an envelope from his pocket with ostentatious bad grace.

So Léger did leave, and with written instructions – the 'soft' minister had given in. Daladier had joked with Léger when they were finally ensconced in the plane: 'So? The guvnor's instructions ...' The two men had exchanged a knowing look. In the end Léger had thought it wise not to read Bonnet's 'instructions' to the President, so familiar was he with the man, his double-dealing and his ulterior motives.

Daladier reflected that Léger, Monsieur Alexis Léger, was a curious character. He liked him, he seemed loyal to him, as much as possible, of course. He was sure at least that Léger would never betray him for his rival Paul Reynaud. He even felt certain affinities with him. They were both *déclassé*. Léger, upper middle-class and from the overseas territories, the son of Creole industrialists who had moved unsuccess-fully to the metropolis; and himself, a deserving scholarship boy. But there was a certain distance between them.

The President was impressed with Léger.

Because he was tall, slender, airy, unlike himself, who was more earth-bound. He had a kind of aristocratic elegance, and that faint Creole accent that no one ever made fun of, unlike his own, which was too Provençal. Not that Presi-dent Daladier was not a handsome man. He was far from hideous, he was pleasing, imposing, but the fashion, it seemed to him, was for tall men. Daladier was short, stocky, solid, well fed. He gave the French every sign of rude health, and that was not something that could be said – he reassured himself – of men who were too handsome, too young.

There were so many things he wished he could say to Léger, but he didn't dare, held back as he was by his shyness, the proprieties, protocol; he wished he could talk to him intimately, as they had talked of Czechoslovakia, about his triple life.

The first life, at the Quai d'Orsay, he knew. He knew the

man's merits, and his shortcomings too: his laziness, his slovenliness when it came to really reading all the diplomatic dispatches; his tendency to hold court in his office with the journalists under his control; and his reputation as a freemason, about which Daladier's secret services had not managed to unearth anything. But none of that was very important. Alexis Léger kept the Quai in order, and he did it rather well.

Alexis Léger's second life, it seemed, was that of an interesting poet, known to a small coterie under an impossible pseudonym: Saint-John Perse. The President had got hold of two of his collections of poetry. He had skimmed through the first one, *Éloges*, published in 1911, and the second, more recent one, *Anabase*, published in 1924. His reaction had been that for a career diplomat Léger had a good style, a little abstract for his taste, since he preferred solid texts, well-structured and backed up with proper documentation. The President had not found the poems displeasing, but had reflected that it was perhaps a little absurd for a senior civil servant of his class to waste his time making rhymes. But in the end, if that was where his fancy took him . . . Why not poetry, or astrology, or even detective novels, if that was what he enjoyed, as long as he remained the great servant of the State?

But what intrigued Daladier above all, even more than the 'Sunday poet', was Léger's third life. The individual lived with his mother and sister in a pretty apartment on the Rue Camoëns, splendid compared to President Daladier's three rooms in the poor 16th arrondissement. And he was, it was said, a bit of a ladies' man. His mistress of the moment was a beautiful Cuban woman; his lifelong mistress was – he knew her well – the influential Duchesse de Flers. She was his close companion, in the eyes of the whole of Paris; and that didn't seem to bother the Duc. Léger lived, so to speak, with the Flers, it was there that he received his visitors, it was there that he hurried to after work at the Quai d'Orsay, he even spent his holidays with them.

The President thought it was curious – and rather flattering – that he and Léger had such a point in common. It was a form of implicit companionship. The President had his marquise, Madame de Crussol; just as Léger had his duchess, Marthe de Flers.

Neither he nor Léger, of course, had ever even considered discussing these associations; ribaldry wasn't their style. And besides, the two women had honourable reputations in society. One, a true aristocrat, née de Cumont, a duchess by her marriage to the Duc de Flers; and the other, née Béziers, as he used to tease her, a Marquise by her marriage to the Marquis de Crussol, himself the grandson of the Duchesse d'Uzès. The President thought it funny that the lovers of the two most powerful women in Paris – with their 'left-wing salons', they made and unmade cabinets – should be on this plane at this moment.

The idea that he was allied to Léger and the Flers, and thus had access to their powerful networks along with those of the Marquise de Crussol, gave him a sense of invulnerability as he set off for Germany. Bonnet could always come with the newspapers he had in his pocket, his friends Berl and Monzie, the Havas agency that he controlled, his handful of deputies in the Chamber! Monsieur Paul Reynaud, a little chap, small-minded too, prepared to do anything to take his place, could go on stamping his feet with impatience, and the Marquise de Portes with him! What was Madame de Portes compared with the joint forces of the Marquise and the Duchesse de Flers?

7

HEADING FOR MUNICH

He would be in Munich in less than three hours. He was glad of the respite. No phone calls during all that time. No signature books to be signed, no ministers to calm, no soldiers to encourage, no journalists to shake up. Especially the soldiers! The President had barely recovered from his rage against them. The previous day, an important military meeting had been held, with him at its centre. The topic was mobilisation, the supply of troops; the officers outlined the problems of passive defence; they lamented the cruel lack of anti-aircraft defence; and they congratulated themselves on the usefulness of the Metro as an air-raid shelter. The President also wished to be informed of the distribution of gas masks to the population. Because France had taken precautions, on this point at least.

The officers were rather undecided. Gamelin turned towards his assistant who, embarrassed, turned towards a less starry general. This man said that it wasn't his affair, and that the gas masks were another department's responsibility. In the face of such carelessness, the President exploded, and everyone started trying to find several million missing gas masks. The civilians in the Cabinet had come to the rescue. The civil servants, the military, the pen-pushers had searched and gone in and out all day. The gas masks could not be found. The President would have fired the War Minister had he not occupied that office himself. Three million gas masks vanishing into thin air! They had to be replaced, as a matter of great urgency. Everyone came out with his own solutions, until one, more daring than the others, suggested that they be ordered from the Czech factories. Their gas masks were reliable, and they were capable of delivering them in time and in the desired quantities.

'That's the state France is in,' frowned the President, stretching out in his Pullman seat, one of the prides of the national airline's MD220.

Even so, he wasn't going to get worked up about it. He tried to go to sleep, to clear his mind. The President maintained that a siesta was necessary to erase anxieties, which he saw, in his peasant way, as wrinkles in the brain. He tried to yield to the rhythm of the plane, to imagine that his soft plunge into the clouds would project him into a protecting universe. He wanted to be cradled. But even though he turned and twisted and tried to find the right position, he couldn't find sleep. There was the whispering of Léger and Rochat. There was the visit from the captain, Durmon, so-proud-to-pilot-the-President-on-the-*Poitou*, specifying the cruising speed, performance, altitude and range of this 'jewel' which had so recently emerged from the Marcel Bloch factories. Then there had been, several times, the diligent steward, determined to give him champagne and something to eat. He had accepted the champagne to get to sleep, he had excused himself from taking any nourishment. But he had started seeking sleep again, with the desperation of a parched man in the desert. He wanted to sleep, not to rest, but to be anaesthetised, to escape all the questions that physically assailed him.

'Why hadn't they been able to contact Chamberlain? What were the British up to?

Might they have changed their minds?

Would they be – who knows? – prepared to intervene to

save Czechoslovakia with us? In that case, with the British Air Force alongside the French, Hitler would have to watch out!

The President wore himself out, first comforting himself, then alarming himself again.

Unless . . .

He sat up in his seat.

Unless the British have suddenly cosied up to Hitler? As they did in the days of Frederick II! It wouldn't be impossible, after all. The British have no pact with the Czechs. Their politics isn't continental . . . And besides, Chamberlain is hardly straight as a die. On the phone, every time we have to talk seriously about the Sudetenland there's interference on the line . . .

. . . And the Germans, is their Siegfried Line really worth less than our Maginot Line?

And the Czech fortifications, don't forget the Czech fortifications . . .

It was with these thoughts, trying to remember the name of the Czech fortification which was, according to Gamelin, more crucial than the others, that the President finally went to sleep.

He was woken over Alsace, on a latitude with Strasbourg. Captain Durmon was keen that the President should see the land of France before crossing into Germany. Daladier allowed himself to be dragged to the cockpit, and asked the captain the whereabouts of the blue line of the Vosges. A horizon was pointed out to him; he saw nothing special and returned to his seat, unsure whether he should be grateful for the attention or furious with this irksome fellow who had dared to drag him from the sleep he had struggled so hard to find.

He couldn't manage to get back to sleep. He tried to busy

himself, and drew from his briefcase a file entitled 'Hitler's Private Life'. It was a note from the French secret service based on dissident German sources. Daladier was used to grubby documents of this kind. He read them distractedly, to complement or invalidate impressions he already had – just as he did with the phone-tap records on which he was so keen. As a result, he told himself, he was better able to judge men and their women, their passions and their weaknesses. But take care, he advised his close colleagues, or the Marquise when she was excessively curious, one must always make moderate and republican use of documents of this kind.

The author of the revelations in question was a former companion of the National Socialist leader, one Otto Strasser. He had been Hitler's confidant since the 1920s, along with his brother Gregor. He had waged many of the movement's early battles, before distancing himself from Hitler, finding him neither 'left-wing enough' nor 'truly revolutionary'. This man Strasser based his statements on a particularly strange relationship that the Führer had had with his young niece, Geli Raubal, the daughter of his half-sister, between 1929 and 1931. He had been over thirty at the time, and was the star of the German political scene; the girl had left the depths of Austria to settle in his apartment at 16 Prinzregentenplatz, in Munich. She wanted, it was said, to become an opera singer. During this period, Adolf and Geli had become inseparable. They went out everywhere together. He took her along to his meetings, he invited her to dinner as if he couldn't live without her. They formed a strange couple, and the young woman exercised, at least at first, a great influence over Adolf Hitler.

According to Strasser's story, one day Hitler had asked the girl to pose naked for him; it wasn't the kind of painting he either did or liked. Artistically, having been cruelly rejected

by the Academy of Fine Arts in Vienna, young Adolf Hitler
was more of a 'postcard-copier'. Within a few months he
had filled whole notebooks in which the young woman posed
in the most unlikely positions. Crude drawings, dirty drawings, filled with crazed violence. Strasser was one of the few
to have held them in his hands. Then the relationship had
become more physical. According to the note from the secret
services, 'Adolf Hitler notably wanted his niece to insult him
and trample on him, and also to strike him with her fists,
her feet and a dog-whip when he was lying naked on the
rug in front of her.'

Daladier, not a prudish man, was stunned. He avidly
continued reading: 'Sometimes Hitler reversed the roles and
struck her too, but never with the violence he demanded of
her.'

The secret note concluded by explaining that it was
probably this 'sado-masochistic relationship' that had led
young Geli to commit suicide in Hitler's apartment on 19th
September 1931, with her uncle's pistol.

Once he had finished reading, the President remained
prostrate in his seat. He didn't even reply to the umpteenth
suggestion from the steward. He was aghast. He sat there
staring at the cover of the file, unable to drag himself away
from those scenes. He saw them over and over again. He
imagined the décor, the time of day for their ceremony, their
revolting gloom, their animal frolics. He couldn't help
thinking about the way he did it with the Marquise.

And what if that was the German's secret, his dark side?
he said to himself, struggling to rein in his imagination. Then
he wondered whether the document might not be a forgery,
a montage assembled by the 'hardliners', a plot by the
Americans or the Jews against Hitler. Why would Otto
Strasser – who wasn't just anybody, who was one of the co-
founders, with Hitler, of National Socialism – why would

someone like that go digging up such dirty stories? And why that story in particular? If Strasser had wanted to damage his former boss, surely he could have come up with something more effective than that. He could have trumpeted that Hitler was impotent, or homosexual, or corrupt . . . But whether or not it was true, the President felt nauseous. He needed to talk about it, to open up to someone about it, or even make a joke on the subject. He thought of Léger behind him, but persuaded himself that it wouldn't be a good idea. He put the file back into his briefcase and tried to go back to sleep.

But he couldn't do it. The spectre of Hitler, a naked Hitler, thin and hairless, suddenly loomed into his head. He was a devil. He yelled, he sprawled. All the emotions he had felt when he had heard that speech on the radio passed through the President's head once more. Particularly fear. Because Hitler didn't talk, he didn't shout, he roared. He was a mad dog, not a political leader. A mad dog . . . Suddenly the President found the comparison troubling: it was the barking of dogs sounding like the roaring of Hitler that he had heard in his dream.

His mind was wandering.

The President wanted to resume control.

All right, so one didn't like Hitler. But one would still have to avoid gossip, and fantasies, and panic. One would have to purge emotion, banish preconceptions, jettison prejudices and even expunge the anti-German racism that he could sense behind the attacks on the Reich Chancellor.

In order to grasp Hitler, one needed a controlling principle.

And there was nothing better in such moments, the President thought with fleeting delight, than Reason. Reason!

Recourse to Reason, examination through Reason, that heady, necessary, life-saving benefit that he had been taught at university. It was the only way to maintain one's course and understand the beast.

He needed to perform a methodical examination.

To find out first of all who Hitler could be compared to – that much was elementary.

Republican, secular, radical and socialist he might have been, but he wasn't thick. He was entirely capable of conceiving of something other than Jules Ferry's Republic. In certain respects he even thought that the British system, for example, was not without its advantages. He envied the stability of his colleagues in Downing Street, who weren't constantly subjected to the infernal war-councils of the French Ministerial Cabinets.

Even Mussolini! The President had finally got to know the fellow. He was a braggart. He was acting out the role of Caesar, but deep down he was old-school, a bit like himself. A defrocked, fanatical, corrupt socialist, it was true. And the President sometimes missed him. Mussolini could have stayed on the right side, our side, if they hadn't annoyed him at the League of Nations over that Abyssinian business. After all, Italy had its right to its own bit of Africa.

Stalin. He was something else. For the President, Stalin was a Georgian first and foremost, and only then a Communist, with all the hang-ups of a great Russian.

The President could understand, identify, pinpoint the others: General Beck in Poland, Salazar in Portugal, and perhaps tomorrow that man Franco.

But Hitler was something else.

The President didn't understand him at all.

Of course he had never revealed any of his confusion in the face of the enigma that was Hitler, not in public or with his ministers, or even with the Marquise. None of his political positions could have indicated the slightest weakness in the face of Germany. Besides, nothing could have given a glimpse, during the Councils of Ministers, of the doubts that assailed him. Wasn't President Daladier the promoter of rearmament, the first of France's defenders? And that was something the Parisian newspapers shouldn't be allowed to forget!

But there was nothing to be done about it. The Hitler question threw him – and the President didn't like that.

Hitler remained impossible to grasp, even with the deployment of reason. He was neither a traitor originally from the left, nor a tsar, nor even a *general de pronunciamiento*.

Hitler was something else.

The President had given the matter much thought. He had read, he had gathered information, he had left behind the Carolingian Middle Ages, his favourite field, to become fixated on the German question. He had considered the idea – on which opinion was somewhat divided – that the master of Germany was a 'new Bismarck'. Apart from German unification, the Reich to which they both referred, that was where the comparison ended as far as the President was concerned. He had also envisaged Hitler as a new Frederick II, a portrait of whom the Führer had apparently hung in his Berlin office. He had turned his attention towards the life of the 'enlightened despot' who had waged the Seven Years War with financial support from England. But Frederick II had protected Voltaire and loved France, while Hitler saw France as 'the hereditary enemy'.

He had listened to various voices. Jouvenel, explaining that Hitler was a kind of 'Teutonic Mohammed'. Louis Bertrand, defending the idea that he was a 'German Napoleon'. The President had nearly thrown him out of his office. Napoleon, Napoleon, Napoleon! He had reflected that this dignitary, who had been head over heels in love when he returned from the Berlin Games to which he had been invited, must have been brainwashed by the German Propaganda department.

He had even heard a British diplomat explaining to him that Hitler was no more dangerous than a 'Gandhi in jackboots' – the expression was said to come from Sir Nevile Henderson himself.

After thinking for a while, the President found all these ideas dizzying and slightly insane.

Then he tried to think differently about Hitler, dismissing the reflex antipathy that darkened the minds of the Parisian editorialists, over-sensitive housewives or over-anxious Jews.

Using empathy, which involved no commitments.

He wanted to think about Hitler without prejudice, that was it, free of all prejudices.

He wanted to think of him as a tough adversary, a rather special colleague.

And basically he was a German colleague.

A German colleague.

He liked that idea. And what was more, it wasn't inaccurate.

Hadn't he and Hitler come to power at the same time, the same day, a few hours apart? On 30th January 1933, the German Adolf Hitler became Chancellor of Germany; while the Frenchman Daladier was being appointed to the Presidency of the Council. The President had often been troubled by that fact.

For the first time, on both sides of the Rhine, in each of the two ancestrally enemy countries, two veterans of the Great War, two men in their forties, two new men reached the pinnacle of their respective states. He had always seen that similarity as more than coincidental. Almost a case of twinship, a great hope, or perhaps a great threat, something which – it was certain – was going to link their fate.

And then there was another reason to remember that day. While in Berlin Hitler triumphed, surrounded by his troops, in a city lit with torches, in the middle of an ecstatic crowd, Daladier was struggling. He had no government, and he was fighting the socialists who refused to join it. They were there, facing him, five stubborn socialists, Auriol, Compère-Morel, Frossard, Lebas and Jules Moch. And he tried once again to convince them. He had dropped everything except the reduced military budgets demanded by the socialists. He had pleaded, tried to demonstrate that he, Daladier, remained true to Jaurès, that they had to abandon their historical isolation. He was busy proposing five posts and a vice-presidency to them when an usher entered the room.

An urgent dispatch.

Adolf Hitler had just been appointed Chancellor.

There had been a moment's hesitation in the little gathering, universal disbelief. The socialists had not seemed to take the affair very seriously, at least as far as the President could remember.

'How could the Germans and old Hindenburg put that hothead, that fairground freak in power?'

Daladier had pleaded again:

'Shouldn't this new fact be taken into account?'

He had pressed the point, to shake them from their dangerous intransigence.

For the socialists, nothing needed changing. Except if he accepted the reduction in military expenditure.

The President and the socialists had abruptly parted.

As he recalled that meeting, an old rage came back to him.

He invited Léger to sit down next to him before they landed in Munich; to make one final point, he insisted. In fact he wanted to share his returning rancour: 'Dear Léger, I've been reading the *Populaire* over the past few days, those socialists have become incorrigible sermonisers. They're claiming to have been the first people to be anti-Hitler. They weren't so clear-sighted in 1933 . . . Those chaps in the Second International didn't want to "change anything about their position", as they said, because basically those Parisians, with their cushy jobs, those birdbrains, didn't give a tinker's curse about Hitler. They were interested in nothing but their Proletarian "base", as they called it, and in letting the workers have the weekend off. Incapable of putting their drawing-room anti-fascism into practice! And to think that these are the same people who, for months now, even this very morning, have been dragging my name through the mud in their newspapers for not having declared war already. They're crying wolf, they're ordering me to slit the throat of Nazism with my bare hands, and save their great friend, while at the same time putting spokes in my wheels. The hypocrites . . .'

And once again he started complaining about the Parisians, the 'soft' politicians, the 'hard' senior officials, the military men and their gas masks, the teachers and their pacifist petition and the workers with their forty-hour week: 'Oh, if only I'd succeeded then! If only they'd followed me on Hitler in 1933! Then Europe wouldn't be here on the brink of war. But I've been hobbled, resisted, defamed. I've been hindered by those impotent republicans. Oh! My dear Léger! There are days when you could envy them, the Mussolinis and the Hitlers! Those dictators send Monsieur Blum screaming, but at least they're free to do what they like. They aren't kept from governing. They don't have to face succumbing to the dirty tricks of the parliamentarians. They alone, no doubt about it, they alone have the means to lead their country, their politics.'

The President abruptly broke off his bitter tirade. He was relieved. A moment later he went on amicably: 'But in the end, my dear Léger, I am a republican, and I am not about to reinvent myself.'

8

RIBBENTROP ON THE TARMAC

Until then, it had been nothing but a dreaded abstraction, front page headlines in the papers, and maps, more and more maps of Czechoslovakia and the Sudetenland. This time he was there. In Munich, the welcome on the tarmac had given him a kind of mental preparation. When he started down the steps of the plane, Clapier held him back by the sleeve. Down below, the company engaged to receive him consisted not of Wehrmacht soldiers but of SS troops. And Clapier wasn't sure that the SS could be considered an official army. They would have to delay matters, they were going to check. The President and Léger exchanged a worried glance. He asked in a muffled voice, but in an imperative tone: 'The protocol, what does the protocol say?'

The welcome committee was waiting below the plane, every second counted. The head of the Cabinet having found no answer to this explosive question, either from Léger or Rochet, Daladier poked his head out of the cabin and immediately drew it back in. The vision of an endless row of men in black, with helmets and boots, all standing to attention, was startling. Behind him, the President heard Léger prompting him: 'Go on . . . go on, Mr President. And anyway, we have no choice . . .' He really did have no choice: the Reich Minister of Foreign Affairs, Joachim von Ribbentrop, observed all this, the hesitation and the whispering.

Finally the President came down the steps.

They noticed that Ribbentrop hadn't changed in five years.

The Aryan type. A real advertisement for the Third Reich. Tall, fair, distinguished, vain-looking, pale eyes that didn't look at anything, a block of ice, but what presence! The two men rapidly shook hands, Daladier forced a kind of prickly manliness, the German remaining distant, barely polite. There was nothing to suggest that the two men had known each other for a long time – and besides, who could have imagined it?

Standing at the bottom of the steps, Daladier tried to regain his composure. He turned round to check that his colleagues were there, muttered pointless introductions, and made as if to sniff the air, fine weather in Munich. The red carpet was there waiting for him, and Daladier still didn't move. He was hesitating because of the SS men. Ribbentrop leaned over to him, then took his arm, almost firmly, and walked him away. The 'Horst Wessel Song' had just come to an end. The 'Marseillaise' rang out, played heavily, pompously, as if unbalanced by the German temperament. Daladier made up his mind to walk past these blond giants with a slow, anxious, uncertain step. His eyes were turned towards them, but failed to see them.

The journey from the airport to the city had been awkward. Sitting in the huge Mercedes convertible, the two men hadn't uttered a word to each other. Daladier knew exactly where he stood. Ribbentrop was the enemy of the day, everyone had told him that. He wanted war, and he was opposed to the principle of the Munich meeting. Ribbentrop had been Minister of Foreign Affairs for only a few months. He was the instrument of Hitler, who had decided to extend his power that year. Like Field Marshal Keitel, who had been placed at the head of the army at the same time, he was an unconditional supporter of Hitler, a zealous servant. Rather as in France, the President had persuaded himself,

the Führer's entourage must contain both 'hard' and 'soft'
... Ribbentrop was among the 'hardliners' of the regime,
perhaps the 'hardest'. And he was after revenge. He had
just been excluded from the triumphal Anschluss six months
previously, in favour of his rival Göring – the chief representative of the German 'soft' stance. Even though he was
the new Minister of Foreign Affairs, Göring bypassed him
while he was on an official trip to London. The humiliation had been great in the eyes of the British, whom he
hated because he had known them so well in the past, first
as a travelling salesman and then as an ambassador.

Where the Sudetenland was concerned, however, Ribbentrop had refused to be messed around. He had even obtained
from the Führer the commitment that Göring would no
longer encroach upon his foreign policies. Once again, he
was an influential warmonger. The previous day he had
almost sabotaged the Munich conference. Knowing where
they stood, the two men eschewed diplomatic manners. What
was the point of wasting time? The President had decided
to confront the Germans; not to stand on ceremony with
them like those bloody British.

Édouard Daladier preferred to contemplate the Bavarian
countryside. The procession of villages, the suburbs of the
city, the denser public gatherings, the sunny weather in the
German south, were his meagre distractions. He darted a
brief sideways glance at Ribbentrop.

The Reich Minister stayed as stiff as an automaton. His
eye was fixed on the road, frozen in his posture as a great
man of the Reich. The President chuckled inwardly as he
saw him like that: 'This man is a genius . . . a second Bismarck
according to Hitler! This former champagne salesman!'

Ribbentrop, before becoming a minister or the ambassador to London, had in fact been the – very well known –

representative of Pommery champagne. He had also become the son-in-law of the magnate of German sparkling wine, the extremely wealthy Henkell. Since 1933, the ambitious Ribbentrop had been a sort of foreign affairs adviser to Hitler. The Ministry and the secret service at Wilhelmstrasse were still a long way from being Nazified at the time, Hitler complained, he didn't trust them. So he relied on Ribbentrop and his networks. The man travelled a lot. Thanks to his professional cover, he was thus at the head of a number of influential Nazi agencies from Paris to London: the famous 'Ribbentrop Office' dreaded by all western diplomatic organisations. For Daladier, Ribbentrop remained Hitler's evil genius. And that was what he would still be today. He would be the obstacle during the conference. Daladier tried to think of the best way of getting round him.

He was lost in his tactical thoughts when, once they had arrived at the hotel booked for the French delegation, Ribbentrop finally spoke, a few sour words.

'If only you had wanted to, five years ago. If only you had listened to Brinon. We wouldn't have come to this!'

The Frenchman reflexively lowered his head. It was something he hadn't expected, that misplaced, almost intimate remark, just as they arrived in Munich. He didn't reply, just a nod of the head, heavy and awkward, indicating regrets, complications of life and a secret shared.

After a moment the President managed to say, 'You're telling me . . .'

1933, THE BRINON MISSION

I gave a start at the mention of Brinon's name.

Brinon . . . Fernand de Brinon . . . The Vichy government's ambassador to Paris, under the Occupation; the most zealous servant of the Germans, who made Pétain and Laval look like 'Gaullist dissidents'. I remembered him as the worst man in the French Collaboration. He had also been in charge during the grotesque and pathetic exile of the government to Sigmaringen, in the summer of 1944! Brinon, wicked Brinon, whose Jewish wife was one of the few 'honorary Aryans' in the Third Reich, condemned to death for sharing intelligence with the enemy and participating in the pseudo-government of Sigmaringen, executed on 15th April 1947 at the Fort of Montrouge.

No, it couldn't be. The President was surely mistaken. Not the same Brinon. What did he have to do with this business?

'Brinon? Which Brinon was Ribbentrop talking about in this car? The French Nazi? Fernand de Brinon!'

'Hang on . . . You've heard of Brinon, and you're an American woman! Oh, Brinon, it's a long story . . . He wasn't just the chief French Nazi in 1945. That's right at the end of it all. I knew Brinon a long time before, in 1922. He was a journalist with the *Journal des débats*, a moderate and pretty harmless publication. Brinon was radical like me, a veteran like me. He was a pleasant man, an aristocrat from the Libournais, in the Gironde, his family must have come down in the world. Very quickly, in the 1920s, Brinon had become a journalist who was especially valued for his deep understanding of German questions, and an ardent partisan of Franco-German *rapprochement*. He spent his life between Paris and Berlin, where he knew just about all the party heads. And he wasn't particularly Nazi. He associated with the German Social Democrat leaders as easily as he would associate with the Nazi bosses.

'Of course, when I became President of the Council in 1933, I was very interested in Brinon's knowledge of Germany. I had followed the rise of Hitler; it had worried me. I was all too familiar with the imperfections of the Versailles Treaty, and I dreaded the party that could pull Hitler out of the humiliation of the Germans. I had told myself we had to get a move on.

'I had just come to power; so had Hitler. Perhaps it was an opportunity. *Rapprochement* was in the air. My attitude then was that "the time had come", and that "if a veteran didn't do it, who would?"

'So as soon as I attained the Presidency of the Council, I entrusted Fernand de Brinon with an unofficial mission along these lines.'

'What do you mean, "with this in mind"? What was the nature of this unofficial mission?'

'Organising an official meeting with Hitler. The great Reconciliation between France and Germany, that's what.'

'As soon as you came to power?'

'You're surprised? I'd become aware of the danger of the situation in Germany. I thought this might be a way of containing it. I have to admit that I'd spent a fair amount of time on the project of meeting Hitler in 1933, and even in 1934, I think . . . That sort of stubbornness really surprises you, does it? People who haven't known war – I mean the Great War – can't understand! And besides, what was so scandalous about wanting to meet Chancellor Hitler in 1933?

'The desire to get on with Germany was on everyone's mind in France. The war veterans, many of whom were in power, said, "Never again." Briand and the poets dreamed of universal harmony, of Peace in Europe. I'd seen – as I told you – a sign in the fact of our coming to power at the same time. I thought that people like Hitler, like me, were the relief guard. For me, at any rate, that was the great theme of the summer of 1933.'

'But why Brinon? You already had François-Poncet in the embassy in Berlin; you also had a good Minister of Foreign Affairs, Paul-Boncour.'

'I didn't want to go through official channels, for fear of leaks. The Quai d'Orsay wasn't involved, and neither was François-Poncet in Berlin. How should I put it . . . I trusted Brinon, and he had lots of contacts. He could get through to Hitler, he'd told me. He'd made the acquaintance of Ribbentrop a short time before, in 1932, at the Polignacs' during a hunt. He had been introduced to the German, who was still in the champagne trade, by an old comrade-in-arms, Guy de Wendel, who went on to become a fierce anti-Nazi. From that point on there was a bond between the two men.'

'So in 1933 people contacted Hitler via Ribbentrop?'

'That's right, and during the summer of 1933, and into 1934, Brinon and I saw a lot of each other. I remember a meeting at Brinon's flat in Neuilly. And there were other meetings, too, probably after I saw to it that Brinon was awarded the Légion d'Honneur. It was in Vichy. I was taking the waters, it's pleasant there in the summer. I had been widowed shortly before. I decided to avoid the Hôtel du Parc and the Hôtel des Ambassadeurs and took up residence in a villa, far from the thermal baths, which were too busy.

I was accompanied by my trusty Clapier and my friends, the Brinons. They were so funny in those days, so popular, so considerate towards me. No hints of what was to come. Nothing to suggest that they would become – ten years later – the most unusual couple in the Collaboration. Because Madame de Brinon, Lise, was Jewish. Which just goes to show . . . I liked her, I called her "the Colonel". I think she's still alive, and that after Brinon's execution in 1947, she remade her life with another extremist in the Collaboration, Benoist-Méchin. She must be addicted to *collabos* . . .

'Our residence in Vichy was discreet. Ribbentrop could stop off there without being seen. I'd done a bit of research into Ribbentrop: his childhood in Canada, his good war in the Air Force, his Social Democrat and Jewish friends, joining the Nazi Party in 1932, and his life as a great European traveller. Ribbentrop was the ideal man for this kind of mission. He wasn't yet an official, but he was very influential. Hitler – and he wasn't close to Hitler – was grateful to him because in January 1933 the main secret meetings – which led to his assumption of power – had been held in his Berlin villa. It was there that Hitler had had to reassure, pamper, lull the German right wing, Von Papen, and the son of President Hindenburg on whom everything depended! That fact, widely boasted of by Brinon, had impressed me.

'During those fine evenings in Vichy, August 1933, we talked a lot, Ribbentrop, Brinon and I. About the Great Reconciliation, of course! I've retained a strange, very sweet memory of it. We were standing in one of those gardens in Vichy planted by the benefactress of the spa, Empress Eugénie, who – it was claimed – had lived in the house . . . Two Frenchmen, a German, three war veterans, three utopians – yes. We were dreaming out loud.'

'What exactly was said during those secret meetings?'

'Precise and important things about the future of our

respective countries. We told the German how terrible we
thought reparation policy was after the Great War, how
intolerable it was to the Germans; that the Americans were
excessively harsh, so un-European, requiring the repayment
of war loans from a destitute France – which led us, alas,
to be intransigent with Germany. Ribbentrop had even – as
I remember – shown his sentimental side and proclaimed,
after a famous and emotional dinner: "The Führer is a quiet
type. Like President Daladier. Neither of them are particularly loquacious." The Brinons, staggered, had loudly
concurred. I had wanted to disagree. I just put on a show
of modesty; but – to tell you the truth – I'd been flattered
by the comparison.

'Besides, our plan was precise. We'd imagined a highly
symbolic meeting between myself and Hitler. A spectacular
reconciliation, the kind that shakes up people's minds, the
minds of the war veterans, and future generations, too. I'd
imagined this meeting on the 14th-century bridge at Kehl,
the first one to be built across the Rhine. Quite a symbol!

'We'd also discussed a whole series of things, apart from
the place, a date, the best time of year, the building of a
gigantic monument to the victims of the war. We had even,
at Brinon's suggestion, gone into details such as the two film
companies we would invite for the occasion – one French,
one German, none Anglo-Saxon. Brinon had started
dreaming of a big Franco-German journal, of which he would
be the editor-in-chief, of course, and all the trips of bosses and
artists that would be organised between the two countries.'

'In concrete terms, what was your battle-plan?'

'We'd opted for discretion, I told you. Ribbentrop and I
were too familiar with the petty jealousies at the Quai
d'Orsay, the low tricks of Wilhelmstrasse, Blum's resistance,
Göring's jealousy. We knew them too well to risk any indis-
cretion. So Brinon was given the task of going to Germany

in early September. When he was there he had two important discussions handled by Ribbentrop. The first with
General von Blomberg, the Reich War Minister, in which
they brought up the delicate question of the restoration of
the Saar to Germany as well as military and customs issues.
The second discussion was more decisive. It was with Hitler
in Berchtesgaden, at the Eagle's Nest. Their conversation
lasted two hours, in the presence of von Blomberg and
Ribbentrop. Brinon introduced himself as a "friend and
emissary of the President of the French Council" and also
as a war veteran. He came to me with a long message:
Hitler's demands.

'The Saarland, "which is German, was to return to
Germany".

'Two: reparations were to be eased.

'Three: the African colonies, part of which was to be ceded
to Germany.

'With my permission, Brinon published an interview with
the Führer in the 22nd November edition of *Le Matin*. I've
found the copy for you. In it, Hitler declared,

If France intends to base her security on Germany's material
inability to defend herself, there is nothing to be done. But
if France allows her security to be found in a freely discussed
agreement, I am prepared to hear anything. [. . .] The League
of Nations is an international parliament in which different
power groups oppose and agitate one another. Misunderstandings are aggravated rather than resolved. I am always
willing [. . .] to undertake negotiations with people willing to
talk to me. [. . .] It is not my intention to attack my neighbours.

'I found all that encouraging. I entrusted Brinon with the
task of setting off for Berlin with fresh instructions. But all

of a sudden, the tone had changed. Germany had slammed the door on the League of Nations. Hitler's conditions had hardened. But I hadn't given up.

'Contacts with Ribbentrop continued throughout 1934. But I realised that my desire for *rapprochement* was not compatible with the regime of the Third Republic. I had to consult Parliament, I had to take the Quai d'Orsay into account, I had to explain myself to my party. And then I started to develop suspicions about Brinon. He was insistent that we should resume the path of Franco-German *rapprochement*. But he was an odd character, a bit of a maverick. And he was very short of money. I knew that he'd started working for the Germans, crassly using this Franco-German committee for which I'd organised the subsidies. Oh, nothing too reprehensible, at least at first: confecting files for the press, a few summaries for Ribbentrop, the organisation of a few pleasure trips for French personalities to the 1936 Berlin Olympic Games.'

'And do you now regret that failed meeting?'

'Sometimes. I've sometimes rebuked myself for stalling, for listening to the ministers who advised me to refuse dialogue with Hitler, who told me that any relationship with Hitler would be a confession of weakness! Why did I need to toe the League of Nations line, when the League of Nations finally disappeared?'

10

THE VIER JAHRESZEITEN HOTEL

The Vier Jahreszeiten Hotel is an old establishment of excellent reputation, the French consul had suggested. The French delegation settled in there before midday. The French President came charging across the hotel hall, shoulders hunched, hidden behind his hat, jacket-collar turned up, a cigarette between his lips. Blinking into the flashes of the international press, he answered no questions, just pulled a disagreeable grimace. He was trying to find his senior colleagues, a way out, a lift, his room, peace to prepare for the summit. He walked on without seeing; he bumped into a group of hotel guests, brushed aside a few hangers-on. He paid no attention to anyone, not to the manager of the hotel, bowed and voluble, nor to the concierges who graciously chorused, '*Willkommen in München, Herr Präsident.*' He raged along like a bull. He was uncommunicative. He barely listened to Léger, who was worried because he had still heard nothing from the British. He was concentrating. He wanted to lose nothing of his strength, that energy that he had been accumulating for a month, of the resolutions he had made the previous day. No one would make him sacrifice his ally Czechoslovakia. The flags of the four nations on all the buildings, the crowd massing all the way to the airport, the horde of journalists and the eagerness of the bellboys seemed to have spurred his determination.

At last he was in Munich.

* * *

Once he was in his presidential suite, Daladier congratulated the ambassador on his choice of hotel. The ambassador blushed with pleasure even though had had nothing
to do with it. François-Poncet was an excellent diplomat.
He was part of that generation when there were fewer than
twenty French ambassadors, they had names like Charles-
Roux or Léon Noël, and enjoyed formal precedence over
their ministers. Moustachioed, nimble, witty, this former
journalist, former deputy, former State under-secretary, was
said to be the best-dressed diplomat in Berlin. He wasn't a
career diplomat – which must have embarrassed Léger – but
in the seven years that he had spent in Berlin, the German
graduate had ended up very close to Hitler's circle.

Now the ambassador to Berlin had become the focus of
the President's attention, that much was clear. He was capti-
vating, he was amusing, people listened to him seriously,
and he wasn't unhappy about that, particularly in front of
Alexis Léger. He was fired up by the boss's interest; the President needed to hear about Hitler and the Germans 'from
the horse's mouth', he had said, thinking that he would
thereby honour the ambassador. Léger, still on the telephone,
and Rochat, hanging around, had abruptly vanished from
the presidential field of vision. Clapier had moved aside;
he was used to that. François-Poncet was the man of the
moment, the man in the know.

To whet his appetite, the President began by interrogating
François-Poncet about his discussion with Hitler the previous
day, the one that had sparked the Munich summit. The boss
had received the dispatch from the Quai, but he wanted
precise details.

François-Poncet told him he had reached the Chancellery
at eleven o'clock. The corridors were bustling with generals.
Hitler had organised a lunch with the commanders of the
invasion unit. He had bumped into Ribbentrop before being

introduced to a Hitler who was 'nervous, tense . . . his expression animated'. The Führer had listened to him respectfully, as he always had done during the five years of their association. He had been particularly attentive when François-Poncet had said, 'You are wrong, Chancellor, if you think you can confine the conflict to Czechoslovakia. If you attack this country, you will set the whole of Europe aflame.' Hitler, turning abusive again, seemed inflexible. But he had replied politely to François-Poncet before lashing out at Beneš, shouting this time. François-Poncet, though, had persevered. The discussion had been interrupted by the unexpected arrival of the Italian ambassador, Attolico.

The President, throughout François-Poncet's story, had been impatient, greedy for details, and proud of his ambassador's audacity. He was concerned, avid, he wanted to know more and yet more . . . He paced around the room, arms behind his back, body bent, his forehead in a frown that some thought concealed an inner ferment. It was the posture of Napoleon before a battle. He rattled off questions at François-Poncet without looking at him.

'In what state of mind did you find him?'

'How long did the discussion last?'

'Was he excited, as he was when he delivered his speech at the Sportpalast?'

'What is the word about his health?'

'How is he getting on with Göring?'

'And with that extremist Ribbentrop?'

The ambassador tried to reply diligently, precisely and in a nuanced manner, weighing up the pros and cons like a good Quai d'Orsay diplomat. At each reply from the ambassador, the President nodded. Sometimes he was surprised and froze suddenly as he learned a fact hitherto unknown to him. For example that it had been Göring who had wanted the conference, and that he had persuaded Hitler 'behind Ribbentrop's back'. The President's intuition was thus confirmed: in Berlin, too, there were 'soft' men on whom one would have to rely and 'hard' ones whom one would have to mistrust.

But time was pressing. The ambassador went on talking for too long. And when an impatient Daladier quizzed him again about political divisions within the Third Reich, François-Poncet began to reply efficiently, in a kind of telegraphic jargon.

'Against war . . . Field Marshal Göring. Against war . . . the former Minister of Foreign Affairs von Neurath. Against war . . . Secretary of State von Weizsäcker.'

A moue of interest from Daladier at the mention of Field Marshal Göring.

'For war . . . Ribbentrop. For war, the regime's extremists such as the head of the SS, Himmler . . .'

The telegraphic method seemed to suit the President. François-Poncet continued:

'But the German population . . . apathetic. They would be inclined against an intervention in Czechoslovakia . . .'

Daladier raised his head. He was radiant. More and more the President appreciated the man and his information. François-Poncet then took advantage of this to slip in another piece of good news; and this time he risked developing it further:

'And it also seems that the Wehrmacht is also against war. It is said that the military hierarchy doesn't share Chancellor Hitler's views. There is even talk of a 'generals' plot'. Colonel Oster of the Abwehr has divulged information to the British. Along with Lieutenant Colonel Gerhard Graf von Schwerin, he is said to have tried to encourage them to show themselves firm against Hitler. He and other superior officers including General Halder, the head of the General Staff, were supposed to be heading up a conspiracy against Hitler. Many

other members of the army were said to have been contacted
on this occasion, including General Beck. Both he and
Admiral Canaris, the head of the Abwehr, said they were
prepared to launch a coup d'état in the event of war against
Czechoslovakia.'

Daladier burst out laughing, François-Poncet blanched.

The President didn't believe a word of this 'nonsense',
which Chamberlain had already mentioned to him in London
on 19th September. He suddenly blew up over this information, which frustrated his meagre certainties. It was a
fairytale, a bad spy novel, worse than that, a trap . . .

The ambassador had committed the imprudence of passing
on this balderdash. He immediately felt his credit with the
President melting away. He wanted to make up for it, and
decided to develop a theme that would make Léger pale
with jealousy. He began in a learned manner: 'And then
there is one factor that should not be neglected. The Austrian
precedent . . .'

Daladier was intrigued. François-Poncet explained that
according to his moderate friends in Berlin, Hitler reproached
himself for not having 'swallowed up Bohemia at the same
time as Austria, six months ago'. That winning without a
fight in Austria had frustrated his desire for military glory.

That perspective suddenly cast a shadow over the President. He paused thoughtfully for a long while.

But like an anxious student swotting up at the last moment,
a host of neglected questions came billowing into his mind
like so many worries.

A chance that he might reason with Hitler?

A way of counteracting Ribbentrop's influence?

The state of progress of the Siegfried Line which – isn't
this right? – wasn't a match for our Maginot Line?

The mood in Austria after the Anschluss? How many
German divisions were there down there?

And the Romanians, would they let the Soviet planes pass over their territory if Stalin came to the aid of Czechoslovakia?

The last confidences of the Russian ambassador to Berlin? Will they move?

Or do we have to forget the Soviets once and for all?

Was the German invasion plan of recent origin? Or did it date back to November, 1937, the moment when the 'French secret service' had warned of the existence of a mysterious 'Hossbach Protocol'?

The President began firing off questions again, and the ambassador took the bombardment without displeasure. For him, it was an opportunity to shine, to make himself as indispensable as Léger, really assure himself of that embassy in Rome – the Farnese palace, a paradise! – that had been promised him; or – one never knows – one day to replace Léger himself at the head of the Quai – if the warmongering Massigli didn't get the job. Weren't people saying that Léger was worn out, stuck in his Briandiste routine, increasingly outmoded?

One last time the President interrogated François-Poncet about the likelihood that Hitler was bluffing. One last time he worried about knowing which factor in Berlin, the 'soft' or the 'hard', had stolen a lead over the other. He had just landed in an unknown, dangerous world. And he was trying with all his might to put Hitler in his own Republican, French, radical, socialist boots. It was a touching spectacle

At the end of this invigorating diplomatic report, the President groaned with pleasure: 'Thank you, Poncet . . . Thank you, Poncet.' He was grateful to him. He had been greedy for information. Now he was sated.

The President suddenly remembered that the others were there. Clapier standing to attention, holding out his coat; Rochat agitated, worried because he had heard nothing from a contact of his from the Quai – and his files – which were probably lost somewhere in Munich. And Léger, indispensable Léger, who had been hanging on the telephone since their arrival. With a jerk of his chin, Daladier inquired whether there was a problem, but Léger didn't reply. He was deep in conversation, and his face was pale. The most courteous Secretary General of the Quai d'Orsay finally blurted a resounding – and very French – insult at the person at the other end before hanging up.

'What on earth's going on, my dear Léger,' asked Daladier, exaggerating his affable Provençal accent.

'It's impossible to get in touch with Chamberlain, Horace Wilson or any Englishmen at all! A moment ago they hadn't even reached the Hotel Regina. Now the hotel switchboard is having problems.'

11

THE *LIKEABLE* FIELD MARSHAL GÖRING

Field Marshal Hermann Göring was standing at the bottom of the big staircase, in the teeming hall, surrounded by his administrators. The President slowed down to get a better view of him. So this was the famous Göring, the second-in-command of the Third Reich, Prime Minister of Prussia, President of the Reichstag, the Reich's master huntsman, and the Führer's designated successor. The head of the terrifying Luftwaffe, the man who kept Daladier awake at night, Daladier and all the French and even the British; who threatened to rain destruction down on Paris or London; who threw everyone into a state of terror with his mysterious long-range bombers. For over twenty years he had seen so many photographs of the man that he almost seemed to know him.

The first time he had seen him was in 1918. His unit had taken an enemy trench, and as they settled into it they found a corpse, taken by surprise while reading a magazine about aviation. On the cover was Captain Göring, successor to the Red Baron von Richthofen. Since then, celebrity had never deserted Göring. The President also remembered that portrait of Göring – that must have been at the end of the 1920s – in which the 'super-ace' posed, in the style of the Harcourt Studio in Paris, like a film star, a cherubic expression, velvet eyes, martial posture, brilliantined hair, something of Rudolf Valentino about him, although in an even more bombastic version. An old hero and a new political leader, from the 1920s onwards he had lent Hitler his legend and a bit of respectability.

Seeing the President coming down the stairs, Göring grew animated. He left his troop behind and came towards the Frenchman, jovial, open-faced, extending a generous hand. Daladier was tempted to close up as the massive Göring hurried towards him; but after Ribbentrop's icy welcome at the airport, the President couldn't help responding to his warmth, his hospitable arms, his humane expression, and finding him likeable. Noting as he did so that the Field Marshal's ceremonial uniform, so white that it hurt the eye, and in which his nineteen-stone body must have been dripping with sweat, didn't exactly suit him.

But more than the many titles of the Reich's second-in-command, an actress wife twenty years his junior, a colossal fortune, dozens of factories that he had taken over all through the country, it was Göring the 'super-ace' who was impressing the President now.

Slightly troubled by these reflections, he scrutinised the only decoration that the Field Marshal – said to be greedy for medals and diamonds – was wearing today: the most beautiful, the most famous, he knew, the Cross of Merit. For a long time the Prussian decoration had been the highest German decoration, and the most prestigious of the First World War. In the Air Force, it rewarded the glory of the knights of the sky. When wearing uniform the recipients had to wear the insignia, a blue Maltese cross with eagles between the arms, engraved with a crown and the gilded words: 'For Merit'.

Facing the hero of 1918, suddenly Daladier found himself transformed. He rediscovered the reflexes of the young officer he had been in those days. The old feelings, the hierarchies of youth long fled, as if petrified in the depths of his soul, had re-emerged. His admiration was intact. Now he was no longer the French President.

He had become once more the earthbound soldier of 1914, the volunteer sergeant in the 258th infantry regiment. Twenty years, a prodigious career, even national borders had been swept away at a stroke. Once again he was the man of the earth, with mud as a second skin and otters for company. The man who raised his eyes to the sky to flee his wretchedness, fascinated by the aerial jousting of those knights of the air who bore names like Guynemer, Richthofen or Göring, and who could sometimes be recognised in flight by their colours and their coats of arms. Because despite Daladier's haughty patriotism, the exploits of Captain Göring had really fired his imagination. He remembered the story told him by a young French airman, former Polytechnicien student and Protestant. In 1918 he had proudly related how he had been shot down over the Somme by Captain Hermann Göring. The French plane was ablaze; the German had flown over, turned to greet him and check that he was alive, and flown off with panache and a beat of his wings, without finishing him off.

Once his initial excitement had passed, the President regained control of himself. He told himself that he was still the French leader. He regained some solemnity when the Field Marshal delivered a kind of 'welcome' speech in singsong French. The Frenchman attempted to reply with the same warmth in florid German. He didn't make too much of an effort. He reflected, to make himself feel comfortable, that Göring was the man of peace in Berlin, and inevitably the enemy of Ribbentrop. Which in these circumstances amounted to saying that he was a friend; in spite of embassy gossip that Göring had compared Czechoslovakia to 'an inflamed appendix requiring operation'. An excess of oratory, certainly, of the kind that one often heard in France, even at the Radical Party conferences where one heard so much nonsense.

Göring chatted away, Daladier stared at him, he wanted to be able to trust him. He was feeling better, but all of a sudden he smelled a heavy, strong, sweet smell all around him. Of incense, of perfume, the kind that a tart would trail through the hall as she passed. The emanations reached him, more and more strongly.

It was Göring, he was wearing perfume.

The President was stupidly troubled. He found that strange. But he had been warned, the Reich second-in-command was a little odd. He liked jewels, he collected paintings and castles, he saw himself as a 'Renaissance man'. He had turned his chief residence into a gigantic mausoleum, in memory of his first, Swedish, wife. He had a personal fleet of ten Condor aeroplanes, an extravagant wardrobe, dozens of ceremonial uniforms cut from every cloth, especially the most garish, which he designed himself, and which he changed, it was said, several times a day. Some even said that in one of his palaces, a residence worthy of a European monarch, he received dinner guests wearing a pink kimono and mules the same colour, and no one was shocked. In Monsieur Hitler's very puritanical Third Reich everything about Göring was accepted, from looting of the worst kind to the use of morphine.

Once the salutations were exhausted, the Field Marshal wanted to chat to the President. And, more particularly, to be seen with him. He led him into the hall, held him by the arm, conversed with him as if they were taking the waters together. They took a few steps like that. Suddenly photographers appeared. Daladier gave a start, Göring waved them away, and the two men resumed their walk towards the cortège waiting in the street.

*   *   *

In the revolving door of the hotel where they were staying, Léger walked towards Daladier. 'There's an emergency,' he whispered. Léger still hadn't managed to contact the British at the Hotel Regina, and what was more they had lost a French embassy diplomat who had his files with her. The Secretary General was convinced of it: the Germans were being obstructive. They wanted to keep the Allies from devising a plan before the meeting . . .

Daladier, who had relaxed considerably now that he had met Göring, donned his sulky mask once more. He was irritable, he grunted at Léger because he couldn't shout; he wondered what to do, he imagined asking his 'new friend' Göring to sort out this problem, which was probably down to Ribbentrop. Then he changed his mind. It would mean breaking the harmony that had just settled in so well.

Embarrassed at making Göring wait on the other side of the revolving door, the President commanded Léger to sort things out. And to meet him at the place where the conference was being held.

Seeing them come out of the Vier Jahreszeiten, in such a friendly pose, the crowd waiting outside exploded. Daladier stopped. He held up his hat to shield his eyes from the dazzling midday sun – 'Führer weather', Göring had said delightedly. Touching cries of '*Vive* Daladier'. He could make out some slogans in German, 'Give us peace', 'Never again', and even bits of the 'Marseillaise'. The President was dumbfounded. So the people didn't want war either. Beside him, Göring was in seventh heaven. He bustled about, he kissed little girls in local costume, he proudly hugged little boys wearing the brown uniform of the Hitler Youth, while old people in Bavarian costume grabbed at him. Daladier felt slightly lost on this unexpected walkabout. Göring quickly caught hold of him. He took his arm and raised it to the crowd, as one does with a champion. Daladier tried to protest. The crowd roared at the top of its voice, the ovation deafened him. He complied and tried to shout his gratitude into Göring's ear: 'Basically your Bavarians are southerners, like my people, the Méridionaux.'

The stroll was endless.

There were more scraps of the 'Marseillaise', portraits of Daladier and the Führer side by side – 'where did they find those?' – cheers, kisses and flowers. The President – who had a quick eye – said to himself that these were spontaneous demonstrations. No regime could manufacture such enthusiasm and such desire for peace. The crowd slowed down the official convertible, cheered them again and again, adored them and begged them to 'give them peace'.

Now the President was impatient to get to the 'Führer's house'.

After a while, the President began to worry about Göring. At this rate they'd never get there. The Field Marshal reassured him: 'No ... None of the three other leaders has yet reached the Führerbau.' Then there was an explosion of laughter and Göring slapped his thigh as if mocking him for being so serious. The familiar, obscene gesture made him stiffen. The President closed up again.

All of a sudden he was finding it hard to bear this procession, the blazing sun that they called 'Führerwetter'.

While the plane was landing, and even while driving away from the Vier Jahreszeiten, he had still had all his spirit, his energy and clear ideas. He was ready. But now he was starting to sweat under his fedora; it was a bad sign. He was too hot and his winter clothes weighed heavily on him. His body felt sluggish. His shirt, already soaked through, kept him from taking off his jacket, as he liked to do during lengthy negotiations. He had to get there soon. The conference had to begin.

The President could no longer hear the cheers, just a rumbling sound. He could no longer recognise the scraps of 'Marseillaise' which, ten minutes earlier, had warmed his heart. He could no longer see anything, not the crowd, not Munich or its classical beauties. There was nothing anywhere but noise and fog. A fog of loving faces, laughing faces, the faces of men in black SS uniforms. It was all an undifferentiated mass. He passed through a vast human hedge, white-hot, adoring, pleading and desperate. He was in the 'toril', the long, blind corridor in which the bull is kept before emerging into the bright sunlight of the arena.

Getting out of the limousine, the President noticed that Hermann Göring's face was dripping with sweat and greasepaint.

PART THREE

1

THE FÜHRERBAU

The President came into the arena at twenty-one minutes past twelve.

The Führerbau was a thoroughly Hitlerian palace.

A building with Greek lines, no ornaments, no curves, all angles but Germanic proportions. The 'Führer's house' looks out on to the prestigious Königsplatz, forming the fourth side of its rectangle. Vast, severe and quite new, it contrasted starkly with the baroque of the city. A bronze eagle, wings splayed, stood out against the pink marble façade. The building was entered through two colonnaded porticos.

The Führerbau was one of the great palaces of the regime. When he came to power, Hitler ordered it built by Troost, his architect of the moment; and as always, the man who dreamed of joining Littmann's cabinet in Munich in 1913 had involved himself in everything: the plans, of course, the materials, the marble, the windows, the conference rooms, even visiting the building site. The place was both the seat of the Nazi Party and Hitler's office, but Hitler hated working in his offices, whether in the Berlin Chancellery or in Munich. In fact, the construction of the new Munich Party Head-quarters was only a pretext. Because for Hitler anything was good if it glorified, beautified, enlarged Munich, his Munich. Nothing was too beautiful, or too expensive, for the 'Athens on the Isar', the other capital of the Reich.

Berlin? It was only a reluctant capital, a foreign city where he lived in a hotel and spent as little time as possible. Berlin the frivolous, Berlin the homosexual, Berlin the red whose care he had entrusted to the former leftist of the NSDAP, Dr Goebbels. Berlin, so unGerman, unlike Munich. Berlin, which he reviled almost as much as he did Vienna, 'that Babylon of races'. For Hitler there was Munich first and foremost, and Nuremberg for the Party Conferences. It was there, in Munich, where he had arrived by train one morning in May, twenty-five years earlier, with a black suitcase, that everything had fallen into place.

And it was to Munich that the master of the new Germany wanted them all to come. To his home.

Drum-rolls. The head of protocol, a tall, red-haired man, bare-headed and in a seventeenth-century morning coat, hurried over to Daladier, who didn't see him at first, busy as he was examining the black-clad SS guards who were presenting arms to him, as motionless as if petrified, pistols in their belts, red armbands on their sleeves.

Inside the Führerbau, ushers dressed in black, with white stockings and buckled shoes, opened the doors and guided in the guests with a quiet flurry. This detail reassured the French President, who found them more civilised than the SS. He couldn't have concentrated during the summit, knowing that those black-clad giants were always standing behind him.

Neville Chamberlain had just arrived, but not Hitler or Mussolini.

'A sorry sight,' Daladier said to himself as he noticed Chamberlain in the drawing room on the first floor. His Majesty's Prime Minister looked as if he had been set there like a knick-knack amidst the Ribbentrops, the Wehrmacht generals and the SS officers. He was still wearing his black overcoat, and clutching his umbrella. He was standing by a

THE GHOST OF MUNICH

cold buffet, which he wasn't touching. No one was paying him any attention. Three men stood self-consciously at his side. Three Englishmen. Same clothes, same overcoats, same umbrella. Horace Wilson, the *éminence grise* of 10 Downing Street, the real brain behind the British policy of appeasement, Sir Nevile Henderson, Great Britain's ambassador to Germany, with a dapper red pansy in his buttonhole, and a young diplomat with a ruddy complexion, Mr Ashton-Gwatkin.

When Chamberlain noticed Daladier, his face suddenly lit up, like Robinson Crusoe spotting Friday. He emitted one of those hoarse, tribal cries that the English sometimes let out at reunions, in their clubs, on the cricket pitch or in the depths of Africa. An abrupt cry of 'hey, Édouaaarrrddd!' that signalled his surprise at bumping into him, his joy at seeing him again, and their old complicity in the face of their ordeal. But that excessive exuberance – because in fact Chamberlain and Daladier had never really fallen into each other's arms – concealed something else: Chamberlain's sense of unease since his arrival, all the little humiliations to which he had been subjected since his arrival in Munich, the lack of protocol, the coldness of the Nazi hierarchs present, their insulting indifference, Ribbentrop's brutal tone . . .

'Édouaaarrrddd,' the Englishman repeated. He took Daladier's hand and shook it endlessly. Chamberlain's enthusiasm, his sudden and demonstrative affection, quite disconcerted the President, who had at that precise moment one sole desire: to grab Sir Neville Chamberlain, His Majesty's Prime Minister and Governor of India, by the collar. Wipe the smile off his face. Give this superior gentleman, who was always round at Hitler's, a damned good shake. And demand, yes, demand that he explain last night's silence, his unanswered phone calls, all his peculiar behaviour since his first meeting with Hitler in Berchtesgaden; and his change of attitude since he had returned, ten days before, from his second trip to see the Führer, even 'harder' than Daladier himself.

Demand that he explain himself about that and everything else, about the essential thing, the thing that was about to happen. About what the two of them were going to say to Hitler. About how the Allies had to act in principle. But the place, alas, was hardly suited to it. The President swallowed back his ire, like a man unhappy with his home life and painfully resigned.

There were more and more generals, SS, Wilhelmstrasse diplomats, Göring's military advisers, black suits and grey-green uniforms, and the two allies were feeling increasingly lost. They stood in the middle of the room, refused champagne and petits-fours and tried to give an impression of composure. They took time to reply at greater length to their colleagues, and to those suited ushers kind enough to take an interest in them. Every now and again they forced themselves to nod, together, at something the other had said, for fear that the Germans might realise that something wasn't quite right with them.

In fact, Göring was studying them with a keen eye.

He came towards them, opening his arms, clutching his Field Marshal's baton. It took only that unavoidable and invasive body, his slaps on the back and a few tourist banalities for the Englishman and the Frenchman to lighten up, and their colleagues along with them.

Daladier finally accepted a glass, but of French red wine. Chamberlain, a mineral water. The ice was broken.

Göring took Daladier's arm as he had done at the hotel, to ask him how he had gained his captain's stripes so quickly in the Great War. The Frenchman, proud as a peacock, was starting to tell him, when Göring became aware that Chamberlain, who had been too old to have gone to war in 1914, was growing bored with the conversation. Then he turned to the Englishman to compliment him on his recent discovery of the aeroplane. The head of the Luftwaffe was interested in the plane that the British Prime Minister had taken that morning. Flattered, Chamberlain replied impeccably, as the great connoisseur that he had been forced to become since his recent aerial baptism, that it was a British Airways Lockheed 10 Electra, which travelled at two hundred miles an hour, at an altitude of almost twenty thousand feet, and most importantly, was the first aeroplane to be pressurised – 'which means that one doesn't notice the journey'.

Göring observed, 'It really is a very good aeroplane.' Chamberlain mumbled his gratitude. The German, so as not to leave the Frenchman out, then took an interest in the comfort and performance of the Air France *Poitou* in which he had flown.

Daladier couldn't help explaining to the two others that the Air France *Poitou* rose to an altitude of nearly eight thousand metres, that it flew at a speed of almost four hundred kilometres an hour, not to mention the marvellous and ultra-modern air conditioning and Pullman chairs.

Göring, visibly very interested, asked him the model of the machine.

'A Bloch 220,' the President proudly replied before it occurred to him that he might perhaps have disturbed Field Marshal Göring by mentioning the name of the aircraft manufacturer, a Jew; but he noticed that luckily Göring had not picked up on it. He had moved on to something else: the FW Condor that had just travelled non-stop from Berlin to New York.

The President found the situation amusing. If only the French knew that! If the French knew that he, Daladier, glass in hand, was innocuously chatting turbines and compressors with the terror of the European sky!

* * *

Then Mussolini turned up. There was a hurricane. The *decano dei dittatori* – the 'doyen of dictators' – had a martial gait, the green uniform of an air force general, black eyes that rolled like marbles in their orbits. He was followed by Count Ciano, a young, vigorous, slightly stout young man, Mussolini's son-in-law and Minister of Foreign Affairs, in the same uniform as himself, as well as a bustling coterie of decorated, gilded and beribboned officers and gleaming diplomats. The Duce inspected the little assembly, which was staggered by his thundering arrival.

Mussolini greeted Chamberlain first, coldly.

Then Field Marshal Göring, fraternally.

And finally President Daladier, respectfully, with gravity and a click of heels. The President was struck at the sight of the Duce, not so much by his small size as by a curious disproportion between the top and the bottom of his body. At the top, a bull neck, that big, open mouth, that athletic, bulging torso; and at the bottom of the body, the contrast with ludicrous thighs, short legs, so short that they sometimes seemed to be wriggling in the air when his pace quickened. Daladier chuckled inwardly: the famous 'Italian stallion' made him think of a failed thoroughbred, too stumpy-legged to run.

With the arrival of the Italians, the atmosphere heated up. The Germans began to compete in their courtesies to the latest arrivals. The conversations with the French and the English, sidelined until now, grew animated. Chamberlain, who didn't dare disturb the Duce – because the disagreement between the two countries was great – recommenced his attempt at charming Count Ciano. He wanted a tête-à-tête with the Duce. He had to reinforce the bonds between the Crown and the Empire that had slackened after that unfortunate affair in Ethiopia.

The Duce and Field Marshal Göring had moved slightly apart from the others. Göring was waiting on the Italian hand and foot. He snapped his fingers at the waiters and buttonholed the Reich diplomats to satisfy his every whim. He was less boastful, more attentive, completely respectful towards the Duce. He treated him with the particular deference that one owed to an ally that one had just severely humiliated in Austria. Göring didn't forget – we must never forget, he repeated to Hitler, who was too incautious for his liking – that in 1934 the Italians had massed their troops along the border at the Brenner Pass, and threatened to declare war on Germany in the event of an attack on Austria, whose natural protector Italy considered herself to be. Times had changed.

Göring called for silence. The private conversations ceased. The Reich second-in-command was anxious to thank, from the bottom of his heart, the Duce for his mediation, for this long journey, for the trouble caused to him, and especially for his tireless quest for peace in Europe.

Chamberlain in turn raised his glass of mineral water. His smile spread across a blotchy face. All of a sudden, he was relieved to hear the magnificent word 'Peace' uttered within these walls.

Daladier nodded, although his nod was forced, then murmured to Clapier a few words that were lost in the hubbub. 'So where has Léger got to, damn it? Where are Léger and those damned files of his?'

As he listened to these tributes, the Duce turned crimson. He quickly regained his imperial mask, thanked everyone with one of those intense looks that were being posted up – at this very time – on every palisade on the peninsula, before matching it with a solemn jerk of his chin. Then in a flash, the Italian dictator's face lit up with unexpected bonhomie. He resumed his conversation with the admiring German generals, boasted to them of the merits of his *chasseurs* who were 'doing wonders for Franco in Spain', and tried to convince them that giant hydroplanes were the best aerial weapon. He took them by the arm to finish a sentence. He slapped them on the back. The Duce's mask had vanished. Now he was the child of Romagna setting out his stall, voicing his impatience at Hitler's lateness to no one in particular, and saying over and over again, rubbing his hands together as if about to sit down to dinner: 'There is no time to lose, gentlemen . . . My train leaves at midnight. There is no time to lose.'

All of a sudden, Göring stifled a chuckle.

Hitler entered the room, surrounded by his aides-de-camp.

2

HITLER, FIRST IMPRESSIONS

'I still have no clear image of Hitler's arrival. I can't describe it. So many images of him blur together. What was your first impression?'

'I remember as if it was yesterday. He arrived, and there was silence. The little gathering, fifty people or so, turned round in a single movement to see him.

'I was the only head of state present never to have met him . . . Mussolini and he had been openly allied since the constitution of the Rome-Berlin Axis in 1936; they had seen each other often since 1934. Chamberlain had been received by Hitler, twice in September, for long visits, as you know.

'At first Chancellor Hitler was very abrupt, barely polite, with Mr Chamberlain; then he made his way towards me. He studied me as he came forward. He was probably sizing me up – and I was doing the same. Once he had arrived in front of me, I realised that he was slightly taller than me. But not more sturdily built. I studied him intensely. Although he was forty-nine, his age would have been difficult to guess. He could have been younger, or very old, more than anything he looked – how should I put it? – sickly, yes, that's it. His skin was grey, almost blue. I thought to myself that this man wasn't in good health. Léger explained to me shortly after-wards that it was due to his diet, strictly vegetarian. He shook my hand for a long time, to my great surprise, almost warmly. I heard him say, in a pleasant, gentle voice, "Welcome, President Daladier." He bowed to me ceremoniously. But all of a sudden, as he was greeting me, his gloomy eyes rolled upwards.

'Then everything resumed its diplomatic course.

'I was surprised and slightly puzzled by his strange appearance. You see, we democrats aren't used to such things ... To this get-up and ... to this kind of face. A unhealthy, sallow, ashen face, with tense features. Looking at him, I tried for just a moment to imagine him as a man in the street, without his uniform, without that strange square moustache and without that famous lock of hair. I couldn't ... That lock was Hitler in a nutshell. It was much longer in those days than in the propaganda photographs. It fell into his face. His neck trembled for a moment, as if he were suffering from a tic, and the lock covered his face. That, added to his apparel, gave him a bohemian appearance.

'He was wearing a khaki jacket, like a private soldier; on his sleeve, an armband with a swastika. He was wearing black trousers, too wide, that fell on rough boots, unpolished, battered, their soles worn through. Yes, I remember his shoes, tramp's shoes. I remember my movement of perplexity and disdain. I said to myself, "So this is the supreme dictator of Germany." He looked like nothing on earth. Apart from Aristide Briand, who looked like a tramp as well, I didn't know anyone who looked like him in our political, diplomatic and even military circles. The man wasn't of our world, or even of Mussolini's, in spite of his eccentricities. Hitler didn't look like any German, not like Ribbentrop the socialist, or even the civilised Otto Abetz whom I had met in Paris with Brinon, before I had him expelled in 1939, or the German soldiers who were Prussian Junkers – country squires, if you will – unpleasant but very well dressed, very well brought-up.

'He didn't actually look like a German. Oh, of course, they aren't all blond and blue-eyed, although that would have been the minimum requirement for the head of the "master race". But he was dark, he really was; his cheek-bones were high and prominent, like those of Hungarians or Slavs with Asiatic blood; his waist, his bent back, were far from athletic. I studied him and said to myself that the French secret services might be on to something.'

'The secret services?'

'Well, some of them claimed that Hitler had Czech blood. According to them, neither side of his family came from Upper Austria, as he claimed, but the Waldviertel in the north-west of Lower Austria, very close to Bohemia. And it is the Czechs who have populated that region since the 13th century. Some of my advisers explain his hatred towards the Czechs, and particularly towards Beneš, by saying that he wanted at all costs to have his own roots covered up. But in the end what he wanted that day was the Sudetenland; that was why we were there. And if he had Czech, or even Jewish blood, as others maintained, that altered nothing about the case.'

'What did you say to each other before beginning the conference?'

'Nothing else. I think he was in a hurry to get down to it . . . And so was I.'

3

FIRST SESSION

Hitler had called to Ribbentrop, 'Bring them to me,' as you might address a beater when hunting. The Führer started walking alone towards his office. Mussolini caught up with him; inevitably, the two dictators had to walk together. As they walked they swapped a few words, two or three laughs and, most significantly, several brief glances. They took care to walk in the same rhythm. They admired one another. They were, in fact, keeping an eye on one another. One must never overtake the other; but neither must fall back by so much as a step. The procession set off. The function room emptied. Chamberlain and the British followed sadly, framed by Göring and Ribbentrop. The rest of the diplomats, the military officers and the experts walked at a respectful distance. The Italian officials lagged behind.

But the French didn't follow. The President moved about restlessly in the big, deserted room. He repeated out loud: 'Where is Léger? Where on earth is Léger?' He shouted at an usher, then at a mute and menacing SS officer: 'I'm not starting if Léger isn't there.' Then, barely a note lower, to his colleagues, he admitted, with a weak and stupid smile: 'I can't start without Léger. He knows these things; I don't know anything about them.'

Finally Léger appeared, breathless and shaken, no longer quite so high and mighty. He barely apologised. And started saying how they'd dragged him all over Munich to keep him away. He asked if anyone had seen 'a certain Mademoiselle Klobukovski who's got all the papers!'

In the end Mademoiselle Klobukovski arrived, equally breathless, handed the famous documents to Léger, and the French dashed off.

The red-haired maître d' in the uncomfortably tight uniform, the one who had welcomed the heads of state on the flight of steps, was still hard at work. By the entrance to the room, he was guiding the flow of dignitaries. He channelled the experts, grouping them according to their area of specialisation, into a first room, where they immediately opened their napkins and sat down. He guided the military advisers – there were many on the German and Italian side – towards a second room where they immediately rolled out their maps. He guided the diplomats, still bobbing about at the rear of the procession, hoping to be admitted into the holy of holies, and authoritatively led them into an antechamber. The summit had been called so quickly, the rules of protocol had been left so vague. They tried their chance. The sole watchword had been given by Hitler: no Minister of Foreign Affairs. An exception had been made for Ribbentrop because he was the inviting power; and for Ciano because Mussolini was being helpful.

The phlegmatic François-Poncet quickened his step to catch up with Daladier. He was firmly held back by the carrot-topped minder. Alexis Léger passed through without hindrance and didn't reply to the insistent look of François-Poncet, the schemer, a representative of the 'soft' line in disguise, a barely repentant Germanophile who openly campaigned against him at the Quai.

Even Göring, the Reich second-in-command, had been stopped by the red-haired maître d' as he tried to rush into the hall in Hitler's wake. The minder dared to give him a confident shake of the head. Daladier observed the scene.

Göring turned crimson, he muttered, he menaced. His jaws were clenched and his Field Marshal's baton was threatening. 'But what about Ribbentrop?' he protested. The redhead stood his ground.

Daladier had understood poor Göring's humiliation. Furtively patting him on the shoulder, he tried to let the Field Marshal know that he was sincerely sorry. The other man didn't even notice.

The only people left at the door to Hitler's cabinet were the Four, their right-hand men and the translator. They deposited their headgear and belongings at the cloakroom, where the caps of the dictators sat next to the soft hats of the democrats and Chamberlain's umbrella.

Hitler entered first, followed by Chamberlain. Mussolini gave his son-in-law a buccaneering wink. Daladier was relieved as he became aware of the presence of Léger behind him. Before entering the room, he tapped – as others might cross themselves – the 'Gamelin note' in his jacket pocket.

The two doors of Hitler's office closed again.

The Führer's study was anything but an office. Hitler hated offices. He hated sitting down at a desk, he hated timetables, he hated formal meetings, never a meeting before midday. The Führer of hardworking Germany hated working. It was a survival – along with his habit of getting up at eleven o'clock in the morning – from his bohemian youth in Munich, where his days were spent haranguing crowds from makeshift trestle-tables, or plotting in the back rooms of beer-houses. Today, the Führer had large numbers of secretaries mobilised all over the country, ready at any hour of the day and night to take notes for one of his speeches. Everywhere, in the Chancellery in Berlin, at the Berghof, his Eagle's Nest, at Party headquarters, in his private apartment in Munich and even at the hotel where he stayed in Berlin.

More than an office, the place recalled a village hall, in its size and rural decoration, a mixture of wood-carvings and floral wallpaper. The room was rectangular, lit by two high windows, of impressive proportions like everything else about the Führerbau. On the left as one came in there was a huge fireplace, then a pedestal table, sofas and armchairs.

Without waiting, Hitler headed for a sofa. He slumped into it as spoiled children do, or exhausted old men. He gestured slackly to the others to do the same. Disconcerted, Daladier opened his eyes wide to look at Léger, indispensable Léger, suddenly the holder of a magical power: decoding, deciphering, translating, guessing everyone's ulterior motives, as the specialist that he was. Léger darted him a cardinal's smile about their host's nonchalant manner, signifying that in a quarter-century at the Quai d'Orsay he had seen others behave similarly. That comforted the President.

The interpreter Paul Schmidt sat down on Hitler's right, close enough to his ear that he might be heard, but slightly behind him so that he could also be ignored. Schmidt was one of the few old-school diplomats at Wilhelmstrasse; he wasn't a Nazi, but he was none the less appreciated for his diligence, his discretion and his experience of international summits.

The rest of the assembly was still standing.

There was a moment's hesitation, as at a dinner without a seating plan. Daladier looked for the seat that seemed most appropriate for the ordeal that he was about to undergo. An armchair, not a sofa. More or less opposite him, but not too directly. He sat down in the armchair facing Hitler, with Léger on his left. This was it. The President methodically wedged himself into his seat. Stay calm, stay calm. He was the athlete about to be put to the test. He fidgeted his body into its best position. He crossed and uncrossed his legs to smooth his muscles. Before noticing, not without pleasure, that he had not lost in the deal by not sitting on the sofa, which was too low, too soft.

It was 12.45.

Hitler began. He assumed the air of a shady dealer in a hurry, leaned forward as if he wanted to create a kind of intimacy between them, and got the ritual of thanks out of the way. They had some business to get down to; for him, it didn't seem like a conference. First of all he paid tribute to the Duce, who had wanted to take 'this very long journey' to act as mediator in this difficult affair. He had insisted on the word 'mediator', matching it with a respectful smile.

Mussolini, stretched out on his seat, arms wide, had the satisfied air of a matchmaker doing his job: bringing the parties together.

Daladier noted the Führer's air of deference, almost submission when he addressed Mussolini. He also noticed that the dictator's voice wasn't the same as the one he had heard on the radio, by turns nasal or hoarse, always violent. Now it was a voice like any other; it was also capable of charming inflections. Daladier, himself a very good orator, wondered, as an adept in the field, about this curious phenomenon.

'Now, gentlemen, I can admit it, we have created a weapon the like of which the world has never seen. In the past five years I have spent billions and equipped my troops with the most up-to-date weaponry. I have ordered my friend Göring to create an air force that will protect Germany against attack from any quarter.'

This tribute to Göring – who was not present – was glowing. Ribbentrop tensed. Hitler observed with amusement the vexation of his Minister of Foreign Affairs, then addressed Daladier directly:

'I have taken a great deal of effort, Mr Daladier. Yes, I

have even declared that there were no remaining problems between ourselves and France, Mr President. That Alsace-Lorraine had ceased to exist for us, that it was merely a border territory for us, because we did not want to go to war with France because of it.'

Satisfied nods from the President.

Chamberlain, holding his knee with two hands, rocked back and forth, visibly bored by this speech that he had already heard twice that month; and also because his French ally was suddenly gaining in importance in the eyes of their host.

But then his voice changed, became more guttural and vaguely threatening, as he said in a singsong voice, for everyone's benefit:

'The world must doubt no longer ... No longer it is the Führer, no longer a man who speaks, but the German people.'

He studied the three other heads of state and, as if they had not understood, he began to develop the same idea at length.

He grew heated as he spoke.

The man metamorphosed.

He closed his eyes, or he rolled them. He clenched his fists, sometimes he waved an arm. He seemed to be obeying the fist that hammered down upon the pedestal table. Finally he drew himself upright, transported, impelled by a driven, vivid rage, his face filled with pain:

'You will be familiar with the question that has moved us most deeply over these past months. Its name is not so much Czechoslovakia as Beneš ...'

He shouted the name of Beneš three times, as if it were a curse.

'Beneš ... That name contains within it all that worries millions of men today, and all that stirs them with fanatical resolution ...'

And then he calmed down again.

Everyone present was in a state of shock.

He fell back into his sofa and closed up again, with nothing to explain either the preceding rage or the despondency into which he seemed to have fallen.

A welcome silence fell upon the assembly. They thought the wrath had subsided, that the chancellor had finally resumed civilised behaviour, but he started hammering the table once again.

He said, 'Beneš,' and it all began again. 'When Beneš created this state by means of a lie, he declared that he wanted to organise it along the model of the Swiss cantons. But he instituted a rule of terror. How long must that go on? For twenty years the German people have witnessed this oppression from the sidelines. If they have done so until now, it is because they were powerless.'

Paul Schmidt did his best with the translation. It had to be utterly perfect; and simultaneous, to boot. For Hitler in German. For Chamberlain in English. For Daladier in French. Only Mussolini had refused a translation, and suggested helping Schmidt. As the Duce had repeated often enough since his arrival, he was the only one of the Four who spoke English, French and German as fluently as he did Italian.

With each phrase, placid Schmidt found himself pressured either by Hitler or Mussolini. When he guessed from a pause or a sigh that he could continue, he was forever being interrupted by Hitler resuming. And when Hitler was being translated, it was Mussolini who involved himself in all the versions. It was a complete hubbub.

Dismayed, the two democrats were forced to listen to Hitler, who went on soliloquising amidst this chaos. Hitler who was to be pitied, Hitler who was moaning, Hitler who was forever weeping as he spoke of the martyrdom of his brothers the Sudeten Germans.

The Führer's entreaty had its effect.

Chamberlain would have agreed to anything if it would only stop; every now and again he nodded unhappily.

Daladier, frowning and constantly on his guard, minutely gauged his adversary. Listening to the translation, he had realised that Hitler was serving up a precise replica of his speech of 12th September, the one in the Sportpalast. He admired the orator but he decided to be wary. Not to be impressed.

So he watched Hitler growing agitated, exhausting himself, losing his calm. He studied his tics, in particular that left shoulder that sometimes twitched at the same time as his knee. He looked for the flaw; he tried to guess the weak points; he tried to analyse the slightest of his moods. He considered his adversary, from every angle. He tried to apprehend the beast.

Hadn't he always been an excellent judge, the best judge of men, of all the people he had met, charmed, commanded in the Vaucluse, in the Radical Party, in every ministry he had passed through? Oh, his knowledge of men! Madeleine, poor Madeleine used to say admiringly that he could read men like an open book. And in fact, bumping into anyone in a market at Carpentras or in the Salle des Quatre Colonnes, Daladier could give him a mental x-ray. He really did know men. He knew in a flash what it was that made them live, love, obey and, of course, vote. Men were Daladier's affair. Everyone. Charming the right wing of the Radical Party, commanding the fascist Cagoulards on his staff, while being able to find himself, during the time of the Popular Front, sharing a platform with Maurice Thorez. Who else could have done as much? So why not today? Was this German cut from a different cloth? Didn't he too have guts, a brain, two arms and two legs? Hadn't he once been a baby before becoming the devil of Europe? While it might have been said that there was something of Parsifal about Hitler, of a 'jackbooted Gandhi' or whoever, he was still a man for all that.

He, Daladier, would find his weak point, the best angle of attack.

It wasn't all that complicated.

1. The German was violent, so he respected strength. He must be strong.
2. The German spoke frankly. So he mustn't stand on ceremony with him, not like the Englishman.
3. The German was a little odd, it was true, but so far he had found no one to contradict him, or even simply negotiate with him. He had had only that drip Chamberlain; and with Daladier things would change, you could be sure of it.

Armed with those three rules, Daladier wedged himself solidly into his armchair.

Hitler was about to continue.

With an authoritative wave of his hand, the Duce interrupted him. It was Chamberlain's turn. The President noticed that Hitler had bent forward, without grumbling, at the older man's injunction; and that he had begun to stare at an ornamental detail in the carpet.

Chamberlain's thanks were more drab. The British Prime Minister addressed Chancellor Hitler in a tone that he always used with him. A tone of patience, of good will, the tone of the Nobel laureate that he would become, without a shadow of a doubt, after the Munich affair. Neville Chamberlain announced that he was not 'party to the conflict'. He said this in a detached, seigneurial way, as if he too wished, following Mussolini's example, to act as mediator in 'this dispute which concerned only Czechoslovakia, Germany and France . . .'

Daladier was dismayed by this display of British spineless-ness. He clung to his chair with his strong arms. Wanting to scream, he muttered. He wanted to take Chamberlain by his jacket collar, he really did; instead he merely turned to Léger, who had also heard.

Despite Chamberlain's best efforts, Hitler didn't look at him. The Englishman was searching for a nod, an acknow-ledgement, some gesture to recall the romantic complicity of their first meeting at the summit in the Alps, in that Eagle's Nest in Berchtesgaden where everything seemed possible, as long as Germany was granted the possibility of 'reunifying'. But nothing came. Hitler continued to ignore the concilia-tory Mr Chamberlain.

The Führer's eyes and Mussolini's settled on Édouard Daladier. The President understood that it was his turn.

But Chamberlain hadn't finished. He raised a finger to continue, like a pleading schoolboy. When he felt he had permission, the Englishman continued with slightly forced enthusiasm:

'And I nearly forgot. I also wanted to say that I agree completely with the Duce, and indeed with the Führer. We will have to get a move on. We will have to finish within the day . . .'

Everyone's attention subsided once more. Daladier didn't need to wait for Schmidt's translation. He blanched again.

'Great Britain has no other aim in this meeting than peace in Europe . . .'

The British Prime Minister left his phrase dangling, still hoping to catch the Führer's eye. Wearily he declared in a louder voice, as if there were still time to attract his atten-tion: '. . . and of course the reunification of the German people upon which Chancellor Hitler and I agreed at our first meeting.'

Daladier stared at Chamberlain. He seemed to see him for the first time; he was discovering him. He began to splutter between his teeth, for Léger's ears, 'perfidious Albion'. He repeated the oath, more loudly, striving to be heard by the British who were facing him.

He couldn't believe it.

He thought he knew everything about this difficult ally. Since his first meeting with Chamberlain in London in April, he had understood that the British policy of appeasement towards Hitler was not exactly the same as the French. He didn't know the differences between the two allies. Obviously he knew that Britain, unlike France, had no commitment of solidarity towards Czechoslovakia. But now he was discovering another Chamberlain. Not entirely an enemy. But no longer an ally.

The President was shaken by this revelation. Groggy, like a cuckold finally forced to confront an ancient truth that he had previously refused to see.

It was the President's turn. So as not to be left behind, he too thanked Chancellor Hitler for his invitation, but no more than that, without Chamberlain's bowings and scrapings. He even, in a sudden impulse of Machiavellianism, tried to linger warmly on the determining role and actions of His Excellency, Benito Mussolini.

Flattered, the Duce, who was slumped in his armchair, sat up. Daladier noticed him. He reinforced his words of thanks with a look of gratitude in the Italian's direction. His British ally had just worried him, the President improvised. He seemed to be searching this sudden desert for an ally, some support, a glance. There was the Duce. Why not? And in the whirl of improvisation he said to himself that after all, Laval, Bonnet, de Monzie, the whole pro-Italian lobby in Paris, might possibly have a point ... That Mussolini wasn't Hitler ... That he was, after all, an old socialist. That it had been madness, after Stresa, to let him side with Hitler ... And that they should have closed their eyes to the Ethiopian affair ...

No one had noticed Daladier's excitement. The diplomatic formulas, and that glance at Mussolini, had enabled him to recover with aplomb. Now he had to get to the nub, that energetic intervention that he had been thinking about since Hitler had taken the floor.

He would have to make the leap, make his presence felt. He would have to make them forget Chamberlain and his spinelessness. Confront Hitler, that wild beast. He, Daladier, knew how to talk to these people.

So he would talk to him, man to man. Warrior to warrior. War veteran to war veteran, since they were both veterans, unlike Chamberlain who, in 1914, was already an old man.

The President made his leap, taking advantage of a slight lull in the conversation. He began without ceremony, but in a resonant voice. As an experienced orator, he knew that his voice carried; he found the appropriate tone, serious, low, filled with menace.

'Gentlemen, first of all I would like Chancellor Hitler's intentions made perfectly clear.'

Then he paused dramatically.

The President was no longer the taciturn, weary, sulky man he had been since his arrival. He had become solid, offensive, even arrogant once again.

He allowed Schmidt to finish the translation of the first part of his sentence; but when the translator had finished he remained silent. He needed everyone's attention. Mussolini stopped chattering to Ciano, Hitler emerged from his contemplation of the patterned carpet, and the British pretended to be interested. His dramatic little moment had had its effect. The President was not unhappy. This way he would win respect; he had no intention of raising his voice. It was up to Hitler to do the shouting, that was his register; but not Daladier, not France.

He went on, with the satisfaction of a teacher triumphing over an unruly class: 'If Chancellor Hitler is suggesting, as I understand him to be, destroying Czechoslovakia as an independent state, and simply attaching it to the Reich – annexing it, in fact – I know what it remains for me to do . . .'

He fell silent again before slowly rising to his feet.

Concern flashed in Mussolini's eyes, which tried to find Hitler's.

The translator began whispering his versions, in German for Hitler, in English for Chamberlain, and avoiding Mussolini. He didn't want to break the solemnity of the moment. Daladier darted him a look of gratitude; and when Schmidt had finished, the President continued, still in a resounding and resolute voice.

'It remains only for me to return to France.'

And he pointed at the door.

No need for Schmidt. They had all understood.

Mussolini sat up, alert now.

Hitler emerged from his torpor.

Chamberlain suddenly cursed, turning to face Horace Wilson.

In a flash, struck by the President's brutal determination, everyone looked at him differently. They couldn't believe it. Nice Monsieur Daladier had become a different man. A maniac, a madman fiddling with nitro-glycerine, the kind you don't want to argue with. A dangerous, unpredictable, important man.

Hitler, staying rather in the background, suddenly appeared

to have shaken off his boredom. He had been abruptly awoken by the danger, excited. He was on his guard again, and handed the reins to the Duce. Mussolini took charge of the operation. He approached Daladier. He looked distraught, unhappy. He wanted to flatter Daladier's vanity, and said to him pleadingly, 'Let's see, Mr President . . . Let's see . . . The Führer's idea has not been properly understood . . .'

Still standing, ready to leave, with Léger standing by his side, the President froze. His body was on the point of departing, but his eye deigned to take an interest in Mussolini's plea. It was like that of a wife, seriously offended but too weak to leave, or too destitute, threatening, secretly still hoping, until the last second. With a slightly forced jerk of his chin, the Frenchman indicated to the Italian that he was listening.

Mussolini announced to him, with cautious enthusiasm, in a curious mixture of Italian, French, English and German:

'But on the contrary, Mr President. The Führer has insisted on the fact that apart from the Sudeten districts, Germany claims no part of Czech territory. He expressed himself badly . . .'

Then he mimed a gesture of reproach in Hitler's direction. He repeated:

'He expressed himself badly . . . He expressed himself badly . . . I tell him that so often.'

He pointed to Hitler as if he were a good-for-nothing. And to the great perplexity of the others the German leader allowed himself to be insulted by the Duce. He was silent, curled over on his sofa, his back bent as the other man gave him a sound talking-to. He looked like a guilty child.

Mussolini wanted to press his advantage home. He demanded that Hitler apologise to 'Mr President Daladier'.

The Duce insisted. He seemed to be taking a certain pleasure in this little piece of play-acting. Daladier observed the little game. He was stunned by the German's sudden docility. He couldn't believe the effect that his threat had produced.

Finally Hitler complied.

Slowly, in a low voice, with the injured pride of the penitent in his eye, he sat up and apologised.

'No, Mr Daladier, I did express myself badly. The Duce put it very well . . . I don't want any Czechs! I want only my German brothers.'

Hitler paused after each phrase. This time he let Schmidt finish his translations. Then, observing that his words had had a calming effect on Daladier, his eye was drawn once more to Mussolini, and his encouraging, coaching gestures: 'Very gently, very gently, that's it.' It appeared that the danger had passed, so he said to Daladier, suddenly facetious:

'Come now, Mr President. These Czechs, you'd let me have them all, and I don't want a single one!'

Daladier felt an impulse of revulsion at this great lie, but noticing that the entire assembly – even the placid Paul Schmidt – were laughing uproariously at the Führer's sudden unexpected *bon mot*, he decided to sit down and smile, just smile, at Hitler's joke.

In his head he turned the jest over and over, examined and dissected it.

He concluded that the Führer didn't want 'the dismantling of Czechoslovakia'. It could not be stated more clearly. He wanted the Sudetenland, but not more than that. Certainly, the Czechs would have to make concessions. There would have to be an amputation, and it's never nice to ask that of a friend, but apparently the life of Czechoslovakia was not under threat.

Clearly, the joke was an acknowledgement that his solemn warning had been received.

All of a sudden, the President felt better. It was as if he

had been relieved by Hitler's undertaking. He even began to laugh openly along with the others. And as the laughter continued, as Mussolini added to it, as Chamberlain spluttered, Hitler and Daladier exchanged a glance. For the first time, a manly look, Daladier said to himself. There was something in the Frenchman's eye that was like gratitude, contentment, something that meant, 'We have understood one another.'

4

'THAT'S WHEN I SHOULD HAVE LEFT'

'That's not a bad version of the scene, Mademoiselle. In fact it was at that point that I should have left. Because I really did want to leave!'

'Leave the conference? So it wasn't just for dramatic effect?'

'No, it wasn't. It wasn't just dramatic effect, as you put it. In spite of Hitler's joke about the Czechs, in spite of the laughter, in spite of Mussolini and his winking, I had sensed a trap. There was no agenda at this conference. I realised I was in hostile territory: Chamberlain wasn't trustworthy, as I had just worked out; Mussolini wasn't really the "mediator" he claimed to be. And as for Hitler, you know . . . All of a sudden I was alone. Yes, so alone that I was ready to leave for Paris. I was oppressed; I knew I was stuck; I had seen enough. It was the right moment. It should have been the right moment . . .'

'So why didn't you go?'

'I was going to go! I was on my feet. The door was just a few feet away. Léger would have followed me. During those few moments, which lasted a century, I had only that one idea in my head. Getting back to Paris, as quickly as possible. I was mentally prepared. I was going back to Paris.

'I had a sense that fate had given me a role that was tailor-made for me. I had worked out how long it would take me to get back, less than three hours. I would be in Paris by the end of the day. I wouldn't tell anyone. And I would turn up at my house once night had fallen. Incognito. No parading, no cheering from the French, who would have been so proud of me. I would just have gone home. I would have seen my sons. At that precise moment I desperately wanted to hug them. Yes, I'd have gone home and spent a peaceful night.

'Of course, I said to myself that a gesture like that would cause one hell of a fuss, but how elegant it would be! I was already thinking about what I would tell the French on the radio the next morning, and the speech I would deliver to the National Assembly which – I had no doubt – would not shower me with roses. But I was ready to cross swords with them, even in front of the political bureau of the Radical Party; ready to confront the right-wingers who took the 'soft' line, Bonnet's gang; ready to knock the living daylights out of the 'pacifists' in the SFIO, the French Section of the Workers' International. I was resolute. The Four would only be Three!

'But you see, life is strange, it would have taken so little, just a few steps, a few seconds. I tried to catch Léger's eye to say we were going, but I couldn't. He was bent over his notes. It was then that I began to doubt.

'While Mussolini tried to ease the situation, I imagined my fall before Parliament. I counted the number of deputies who would vote for me. I saw myself politically dead, fallen in the field of parliamentary honour. I could easily see the next day's press. I even heard the calls of the newsvendor, the one in the Place de l'Opéra, cheekily saying over and over again: 'Munich: Daladier withdraws'. I also saw, perhaps in that moment of super-lucidity, the incomprehension of Jean, my son, as he saw me arriving at the house. His father had deserted the battle against Hitler. It all formed a commotion in my head.

'I was on the point of leaving, but I could hear the sniggers in Paris restaurants as I arrived, the harsh comments of Pétain, the revenge of Laval, the great speech that Blum

would deliver against me, the Communist street demonstrations, the rebukes of old Herriot, taking his revenge after
so many years. It all ran through my head. I imagined the
joy, the delight of Madame de Portes in her salon that same
evening; and her little schemes, inevitably; and the
summoning of her protégés, Paul Reynaud, her lover, and
Bonnet, their great friend; their plans drawn up in the night
to replace me. They were strong enough. I gave them the
chance. But they didn't agree on anything. Reynaud pursued
a 'hard' stance, Bonnet a 'soft' one: certainly, the clever
Hélène de Portes would know what to do.

'I also considered – and this was important – the great
sorrow that I would cause the Marquise. She would never
get over the humiliation, seeing her rival Madame de Portes
triumphant, her enemies in power and her salon deserted,
no, I couldn't do that to her.

'Ah! Not that, to have left like that would have been
death.

'Yes, in those few seconds, I saw the mob upon me. Mine
first of all, already working towards my ruin. The left wing
of the Popular Front, my old friends who would have trampled on me in the name of their anti-fascism. And also the
far right, with its newspapers howling "desertion". They'd
have turned me into a new Salengro.

'A "deserter", and this time for real.'

'But why a "deserter"? Why not part of the "Resistance",
even if the term didn't yet exist?'

'You know very well, Mademoiselle. The political death
that I had experienced four years earlier. And I had thought
I would never recover. After 6th February 1934 . . .'

'What does 6th February 1934 have to do with it?'

'You may remember that I was President of the Council.
After the Stavisky scandal, the far-right leagues had called
for a big demonstration, the Communists too. The political

climate was terrifying, the Republic was discredited. We expected rough weather ahead. But that famous 6th February was even worse . . . I was a young President of the Council, certainly, but I'd been working all night. The Republic had resisted. The riot squads had blocked the insurgents on the Pont de la Concorde, driven back the assaults from the "Camelots du Roi", the right-wing monarchists, in the Rue de Bourgogne. And alas, in the early morning, there was a heavy toll: eighteen fatalities, 1435 injured. But by being firm, I think that that evening I saved the Republic.

'I had been helped in the task by my Minister of the Interior, the socialist Eugène Frot. He too wanted to hold out, at least for the 6th, and afterwards. Together we spent much of the night consulting people like Dalloz, consulting the public prosecutor to find the most legal way of decreeing a "state of siege".

'On the morning of 7th February 1934, calm had been restored to Paris. The road maintenance service was erasing the traces of battle. I thought the storm had passed. But in the morning a wind of panic began to blow through the Republic. The morning papers ran headlines about the casualties; they had exaggerated the numbers; they had turned me into a "murderer". It was cranked up beyond measure. No one spared me: neither the left who didn't think I was firm enough, nor the right who accused me of having blood on my hands. Rumours were beginning to circulate about an "even worse blow" to come, about massive arsenals of weapons ready to be used on the periphery of Paris, about seditious battalions and generals who were going to take charge of the revolution. People were talking about Marshal Franchet d'Esperey. The ministers were preparing to abandon ship. The deputies were weakening visibly. Even the most hard-line republicans laid siege to me.

'We were heading for "civil war". I had to resign.

'It was unbearable.

'I had understood. If I stayed, I would have to call in the army the next time a riot occurred. I would have to make them shoot at the crowd – at least if they obeyed me. My cabinet predicted ten thousand dead, and I didn't want that and neither did President Lebrun. In my childhood, I had heard of Draveil, of Villeneuve-Saint-Georges, of the troubles in the Midi and regiments that had been made to fire on the crowd.

'Late in the morning of 7th February, I handed in my resignation to President Lebrun.

'So you can imagine that after resigning on 7th February 1934 in such a stupid way, one might say, I wasn't going to do the same thing again with Munich.'

'Can you really compare 6th February and Munich?'

'I don't know ... It's true that the fascist and military plot which had panicked the deputies, the ministers and even the President of the Republic had been greatly exaggerated. Later, returning to power, I discovered a certain amount of information. The seditionaries had circulated erroneous, alarming information. They had men at the police prefecture, in military headquarters and even in my own Ministry of the Interior; I learned that it was part of a conspiracy called "the Acacia Plot", which was supposed to replace the Third Republic with a regime of Public Safety.

'So, you can imagine, four years later in Munich, I wasn't going to leave the country in those people's hands or, even worse, in the hands of Paul Reynaud and Hélène de Portes. I'll even admit one thing which may shock you: if I had been in power in 1938, if I had had the powers that your de Gaulle has today, if I'd been a bit of a dictator, shall we say, well, I think I really would have left Munich at that moment. And I wouldn't have regretted it.'

5

THE DUCE HAS AN IDEA

'*Those Czechs, you'd let me have them all, and I don't want a single one . . .*'

They had all just laughed together, like men, and by laughing they had already defused the crisis, or nearly. Mussolini felt that this was the right moment, the one when the insurance broker moves into action, the future client's defences having been gently broken down. He waited for the laughter to subside before saying modestly, tapping his uniform with his hand:

'I have drawn up a brief compromise plan that I would like to submit to you . . .'

He looked in his pocket, and casually took out a crumpled piece of paper. The faces of the two democrats brightened. Something serious at last! Hitler became interested, rose to his feet, even tried to read over the Duce's shoulder, but the writing was in Italian. Mussolini brandished his piece of paper before circulating it. Chamberlain's expression was most respectful, but he couldn't read Italian either. Hitler seized the crumpled piece of paper and ran his eyes over it again without understanding a word, then made the effort – which was noticed – to get up and pass it to President Daladier, who was sitting opposite him. The Three seemed to be grateful for this note from Mussolini, which was incomprehensible to them, but such a generous gesture.

Translator Paul Schmidt offered his services. Mussolini imperiously declined. This was his business. The former schoolmaster was returning to his old habits. He seemed to be giving a class to his audience, which was hungry for knowledge.

1. The evacuation will begin on 1st October.
2. The United Kingdom, France and Italy agree that the evacuation of the territory shall be completed by the 10th October, without destruction.
3. Conditions governing the evacuation will be laid down in detail by an international commission composed of representation of the four powers and Czechoslovakia.
4. The international commission will determine the territories in which a plebiscite is to be held. The final determination of the frontiers in the "uncertain" territories and occupation of those territories will be carried out by the international commission.
5. The occupation by stages of predominantly German territories by German troops will begin on 1st October.

The text was precise. The tone authoritative. The terms considered. The Duce, as he delivered each of these propositions, was straining his talent. In fact, there was nothing Italian about the proposition. It had been written the previous day by Göring, Neurath and von Weizsäcker, following the decision to hold a 'last-chance conference'. Hitler had read it, and added the word 'acceptable', and then Schmidt had, as a matter of urgency, translated it into Italian and transmitted it to Mussolini. The Duce and Ciano had prepared for this little game with great delight. So had Paul Schmidt. So the 'Mussolini proposition' was a decoy, the reply to Hitler's unacceptable proposition, the one made at Bad Godesberg, repainted in Italian colours.

The decoy worked wonderfully well.

Daladier, who dreaded the Bad Godesberg Memorandum

more than anything else, felt rather reassured. Oh, of course, they would discuss it, they might make mincemeat of each other, Hitler would split hairs, but at least it wasn't the German *Diktat*, it wasn't that! Chamberlain who dreaded discord, a new quarrel, more than anything else, was delighted that here was a platform for discussion. For the time being, each in his own way, they all avoided going into the five points of the 'Mussolini plan'. They had not had time to analyse it, to refer it to Paris or London; but together they agreed that it might constitute an interesting basis for discussion.

All of a sudden Mussolini was radiant.

He pretended to consult Hitler about his plan. Acting away, he tried to look prudent. He wished to add that there were some things that were very interesting, but that there were details which would have to be revised.

Hearing these reservations, a veil of anxiety passed across Daladier's eyes. And Chamberlain didn't conceal his alarm.

The two dictators looked at one another. They knew what was what.

Everything was going splendidly. Immediate war seemed to have been averted. Shamelessly, Mussolini actually rubbed his hands. He joyfully announced that they would be able – for sure – to leave at the appointed hour. So they were preparing to go for lunch when Neville Chamberlain intervened:

'I repeat, your proposals, Duce, strike me as an excellent starting-point. But this agreement, notably some of its clauses, can be meaningful only if we invite the representatives of the Czechoslovak government to sit down in session with us . . .'

Daladier vigorously agreed, all the more so because he himself had forgotten those poor Czechs. The issue of their participation in the conference had been brought up the previous day by his colleagues. Beneš had bombarded him with phone calls and oblique interventions. The Czechs in Paris, Blum and his entourage, that madman Kérillis, and even General Faucher, had choked on the idea that the Czechoslovaks had not been invited to this conference. The Czechs . . . That's right, the Czechs . . . He nodded his head, still agreeing, while Chamberlain went on.

Hitler replied to the British Prime Minister, in a commanding tone that had nothing to do with his earlier rage, or indeed with any sort of humour.

'If we have to ask the Czechs their agreement on every detail, we won't have finished before a fortnight's out.'

Mussolini noisily approved. Waving a threatening finger, he added, 'And whatever you do, don't forget that my train leaves at midnight whatever happens . . .'

And the Führer went on, 'In the current state of tension, the slightest delay involves terrible dangers. And besides, gentlemen, it is not a German-Czech dispute that we have to resolve today, but a European question . . .'

Daladier was not unhappy with the European argument. He didn't want to abandon Chamberlain mid-campaign, but he said to himself that the German's reasoning made sense.

'If Beneš is capable of calling into doubt an agreement based on the moral authority of our four signatures, that must mean that he has decided not to accept anything. Except by force.'

Mussolini added, pretending to be reasonable: 'We can't wait for the arrival of a qualified representative of the Czech government before deliberating. It is up to us, the great powers,' – and he stressed the phrase – 'to give Germany the moral guarantee that the evacuation will take place without destruction.'

Daladier had heard 'great powers'; he thought it was the right expression. Mussolini and Hitler had just talked about a 'European question', and that was correct. He was fed up to the back teeth with the Byzantine games of French diplomacy since Aristide Briand, that dreamer, that false prophet, that hothead who had thrown France into the arms of a limited company, their League of Nations, and into the hazardous combinations of the 'Petite Entente' where, according to him, the future of France lay. In principle, of course, Daladier had nothing against the participation of those poor Czechs. Quite the contrary! But on a practical level, Mussolini and Hitler had a point. With the Czechs there things would go on for ever. They would never be happy. They would turn up and spoil the civilised atmosphere that finally reigned among the Four. They would make everything tense with all their jeremiads and supplications. They would slow them down by making more and more demands, refusing to let go of a few scraps of the Sudetenland that were causing all the problems. They would even risk ruining everything, on the pretext that some fortification or other, which wasn't really all that important, was absolutely vital.

But the Englishman pressed on. He might have been the high priest of appeasement, but he was fond of those Czechs. The Three all looked at him, as if with a single eye. They hadn't consulted one another, but they suddenly looked at him as an oddball liable to shatter their budding harmony. Daladier felt a twinge of anxiety. Mussolini, one of horror. And Hitler, contempt for this troublemaker who, just a few days before, seemed to be, if not his best friend, then at least his best future ally.

Daladier broke through his reserve. He tried to support Chamberlain, although without much enthusiasm.

'The presence of a Czechoslovak representative, whom we could consult, if necessary, would be useful ... If only to prevent the chaos that can always occur in the event of a cession of territories.'

*　　*　　*

Now they had all exhausted their arguments. They were each in their corner. Hitler quietly spluttered '*Nein, nein, nein,*' gently tapping his foot.

Mussolini swore between his teeth, his face contorted with fury. He seemed to be cursing the Englishman.

Daladier was pretending to be elsewhere. In fact, he was enjoying a new and unexpected situation: this time he wasn't the troublemaker. Which didn't keep him from dreading the worst, more complications, the return of the storm, Hitler's explosions, Mussolini's skilful pressure, and finally the derailing of a conference which was at long last becoming interesting.

An interminable moment seemed to pass before Chamberlain whispered, with the awkward air of someone who has just realised that he has disturbed his hosts, 'It might be enough . . . it might perhaps be enough . . .'

General alarm among the three others, all hanging on the Englishman's word: '. . . if this representative was in an adjacent room . . . at our disposal.'

Daladier was stunned. He really didn't understand the Englishman at all. He had feared the worst, the final rupture, the final polemic that would send everything flying. He was impressed by his ally's practical mind.

As Chamberlain's suggestion was uttered, a tic crossed Hitler's face. He had been impatient, tense, threatening; he had been so bored since the beginning; he was listening again, his eye bright, almost benevolent.

Mussolini nervously tapped the back of his chair. He was preparing to refuse when Hitler gave him a gesture urging him to moderation. Faking exasperation, Mussolini came out with a resounding, 'OK, OK, OK.'

6

THE ARRIVAL OF THE CZECHS

A long corridor in the Hotel Regina, the palace where the British delegation was staying. Two men stepped forward, with uniformed members of the Gestapo on either side. Dr Vojtěch Mastný, the Czechoslovak minister to Germany, and Hubert Masařík, a young Czech diplomat who had come from Prague. Their plane, which had flown from the little Czechoslovak town of Ruzyn, had just landed in Munich. Upon their arrival, they had been treated like suspects. The Gestapo was at the airport: the Germans had sent a police welcome committee rather than a diplomat from Wilhelm-strasse. The two men had been bundled into a police car and driven in silence to the hotel. In fact, since they didn't legally exist as far as the Germans were concerned, they were part of the British delegation.

The two men were accompanied by a British diplomat, Mr Ashton-Gwatkin, who had hastily joined them. They knew him. He was a colleague of Lord Runciman, whose mediation mission had left the Czechs with such an unpleasant memory. Lord Runciman, Lady Runciman and their socialite cohorts had shown themselves particularly attentive to Konrad Henlein, the head of the pro-Nazi Sudeten Germans. They had spent most of their time associating with the Germanic squires, decrying the 'Czechoslovak oppressor'.

The two Czechs didn't reply to Ashton-Gwatkin, who chatted non-stop, whispering and wiping his brow. They stepped forward stiffly and in silence. Dr Mastný, the elder of the Czechs, betrayed his nervous state by fiddling with the handle of his briefcase, which contained President Beneš's secret proposal concerning possible territorial cessions to the Germans. The other, Masařík, walked with a kind of insolence. The two Gestapo guards came to a stop by a doorway and performed a sort of goose-step as they lined up on either side of it. Speaking German and making no concessions, they invited the two Czech diplomats to enter a small room; the British diplomat followed them. He was nervous.

The room was windowless. It wasn't a bedroom, or even a garret; more one of those nooks where, in large hotels, the chambermaids change their clothes and store their equipment. The place had been emptied, but it smelt of cleaning products, an acrid mixture of perfume and bleach. Two Gestapo guards were stationed by the door. The light coming from the ceiling was white and too strong.

Mastný questioned Ashton-Gwatkin about their presence at the conference: 'When are they going to see us? Has the conference begun?'

Ashton-Gwatkin: 'Unfortunately we couldn't wait. And besides, Chancellor Hitler is inflexible . . .'

Mastný: 'But how can they hold a meeting like this without us?'

Ashton-Gwatkin: 'There were last-minute complications. But don't worry, along with the French, we're doing our best to defend your interests . . .' (A silence.) '. . . and also to avoid war breaking out in Europe tomorrow.'

Mastný: 'How can you take that decision without the main parties concerned? We have no idea what's being hatched here. We don't know what starting-points you will be working from. The ones from the Franco-British plan of 16th September, which were already intolerable to our nation? Or those of Hitler's unacceptable *Diktat* at Bad Godesberg?'

Ashton-Gwatkin, embarrassed: 'I can't tell you anything yet. But alas, given the state of progress of the crisis we can dread the worst . . .'

Mastný: 'The worst? What do you mean?'

Ashton-Gwatkin, evasive and more and more embarrassed: 'The situation is difficult . . . Very difficult, yes . . .'

The faces of the two Czechs fell as Ashton-Gwatkin delivered his confession. President Beneš had told them the situation was dangerous. The generals in Prague and the generals at the fortifications had urged intransigence. The Prime Minister, the Minister of Foreign Affairs and lots of geographical experts had prepared them, with rage and tears in their eyes, for the ordeal that they would have to undergo. But now they were actually being kept out of that ordeal. They wouldn't even have to defend themselves; the French and the English would take charge of that. Mastný's rage was cold and impressive, and the emotional Ashton-Gwatkin tried to leave. The ambassador held him back by the sleeve. Masařík then unrolled the map of his country, crossed with big red lines.

Mastný: 'You see . . . These are the areas vital to the survival of Czechoslovakia! On this map you can clearly see that the idea of touching what we call the "Moravian corridor" is utterly unthinkable. If that were to be affected in any way our country would be cut in two. That would be the end of Czechoslovakia.'

Ashton-Gwatkin wore an expression of condolence. He nodded severely, without a word, his eye gloomy and compassionate, but without looking at the map of a far-off country of which we know nothing, as Chamberlain put it. He knew nothing about Czechoslovakia, or of the subtleties of their *Mitteleuropa* and that ridiculous 'Moravian corridor' of which the other man spoke as if it were the Indian Empire.

Ashton-Gwatkin really had to go. People were waiting for

him, they were calling for him at the Führerbau. He slipped outside, leaving them and promising to come back soon.

He slammed the door, and there was the sound of a sliding bolt.

7

'WHAT THE HELL AM I DOING HERE?'

Hitler was the first to leave his palace and dive into his car. Chamberlain followed him and disappeared into the crowd. Next came Daladier, a little gruffer than usual. He made a mistake and tried to get into the Duce's car. A black-clad guard pointed out his error. He stepped irritably aside with a shrug to make way for Mussolini, who was joining Hitler for lunch. Mechanically he lit a cigarette. He was heard muttering: 'What the hell am I doing here?' Then he got into his own car, which had come forward.

The crowd was dense. The President's car was already in gear when Field Marshal Göring tried to get in. He struggled, puffed and finally slipped heavily in, weighed down with the gold dagger that he wore in his belt, and the Field Marshal's baton that he held in his hand. He asked if he could be dropped at the Vier Jahreszeiten Hotel, and burst out laughing when he managed to wedge himself in beside Daladier. Without even looking at Léger, he pushed him on to the opposite foldaway seat. Léger stumbled; he blanched at the insolence, unparalleled in his long international career. He didn't dare protest, and anyway, what would have been the point? The Field Marshal was already, after his exhausting boarding manoeuvre, deep in conversation with Daladier. He had been utterly perplexed by the incident, but had quickly decided that the Reich second-in-command's sympathy was worth the small dent to his colleague's self-esteem.

'Well, Mr President, how did the first session go?' asked Field Marshal Göring with a bitter expression on his face. 'I hope my great friend Baron Joachim von Ribbentrop,' he guffawed at the name, 'wasn't too nasty to you.'

'Mr Ribbentrop didn't open his mouth,' Daladier protested ironically. Göring wasn't afraid of words! So he made no secret of his pique at having been excluded from the conference in favour of his rival. So François-Poncet was telling the truth. Since Ribbentrop had succeeded von Neurath, Göring had been sidelined from foreign policy, except in terms of the Balkans, which had numerous resources relating to the four-year plan for which he was responsible.

'And it's all the better that Mr Ribbentrop didn't speak! You must be careful, Mr President. Ribbentrop exerts a very bad influence on the Führer. Even yesterday, at the very last moment, we had to be very – how should I put it – inventive to keep him from sabotaging the conference. When he learned from the Führer that it was being held today in Munich, and the announcement of his proposal was made public, Mr Ribbentrop exploded with rage. You should have seen him!'

Like the sly peasant he thought he was, Daladier feigned indifference to what he thought of as a first-hand revelation. He decided to let the exuberant Field Marshal speak, to push him a little, just a little, let him spill out his bitterness. He would find out more about the German game. Then, he nodded painfully. He spoke in short sentences so as not to interrupt the German's delivery:

'Yes, this morning at the airport, he looked as if he was having one of his bad days.'

'Ah, but Mr President, Joachim von Ribbentrop always looks as if he's having one of his bad days.'

They couldn't help laughing together. Göring continued, more seriously:

'You know, Mr President, this man is a fanatic. One might have imagined that associating with the English would have civilised him. Not a bit of it. Do you know what Mr Ribbentrop dared to do a few months ago? When he was presented at court, to His Majesty the King of England in person ... Do you know what? He had the affrontery to give him the Nazi salute. Yes, Mr President, you heard me correctly, the Nazi salute. To the King! The whole court was severely shaken. It was my great friend Ambassador Henderson who told me. No, some things are not done!'

The Field Marshal seemed so sincere, so indignant; he said everything so naturally that the President forgot that Göring himself had, in the past, caused a scandal by presenting himself before the Pope at the Vatican with a Nazi salute.

'You see, the man doesn't know how to behave. He doesn't, and no more do the new German diplomats. This fake aristocrat, this fraud. You can't have any idea what the functionaries worthy of the name are saying about him. That such a man should be a minister! And what's more, he wants war. He dreams only of that.'

'That's what I thought,' Daladier replied, and said no more, noticing that his strategy was working.

'War ... war ... It's all he can talk about. And do you know why?'

Daladier was obliged to reply that he didn't actually know.

'Well, Mr President, because Joachim von Ribbentrop has never been a soldier. He doesn't know what it is. This fake German – he was brought up in Canada and England – is also a fake soldier. Just think, he ended his war in the cavalry on the Turkish front. The cavalry on the front!'

Nods from Daladier, more vigorous, sincere this time.

'He isn't like us,' Göring said, suddenly more serious.

He had said 'us' ...

Göring, the hero, the terror of the skies, Göring, the true

successor to the 'Red Baron', had said 'us', thus wrapping him in the cloak of his own legend, Daladier, an obscure infantryman. He had said 'us' as if they were equals, brothers in arms, as if they had had equal shares of blood and glory during the four years of hell. He had said 'us'. Göring had fallen silent. The limousine crossed a still joyful Munich; nothing mattered now, not the conference, nor the ulterior motives, not even this poor Léger who had been thrown on to the jump seat. Once again, he stared at this peculiar Nazi who seemed, like him, to be touched at the mention of 'their' war.

After a long silence, Göring sighed:

'You must have suffered in 1917, with the battle for Mont Cornillet.'

'Oh, just as much as those on the other side, shut up in those tunnels where they died such terrible deaths! Field Marshal, your compatriots fought valiantly. They suffered just as we did. It wasn't just Mont Cornillet. In other places, too we ended up meeting one another. In the moments of respite, we spoke from trench to trench. Sometimes we passed each other tins of food across the lines. Other times we joked. Once we even held a celebration for a soldier in the opposite trench, when a child was born. You don't forget things like that. I even heard about one Christmas when the French and the Germans fraternised, in defiance of orders from above.'

'How right you are, Mr President! You don't forget that kind of thing, you can't. And it's because you and I have been through it that we must speak and act to ensure that it never happens again.'

'Never again, Field Marshal . . .'

'Thankfully not everyone is a Ribbentrop, not in Germany, or . . . in France, Mr President. Luckily there are, in Europe, people like you and me.'

The President didn't know what to say in reply. He was touched. He remained thoughtful, reflecting that he might have made an ally.

Together the two men responded to the acclamations of the crowd, as the situation demanded.

Göring was wedged tightly into the seat. He merely jerked his chin, and smiled from time to time when they reached a crossroads. His face was always turned towards the people. The President noticed that the German never responded to the cheering with his hand or his hat, as he himself had begun to do. It was difficult. He had experienced it before. It forced you to keep your arm raised all the time, to lean slightly forward, always in an uneasy balance on the seat, which meant you were thrown back at the slightest touch on the brakes, making you look ridiculous. The President, suddenly frivolous, was amused to think that there was a skill to being cheered.

Göring back at him.

'Listen, Mr President, you know I have a dream that I've never been able to fulfil . . .'

'And what is that, Field Marshal?'

'Ah!' said Göring, almost shyly but with his eye bright, his mouth in a greedy moue. For a few second he said nothing, resting his hand on Daladier's arm as if bringing him solemnly into his confidence. 'Listen, because of the war a little while ago, and events in the Sudetenland now, I have never been to Paris. And I would so like to go.'

'Really? Paris?'

'Yes, to walk in the streets of Paris, to go to Versailles one day, visit the Louvre . . . yes, the Louvre, the finest museum in the world. Did you know that I was a collector, Mr President?'

'Of course I did, Field Marshal,' exclaimed Daladier, who

didn't. 'But are you serious, Field Marshal? Or rather, forgive me, is your wish really serious? Really, Paris?'

'Entirely serious, Mr President. I could even go there by boat. On the Seine in my *Karyn II.*'

'Good heavens. That is something we could do, isn't it? Léger, what do you think?'

Léger didn't hear; he was too far away, on his jump seat.

'I'll discuss it again with Léger,' cried Daladier, slightly irritably. Before asking Göring, bright-eyed, 'Field Marshal, do you know what would be terrific? If you came with Chancellor Hitler . . .'

'What a great idea for peace! He's never been able to get to Paris either. Oh, if only I could persuade him. A great idea . . . A great idea . . . Oh, if only Ribbentrop didn't exist. It's really a magnificent idea. An idea for men of the war generation . . . Yes, I'll try. Particularly since I think you're in the Führer's good books. As long as he accepts the Duce's plan this afternoon! But it won't be easy . . .'

They had reached the Vier Jahreszeiten Hotel. Once again the President refused the Field Marshal's invitation to lunch. He went straight to his room. And Göring ran to honour his banquet with his presence.

PART FOUR

1

LUNCH WITH HITLER

Entering Hitler's private apartment, where lunch was to be held without the democrats, the Duce studied the German as if for the first time. He remembered that day in 1934 when he had first received the young German leader. He had seemed to him like a petit-bourgeois in a raincoat made of putty, felt hat in hand, floating in a civilian suit, neither handsome nor ugly, with a lumpy nose, a thin mouth and, in those days, a thick moustache. He had seen that German who so admired him as a poor relation.

How could the Führer of all the Germanys live in a place like this! An ordinary apartment, in a block shared with other tenants, low ceilings and mean windows, no real colours, no class or grandeur. What a lack of taste! After all, the Reich could afford to give him a palace, and there was no shortage of those in Bavaria. They could have found him, as they had for the Duce in Rome, a Villa Torlonia belonging to a prince who would hasten to rent it out to him, and for a paltry sum!

The walls were papered with a sad pale green fabric; in the dining room the table was already laid as if in a lawyer's house; passing into the Führer's bedroom, Mussolini happened upon a muscle extensor behind a door, the same kind that he used to strengthen his arm before keeping it stiff for more than an hour during processions. The only luxury items in the house were old masters; rural scenes most of all, the same ones that would have been found, pompously framed, in a *völkisch* bourgeois household, except that these were originals.

Hitler lingered over each of the paintings: Titian, Bordone, Lembach, Dürer, whose engravings adorned his office at the Chancellery; Brueghel, his passion; Vermeer, whose master-piece, according to him, he did not possess, that *Artist in his Studio* that he would do anything to acquire, and thus enrage that dear Göring who flattered himself the greatest collector of Vermeer. He wanted to laugh, but he could only snigger. Hitler's laughter was never clear-cut; there was always a background of bitterness.

The visit was endless. Taking advantage of Hitler's tirades, Mussolini tried to distract himself without the Führer noticing. He turned towards Ciano, his son-in-law, his minister, his whipping boy and accomplice, to make fun of the German. He enjoined him, with a vigorous nudge of his elbow, to notice the tic in Hitler's shoulder which, he murmured, 'has got worse since last year'. At the fifth painting, no longer capable of enduring an art history lesson, the Duce said, in Italian, and almost out loud: 'Soon he'll be telling us it was the Teutons who created civilisation and culture from the depths of their caves . . . *Ma che stronzo.*'

Mussolini was used to the German. During the course of a few official journeys and a stay in the Berghof in Berchtes-gaden, he had got to know him, and perfected an infallible technique. It could be summed up in a single instruction: 'Let him get it out of his system.'

That was his method when, alone with Hitler, the Duce wanted to get something, or avoid something else, or just have a bit of peace. Managing Hitler was a simple affair. You had to let him talk, talk, talk. Never interrupt him, except in high-risk conferences, like the one a few moments ago. Study the cycles of his discourse, being careful not to mistake a break, or too long a breath, for a conclusion. And most important of all, never interrupt him in full flow. That was dangerous. If you did, he would start all over again from the beginning. And then he put you through a new ordeal. Slowly, he brought his *idée fixe* back to the centre of the conversation. The nervous torrent quickened. Then would come exhausting digressions, sometimes even traps like those questions that one should never – repeat, never – answer under any circumstances. Let him relieve himself . . . The image had the merit of both clarity and efficiency. That was how Ciano and Mussolini prepared themselves before they saw him. Because the master of Italy, in spite of the Axis, his presence in Munich and the recent warming of relations between the two countries, remained doubtful. He almost considered Hitler slightly deranged.

The Führer lingered over a contemporary painter, Wilhelm Löwith, whose admirable painting looked like the work of an 18th-century artist. He waxed lyrical over the *Pregnant Woman Reading a Book*, which the Italian studied distractedly. Hitler noticed that Mussolini didn't look convinced, and then set about revealing the hidden meaning of the canvas. He was inexhaustible, explaining at length why the light came from above, enthusiastically praising the artist's incomparable technique, before regretting that the painter was Jewish.

'He's the only Jewish painter I can bear,' he announced proudly. 'All the others are forbidden, or will be, because we won't tolerate "degenerate art" in the Reich. But Löwith isn't like that . . .

'Observe, Duce,' he continued in a lower voice, taking his Italian friend's arm. 'Observe, Duce. Everyone has his Jew . . .'

Hitler paused before continuing, enigmatically, almost bawdily: 'Or his Jewess. Isn't that so, Duce?'

Mussolini didn't react. But the insinuation struck him hard. Hitler was alluding to Margherita Sarfatti, Mussolini's mistress of over thirty years – the one that Ribbentrop's secret service had nicknamed 'the Jewess' – who had recently been replaced by the young Clara Petacci.

Suddenly Mussolini felt uneasy about this obscene incursion. All complicity with the German on this point, on the matter of love, struck him as – he sought the right words and could find no other – 'disgusting'. You could laugh at anything, but not, curiously, with Hitler. There was something repugnant about him, something physical, something indefinable. He didn't know if it was all the things that people said about his love affairs – or rather about his complete lack of love. The unhealthy, sickly side of him; that grey skin, so grey, almost corpse-like. Or that smell, the slightly toxic smell in which he was always enveloped.

At the table of Hitler's little *Speisezimmer*, canapés of woodcock were being served. The venison was first-rate. The Duce, alert to this attention at the Führer's table, wanted to cheer up the gathering with a touch of humour: 'These woodcock are, we might say, the citizens of Mr Hermann Göring.' Since Göring was absent from lunch, Mussolini had sensed disgrace. With his reference he was making a joke at the expense of the man who was also the Reich's master huntsman, and as such reigned over the forests and all the creatures that lived in them. Mussolini burst out laughing all by himself – Göring's citizens – all the more so in that he was a huntsman himself – it was indispensable to anyone with an ounce of manliness – and knew that his German partner was touchy on this point. Ciano smiled. He was the only one at table who did. Himmler, Hess and Ribbentrop pretended not to have heard. They had blanched. Talking 'game' at the Führer's table was taboo, it was a blasphemous topic of conversation even if

Hitler had chosen to honour the Duce with the little birds that day. The three hierarchs grunted, mumbled their indignation, noisily made it known that they too required the Führer's menu rather than the superb venison that had just been placed in front of them. Passionately and concertedly they sought the boss's benevolence, to no avail.

Hitler's mind was elsewhere, he showed the concentrated agitation of a child waiting for his dish. He was on the alert; he watched the bustle of the servants; he became impatient, from time to time, tapping his cutlery. When the soup – mushroom soup – finally arrived, he didn't wait for anyone. He began ceremoniously inhaling it. He swallowed it, alone and concentrating, as old men do when they stir their soup, eyes fixed on their plate, studying the liquid as a fortune-teller stares at coffee grounds, sometimes pausing on a spoonful, considering it for a long time before chewing strangely on it and swallowing it down. Hitler stayed like that, indifferent to the conversation, absent for many minutes, in that state of dazed lethargy.

When Hitler finally did lift his head, it was to say, 'You saw that nigger . . .'

Mussolini nodded with his chin, but he didn't know what nigger the Führer was talking about. He didn't really try to find out; he guessed it must have been an old conversation that the two men had once had about Ethiopia – now the 'jewel of the Empire' – which was now resuming; that in fact the nigger was not his own personal nigger, the late Emperor of Ethiopia, the Negus who travelled from capital to capital of the democratic world with his martyrdom on his sleeve. Mussolini discovered that he was completely wrong when Ribbentrop, always the swiftest, the most zealous, the most likely to understand the Führer's deeper thought processes, intervened:

'You are right, my Führer, it is the sign of a profound decadence in France that it should have at the head of the Foreign Ministry a nigger,' (he stressed the word), 'a Martinican . . .'

Ciano, wanting to add a skilful touch, added with – he sensed – the implicit permission of his boss and father-in-law, 'That tells us a lot about the diplomatic service that France inherited from Monsieur Aristide Briand.'

And so went the chat about the impudence of the 'Nigger', that insolent creature who dared to speak in the place of the somewhat 'outdated but not unsympathetic' Daladier about the comparative qualities of Ambassador Attolico, who was always anxious, the British Ambassador Henderson with his pansy in his buttonhole and François-Poncet who, it was said, would shortly be appointed to the embassy in Rome. They discussed the audacity and significance of the presence of Alexis Léger in such a meeting, until Hitler concluded peremptorily, speaking severely to his Minister of Foreign Affairs:

'Such incidents must not happen again, Ribbentrop. These coloured people should not be permitted to concern themselves with European affairs. Nor should Reich diplomats have anything to do with such people. You have understood, Ribbentrop.'

The impeccable Minister of Foreign Affairs had failed this time. He had wanted to draw the Führer's hatred to the subject of Léger; he had provoked him, had stirred him up, and the flames had just flared up with great force. To hide his humiliation, for he had never been rebuked by the master since his appointment as head of foreign affairs, Ribbentrop nodded. He pretended to take note of the Führer's order.

Only then did they move on to the Englishman, Chamberlain.

Hitler launched in greedily:

'You saw his degenerate face, Duce. Well, just think, I've had to put up with it for at least three days. Once at the Berghof, where he arrived as pink-faced as a girl, so happy at having enjoyed his first flight. And then again for two days and two nights in Bad Godesberg, where he turned into my private secretary, to whom I dictated the conditions of the peace. He was servile, obedient, diligent, ready to do anything, at any time, as long as I didn't do anything to affect the interests of Empire and the City! But never open. Not that. In spite of his declarations: sly, like all English people.'

Mussolini, who was bored when he wasn't talking, thought this was just the moment to develop his theory about the English:

'How right you are, Führer! Look at the Englishman and you will understand! When the people of a country are so enamoured of animals that they build cemeteries, hospitals and houses for them; when the people of a country set up foundations for parrots, it is a clear sign of decadence. What's more, apart from these countless reasons, it also depends on the composition of the British population. A surplus of four million women! Four million sexually unsatisfied women who create all sorts of problems to excite or appease their senses . . .'

A sardonic little smile brightened Hitler's face. Hammering the table, he thundered:

'Alas for Britain, she has not wanted to understand.'

Ciano gave a start and Mussolini settled into the pose he liked to adopt when listening to Adolf Hitler. An imperial mask, eyes narrowed, chin in hand, nodding with one finger pressed under his chin at each of the sentences of his younger ally, taking the others as witness on any particularly pertinent or visionary point, most often drowsing.

'England is not the hereditary enemy of Germany as France has been. Hence,' added Hitler, a tone higher, 'she is not the hereditary enemy of Italy either. But England will be punished for refusing our offers of alliance.'

Mussolini wanted to return to the subject of the day, Czechoslovakia, because, in spite of his 'wrong note strategy, he still didn't know Germany's precise intentions, and that fed into the bad mood that he was just managing to suppress. He had a practical mind, he was methodical, serious and dogged, and fundamentally he had retained his respect for diplomatic practices until the Ethiopian affair, however filled with goodwill he might have been, turned him into an international pariah. He was the opposite of the Führer, whom he found muddled, vague and dangerously fanatical. He sometimes judged him harshly.

'And so to Czechoslovakia . . . What are we going to do this afternoon?'

Then Hitler looked Mussolini up and down as if he were a real simpleton, a tiresome individual who had come to talk to him, brutally, about something completely irrelevant. One might have thought that he had never heard of Czechoslovakia. He sought to check himself, soften himself so as not to offend Mussolini. He said unctuously, 'Ah. That will all be sorted out, Duce, I trust you.'

A smile of satisfaction crossed Mussolini's face. Of relief, too. He preferred this tone.

'But you know, Czechoslovakia isn't a mere trifle, Duce.'

In a lower voice, hoarse again now, he told his mentor of his final ambition, as if confiding a secret:

'Yes, Duce, a day will come when we will have to fight, side by side, against France and England. The democracies hate us. They want us dead. They want us economically and vitally stifled, and they have demonstrated as much by refusing to allow the cession of the Sudetenland to the Reich.

They hate the German people because they know we have a social organisation which . . .'

He paused and rose half out of his chair, pointing at Mussolini:

'. . . you alone, Duce, can match. That's why they are preparing to strangle us . . .'

He rose completely, this time to bellow with anxiety: 'But we won't let them do it, will we, Duce?'

He had once again become the apprentice humbly begging help from the inventor of fascism, the sovereign's protection.

Taken aback, Mussolini turned towards Ciano and gave him a look at once boastful and unhappy, pleading for a phrase, a U-turn, an escape route, some sort of diplomatic magic that might help him out of this tight spot. Ciano's face remained blank. He had been the furious craftsman of the Axis, one of the privileged interlocutors of Hitler, Göring and Ribbentrop, coming and going between Berlin and Rome; he had spent more time with them all than the Duce, he had instigated the Italian *rapprochement*, but now he was beginning to have his doubts.

Mussolini was obliged to murmur, without any real conviction, 'No, no, Führer, we won't allow ourselves to be strangled in this way.'

That was all Hitler needed:

'How right you are, Duce. The next war will be terribly bloody and cruel. We will demoralise our enemy with a war of nerves. Yes, we must be cruel. We must be so, with a clear conscience.'

At these words, at the idea of conscience-free cruelty, Mussolini nodded vigorously. Because he recognised these themes, his own words. Cruelty, sacrifice, the New Man, the Roman Mediterranean. Yes, Hitler really was doing a Mussolini. So there was nothing in those slanders about him, about his Austrian treachery, his desire to outdo the Italian

Empire. No, Hitler remained a fascist and an ally. Apart from his arrogant talk, wasn't his sole focus of interest Eastern Europe? Well then, he could have his Eastern Europe, as long as the Mediterranean (and a bit of Africa too) turned Roman again!

'War, yes, war,' Hitler went on. 'It is, as you well know, Duce, the most natural thing in the world. It is of all times and all places; it is an everyday matter. It never begins, any more than there is ever peace. War is man's natural state . . .'

Another nod from Mussolini. He was enthusiastic. He loved the vigour, which reminded him of his roots and restored a meaning to the beautiful word 'fascism'. Because the Italians were becoming bourgeois! He rose to his feet to toast the genius of his friend the Führer, who, slightly puzzled, picked up an empty glass and clinked it against Mussolini's, without losing his thread:

'What is war, Duce, if not cunning, deception, strategy, attacks and surprises? Yes, we are barbarians . . .

'And we want to be barbarians, it's a title of honour. We are, Duce, the ones who will rejuvenate the world. The present world is approaching its end. Our task is to devastate it . . .'

Delight from Mussolini at this happy formulation. Slight weariness too, fear in spite of everything that, beyond the lovely formulations, Hitler might once again set off on an interminable speech.

But no. Hitler, suddenly more sober, utterly calm, seemed to be reaching his conclusion:

'If we must one day declare war, will we delay, will we worry about the fate of ten million young Germans and young Italians that we will be sending to their death?'

The spectre of those ten million young Italians being sent to their deaths terrified Mussolini. Even so, he didn't turn a hair. He just wondered how many lives he was willing to give for this war. He tried to find the number. The reasonable, acceptable, bearable limit . . . A few dozen Italians a month, as in Spain at the moment, where the Italian air force was 'working wonders'? Or thousands? Tens of thousands? Hundreds of thousands? He raved inwardly as Hitler went on talking.

Even more than all those thousands? A whole generation of young Italians? The possibility of a million horrified him. He banished that deranged hypothesis from his mind, and returned to Hitler. He was shocked by the idea. Mussolini would not put a generation of Italians on a Teutonic pyre.

Nonetheless, he didn't correct Hitler. He might come across as a petty dictator, when in fact he had been the first, the inspiration. Hitler had to be calmed, manoeuvred, guided. One had only to be a match for him. So the Duce said nothing. What could he do over lunch, right in the middle of the summit? So he just trusted to fate and crossed his fingers behind his back, hidden from view.

'And then, Duce, we will provoke a revolution in France; we have agents there; the country is fragile; we shall use all possible means. And then . . .'

With a snap of his fingers at Rudolf Hess, the setting changed. The dining room table became a military desk. A vast map was unrolled.

Mussolini and Ciano noted with unease that it wasn't a map of Czechoslovakia.

It was a map of the Western front.

Hitler paused before saying, hands on his hips, as proud as a child waiting for a reward, 'And then we will invade Great Britain.'

The Duce was flabbergasted.

He hadn't seen this coming. Why would we want to take on the British, attack the very people who were letting us have a free hand in Europe and the Mediterranean? Why them, when they were the very ones willing to let everything go, or nearly? Mussolini wasn't wild about the British, but invading England! Where did that incomprehensible strategy come from, when they had just participated, fraternally and with an English Field Marshal, in the great German man-oeuvres on the Baltic? Mussolini darted a worried glance at Ciano, but let Hitler continue.

'So, Duce . . .'

Mussolini immediately rose to his feet, heavily, almost reluc-tantly. He regained his martial pose, legs parted, planted firmly on the ground, hands linked in front of him; his wisest, most valiant posture, the pose of the older brother wondering what the younger brother's been up to now; the pose of someone thoroughly in charge. He pretended to take an interest in the details of the map that had just been placed under his nose, but with detachment, scepticism, weariness. While Hitler said by way of conclusion, 'Better for this eventuality to come about while you and I, still young and full of vigour,' he looked at him admiringly, 'are still the heads of our respective states.' Then Hitler began to set out his plan for the invasion of England.

This last phrase – 'while we are still young and full of vigour' – hit Mussolini like an electric shock. He was shaken, but went on, as if nothing had happened, running his finger along the Maginot Line, the Alps, the Savoie. He tried to come up with a reply to this startling invitation; how to remain equal to it – he, the pioneer, the master; how to avoid being overtaken by his pupil, how to contain him.

He found the dodge he needed.

He pulled up his trousers, struck himself on the stomach several times, and threw himself on the floor. He did a series of press-ups, then got back up, sweating and strident:

'But my dear Adolf, I'm in very good shape. I have all the time in the world. I'm still young and vigorous. And I hope I shall remain so for a long time to come . . .'

His feat had not amused Hitler, who had difficulty

concealing his impatience. He chewed his moustache, his left leg tapped against the leg of the table. He wanted to take his idea to its conclusion:

'I will shortly turn fifty, Duce. You are fifty-five. And even if we are both in good health,' he broke off and drew himself up slightly, he was now a few inches taller than the Duce, 'we will not live for ever . . .'

Mussolini made a fatalistic gesture:

'Duce, it will take us years to conquer Europe, to construct and consolidate these two empires that we are building . . . and also . . .'

Here Hitler assumed a mischievous expression, the kind seen in Munich beer halls:

'And also to reap the benefits.'

He imagined that his punch-line might please the Italian gambler.

But this prospect didn't make Mussolini smile.

He had suddenly faded away. He was floating, he was absent. What he would really have liked to do was flee, leave this wretched apartment, these lugubrious old masters, get away from Hitler and monkey-faced Hess, Himmler with his satyr's expression, escape Munich and the prospect of war with England, go home to Italy. He would have liked to forget the Axis, retract the vows he had made to Hitler, absolute power over the Mediterranean, the scraps of Africa, the Balkans, and also all those drunken promises they had made to one another. He could no longer stand being there.

He and the German clearly didn't have the same concept of barbarism. He, Mussolini, dreamt of a barbarism that would reimmerse Italian blood in the glorious Roman Empire; while Hitler was only one of those Eastern barbarians, the descendant of one of those Visigoths who had brought down Imperial Rome. There was barbarism and barbarism . . .

*   *   *

'While you and I, still young and full of vigour . . .'

The Duce was suddenly prey to an even greater anxiety. Hitler couldn't have uttered such a phrase without knowing. Was the German aware of the unpleasant rumours? He knew. He must know. His ambassador in Rome was far more resourceful than that ass Attolico . . . But what exactly did Hitler know? Yes, he must have heard of that 'stomach ulcer', and what of it? The whole of Italy knew, in spite of censorship, the whole country wept, pitied the Duce, sent him witches' remedies, blessings, even chemists' prescriptions.

But did he know about everything else? About those attacks which now left him confined to bed for days at a time, contorted with pain until he was relieved with morphine. 'It's your stomach,' diagnosed the ten or so eminent doctors of the Italian Academy. But the illness afflicting the Duce remained inexplicable, unpredictable and incurable. That tormented him, but the sickness in his stomach remained a genuine state secret. Officially, Hitler couldn't possibly know.

Mussolini tried to tell himself that according to his own secret service, the Führer wasn't exactly in tip-top condition either. He tried to bear in mind that for his 'gastric pains', he had a myriad of doctors all around him, Dr Brandt and also the enigmatic Dr Morell with his drugs. He also knew about the chronic constipation revealed by the recent analyses that Ciano had organised for him. Moreover, he had heard of a 'genetic cancer' of which Hitler's mother was said to have died at the young age of 47. He knew all that, the daily injections, the dabs of cocaine in his nostrils, his strict diets. There was nothing he didn't know. But all of a sudden, at the mention of his own old age, Benito Mussolini had felt stripped naked by his disciple. Outdated.

And he had begun to ruminate. He is younger than me . . . His people are younger, too . . . You only have to see him in the stadiums, in Nuremberg . . . More vigorous than my fat, dozy Italians . . . To think that I've been ruling Italy for sixteen years. Perhaps – it's true – perhaps I've grown old . . .

Mussolini emerged from his thoughts to assent to what – he was the elder man, wasn't he? – was plainly obvious.

'Of course, this war will take place. One day. One day.'

But that wasn't enough for Hitler. With a grim expression, his fist on the map, he suddenly pointed unpleasantly at Mussolini:

'Perhaps, you say, Duce . . . Perhaps . . . Perhaps? No, there's no doubt about it, the war will take place. It will be us or them. You know that very well.'

Mussolini cautiously objected, resting his finger on the eastern side of the map.

'It will be hard to fight on two fronts; our enemy is Bolshevism and also . . . if you like . . . and also France, which you have identified – rightly, in *Mein Kampf* – as our hereditary enemy . . .'

The Italian feigned indifference, but he was thinking, of course, about the Savoie, about Corsica, about Nice, Tunisia, the Roman Mediterranean.

He continued, almost outraged: 'But antagonising England, Führer! And tomorrow the Americans! Is that really wise? Particularly since England intends to leave us in peace as long as we let her keep her Empire.'

'Duce, this business about the two fronts: Bolshevism and the democracies . . . Don't worry. I have my own little idea about that.'

The Duce frowned; his eyes rolled with impatience. What could he have come up with? The Führer's 'little idea' had whetted his appetite. Renewed joy and energy surged through him as he remembered what people said about Hitler: that he was infallible. Since 1935, Hitler had surprised him on many occasions: he had conned the English by acquiring a new navy; he had walked all over the French by re-establishing military service in 1935; marching into the Rhineland in 1936; leaving the League of Nations. He also remembered the Führer's steadfast friendship when things were going badly, during the Ethiopian affair. And besides, he had to admit that he had been impressed by the Anschluss.

Mussolini was regaining trust. He was tempted. So Hitler had a plan that he wasn't going to tell him about. He pricked up his ears; he flashed him the complicit look of their heyday; threw him a line, ten lines. Hitler said nothing of 'his little idea'. He seemed to be enjoying the situation in silence.

Don't show anything, ever. Mussolini turned to face a window. He stood in profile to avoid revealing his turmoil, and in the voice of a traveller on a station platform, he asked, 'And when do you see it coming, this war?'

Hitler didn't reply immediately. He seemed to be thinking.

Mussolini tried to see the Führer's silence in the best possible light. He wasn't as mad as all that; so he had a plan worked out; he even seemed to be counting in his head. The Italian imagined that Hitler was calculating the number of armoured vehicles, chasseurs, long-range bombers, secret or miracle weapons that would be needed to undertake a victorious war. He was waiting for an assessment, and then a date. A far-off date.

Finally Hitler announced:

'Not before 1942. By then we will really be ready.'

The Duce nodded several times.

He had said '1942' . . .

2

'I HAD TO GAIN SOME TIME.'

1942 . . .

So Hitler wasn't ready. He wanted to wait until 1942 before starting his war. The democrats had been deceived. I discovered the information the day after a conversation with Daladier when, curiously, he too had told me of the same intention on the Allied side: wait till 1942 so that you can be ready to win.

'Mr President, if you had one crucial argument for staying on in Munich, what would it be?'

'Well, if I had to sum up my position: in Munich, my retreat from war was tactical. I had to gain some time . . . I had seen. I had understood that Germany had warmongering intentions in Europe. For me, accepting Munich had only been a justification: gaining time. Waiting for 1942. For two reasons.

'To wait for a possible American intervention that could only occur in the event of a possible third mandate from President Roosevelt. It was only if he was re-elected that he would have a free hand, given the isolationist state of American public opinion.

'And most of all to rearm. I had commissioned a study of the question. We needed four years. We had concluded that France and her ally, England, needed as long as that if they were to catch up with Germany. Essentially because of our inadequate air force. By that date we would have won without any difficulty.

'We had put in place a plan for the air force.

'We also needed some planes that America was supposed to be delivering to us. And I hadn't waited for Munich before thinking about it. I'd put in orders with Curtiss and Glenn Martin. In May 1938, and then again in October when I got back from the conference, I had persuaded my friend Ambassador Bullitt to intercede on our behalf with President Roosevelt to avoid any problems raised by our orders from the American factories. Roosevelt's intervention was crucial. Moreover, one of Roosevelt's ministers, Mr Stettinius, declared after the war that it was thanks to the French orders in 1938 that American industry was able to equip the Allies from 1942 onwards.'

'You're talking as if you only came to power in 1938. But you'd been War Minister four times since Hitler was in power!'

'Yes, but my hands weren't free, and there were intervals when I wasn't responsible for war. So in 1934 Marshal Pétain, the then War Minister, had had the funds allocated to the military by the budget reduced by twenty per cent. Pétain himself! I was the one who did my duty, not the others. In three years, between 1937 and September 1939, I devoted more than 69 billion francs to national defence, including 39 billion to the air force. If only half of those funds had been devoted to our weaponry by the other Presidents of Council or War Ministers between 1934 and 1936, the situation would have been very different.'

'Listening to you, you'd think that the rearmament of France was your decision immediately after Munich. And yet rearmament was a political decision by the Popular Front of which you were a part, isn't that right?'

'Mademoiselle, do you think that in 1936 you just had to press a button for modern weapons to come out of our factories! When rearmament was decided upon in 1936, our industrial potential was three times lower than that of Germany – which had made considerable efforts in that direction, even before Hitler arrived. Most of our machines dated from the Great War. And there was also a serious manpower problem. The Popular Front wanted rearmament, but couldn't afford it. We didn't want to confront the unions, or fall back on the forty-hour law. Everything was halting production. That was why, for example, the Renault factories that produced two tanks a day in 1935, before re-armament, were only bringing out one a day in 1937. And then there were the aberrations in the issuing of military commands. Rival authorities were short-circuiting one another. Military command was falling into complete chaos.'

'It's always other people's fault as far as you're concerned. Pétain, the Popular Front, your predecessors, graduates of the Grandes Écoles ... So what were you up to when all this was going on? Playing a bit-part?'

'Basically, if I had to analyse things with a bit of hindsight, I would say that the blame lies first and foremost with Pétain, with his military conceptions, particularly that 1927 law which established his defensive doctrine: "The essential object of military organisation is to safeguard national territory." That said it all. You can't imagine what Pétain was like in those days! During those years no one remembered that Foch and Clemenceau saw Pétain as a "defeatist". For us, he was a legend, the most illustrious of our soldiers. The ideologue of the Maginot Line, you might say. We were all under his legendary influence, all of us were. Even Blum, your sainted Blum, saw him as a "republican general". That military philosophy was a defensive one. So everyone listened to Pétain when he said: "When you've spent billions on sound and solid fortifications, you don't do something lunatic like going in front of those fortifications in the service of some adventure or other." That said it all. France couldn't afford two strategies, one defensive, the other offensive. In 1921, Pétain had defined that orientation: "The defensive is a situation infinitely superior to the offensive, because fire kills.'"

"'Because fire kills.'"

3

LETTER TO IDA

Dear Ida,

I had a very short lunch. My colleagues have just left me. I wanted to tell you about a serious conversation I had with Mr Joachim von Ribbentrop at the end of the first session. He is still just as unpleasant (as he was when we met him in London), but he is increasingly influential. He told me of a strange and delicate affair, one that we might even call confidential. The Minister of Foreign Affairs confided in me that the Führer has been severely affected by an affair of British origin. An affair that touched him directly, personally. They are planning to make a film about him. A sort of low farce is said to be in preparation. And the Führer is said to consider that the responsibility for this insulting film lies with us, since the director, and also the performer, of this insane project is a subject of His Majesty. Ribbentrop told me that this man is none other than the clown Charlie Chaplin.

According to Ribbentrop, who was clearly very worried, the film project is well under way. Two notorious Marxist colleagues of Chaplin's are supposed to have been taken on this summer, Robert Meltzer and Dan James. The film is, Ribbentrop tells me, financed by Jewish capitalists on Wall Street, probably keen to come to the aid of their co-religionist Chaplin. It is plain that such an enterprise could severely damage – I could tell by the minister's tone – the good relations that we wish to develop between the Crown and the Third Reich.

Charlie Chaplin playing Hitler! Dear Ida, it is a grave insult. The Germans are quite right to be indignant. Imagine if they in their turn decided to make a burlesque film about our King, or – if my modesty were not suffering enough already – your honourable brother. England would not allow them to do so.

I promised to do everything to prevent this provocative project.

Together, we came up with two possible ways. Put pressure on the film distributors in England and the United States to ensure that they do not 'bring out' – pardon the jargon – Chaplin's film.

The other way is to address myself directly to a man with great influence in Hollywood. The new United States ambassador, my friend Joe Kennedy. Wouldn't he be best placed? I'm sure he will help us in this affair. He will understand its importance; he is one of those Americans who, like Mr Lindbergh, have a clear vision of things and are seeking to establish peaceful relations with Germany. Kennedy will be able to intervene at the source of the problem. He still has friends and powerful interests in Hollywood, from the days when he was a mogul, when he left his large family on the coast and had an illicit relationship with a famous actress, Gloria Swanson.

Ribbentrop was right to talk to me about this business.

How is it possible, at a time when world peace has never been more fragile, that irresponsible fools like this man Chaplin can threaten it with impunity?

I shall have to deal with this affair upon my return to London.

Your affectionate Neville

4

DALADIER SACRIFICES HIMSELF

His colleagues were waiting to have lunch with him, in suite 42–44 of the Vier Jahreszeiten, where food had been prepared. Rather rudely, like a farmer who hasn't finished bringing in his harvest, the President told them he was busy. He took his leave of Léger, François-Poncet and Clapier, promising that he would see them again later. The three men left; he thought they looked a little downcast, wondered if he hadn't been too brutal, whether he might have upset them, but in the end he didn't greatly care. He needed to be alone.

He hurried into the vast, modern bathroom to take a cold bath, as cold as possible. He had been dreaming of it since arriving in Munich. He desperately needed it: it would stir his blood. It was his support, his secret, his drug when the pressure grew too intense. A recipe from his grandfather Mouriès, who used to throw him into the River Durance in the winter to harden him up; a recipe as infallible as the clove-water he was given to drink, which he still remembered as a taste from childhood.

When the President emerged from his bath he was alert but not really fired up. He asked the hotel switchboard to put him through to the Marquise de Crussol in Paris.

As he waited for the call, the President began pacing around his suite. He looked himself up and down in the mirror, turned round and then around again, found himself solid, perhaps a little full-bellied, but slimmer since the diet prescribed for him by the Marquise. He tried to imagine himself with still less of a belly, but wasn't convinced.

Now it was the Marquise that he wanted to talk to. He needed to hear her, to know that she was there, to consult her. She was so precious to him, and so elegant in every situation. Of course he could have discussed his doubts with Léger, but Léger was so unstable. There was François-Poncet, but he was too witty. There was Clapier, loyal Clapier, but he was too docile. He needed something else, the flair of the Marquise, her opinion, her antennae.

He needed to sense, through her, the smell and the noise in France, in Paris; he needed to know what Paul Reynaud and Hélène de Portes were up to, what reports were being delivered in her salon by Odette Bonnet, the spokeswoman for her husband the minister, who was known as 'Soutien-Georges'; what venom Pertinax had spat in *L'Ordre* and Geneviève Tabouis in *L'Oeuvre*; what Lazareff would run on the front page of *Paris Soir*; and what sentence would be passed tomorrow by Blum, in *Le Populaire*. He needed to know what the Party would be cooking up, the left wing, the right wing, and especially Herriot, his former teacher and not his rival.

And more than anything he needed to open up his heart to the absent Marquise; to weigh up the pros and cons, to go through his doubts with her, to hesitate again, without being held up to the judgment of others, to the eyes of Léger, François-Poncet or Clapier. He needed her to put in their proper balance the Heart, meaning his Czech ally, and Reason, meaning peace.

Bereft of intimates, the President desperately needed her.

The receptionist rang him back to tell him that the person requested from the Paris exchange was not available.

The Marquise, unavailable at that time of day, and in these circumstances. The President was frustrated.

Stupidly, intensely, he wanted a few moments of her time. Then he calmed down, saying to himself that he was too sentimental.

Very quickly, his lost and worried mind managed to settle elsewhere.

The image of Madeleine came to him.

It was five years, eleven months and fourteen days. He wondered what Madeleine would have said of the situation; what she would have thought of the course of the conference; what that scientist, with her elevated mind, a stranger to political pettiness, would have advised him to do at that crucial moment.

Leave, not leave . . . The dilemma assailed him once again. He hesitated between war and peace, between staying and going, between the Czechs and the tranquillity of the French. What would she have said?

He remembered her, last time, on her death-bed, that terrible night in Carches in 1932, in their country house. He had arrived too late, just a few hours too late, hours that seemed, after all those years, like a betrayal. While he had been held up in Paris by the Party, the minister, the Colonies of which he was in charge, and all the bores, she was dying. The President had never been able to shake off that guilt. He had been told of her strange death-throes. At exactly midnight, Madeleine had called for the children to be brought to her, Jean who was ten, and Pierre who was only seven. She had talked to them as if nothing was wrong, had told them in the most ordinary way of her last wishes, and then just as calmly she had told the two children that four hours later she would be dead. She had kissed them, and they withdrew. At exactly four o'clock in the morning, Madeleine Daladier was no more.

Once again the pain was acute. The same knife-blow.

Why her? Why not him? Why the admirable Madeleine? Had he been able to choose, it would have been better for him to go and not her, for his children brought up without a mother, without real love, without a home, Jean with his gloomy expression, Pierre always missing the point slightly. It would have been better for science, too. Definitely, Madeleine would have won the Nobel; she would have been, even more so than Madame Curie before her, the Pasteur of the 20th century. While he, poor doubting devil that he was, with the weight of France on his shoulders, what good had he done?

Madeleine's face was in his head; fixed and dazzling, it wouldn't leave him.

He was raving. Why had he been the survivor? Yes, that was it, the survivor?

Then another face came to him at the same time as his 'trench headache' came back. That face blurred with Madeleine's. It was Cheminade. Jean, who died in 1917, the ghost of Jean, always the same apparition, Jean's face shortly after his death, caught in a strange rictus.

That day, too, why had Cheminade died in his place? Why had Providence – as they say – and that shell decided to take Cheminade, so good, so admirable, so Catholic? And why had he himself been condemned to live, to bear that pain and guilt?

At that moment the President understood. This time it would be his turn. He could no longer escape. It was his turn to sacrifice himself.

He thought he felt a kind of mystical fervour, unfamiliar to him, non-believer that he was. In it he found the strength to choose.

Leaving the conference, as he had wished to do, he would quite definitely have become a star. It would have been his political downfall; he would have been defeated in the Chamber, in the Party; but he would have triumphed in legend, in the newspapers and the history books. He would have left like a rebel. No one would forget that gesture. But what would the point of it have been? To let the Three others get on with their dirty work?

Certainly, staying didn't let him escape political death, but at least he was making himself useful.

He would sacrifice himself, he would stay to avoid the dismantling of Czechoslovakia, save their fortifications, their networks, and also that bloody Moravian corridor. To prevent the adoption of Hitler's Bad Godesberg plan. To keep war from breaking out tomorrow, at eight o'clock in the morning. So that they could rearm, and rearm again, and wait for the planes promised by Roosevelt. To gain some time. So that his soul would not bear the curse of war. So that his Jean would not end up like Cheminade.

He was staying to die a little, he said to himself.

Hesitation was no longer an option.

He had to assume.

A phrase came back to him. He had heard it uttered by Léger or someone in the Quai d'Orsay during a cabinet meeting. He had been struck by it:

'OK . . . You can't ask a fellow country to commit suicide. But you can, perhaps, ask it to cut a leg off.'

Cut a leg off, that was it.

At the time, the expression had shocked him. But he had to get it over with. He had to go through it, through the little sacrifice on the part of the Czechs as much – he was convinced of it now – as by his own sacrifice.

He sent for Léger, François-Poncet and Clapier.

Coming back into the suite, his colleagues thought that they were – finally – going to be able to take their bearings before the afternoon session; to consult one another and consult the files that Léger had found again, establish a battle-plan once and for all. They wanted to keep him up to date with all the latest information; Léger had had the Quai and Prague on the telephone. But the President didn't want to listen to them. He was frightened of changing his mind, he dreaded their influence, a Byzantine discussion with the formidable Léger, who would undermine his determination, and the loss of energy that would inevitably follow.

Thumbs on his lapels, he preferred to walk around in the drawing-room, in front of his three colleagues standing in a row. He had bucked up. He was like a surgeon just before an operation. Daladier was determined. He returned to the 'Gamelin note' to make a final point. Turning towards Léger, he explained to him that if Czechoslovakia were to agree to cede the Sudetenland, they would still need to stay firm on the subject of fortifications.

Before leaving his room, he tapped the 'Gamelin note' . . .
Everything was ready for operation 'amputation'.

PART FIVE

1

BACK FROM THE BANQUET

Four-thirty p.m.

After lunch, it was no longer the conference it had been at midday, solemn, extremely tense, ready to shatter at any moment. It was diplomatic bedlam. A summit like any other, where some people came back from a banquet at the Vier Jahreszeiten Hotel, joyfully led by Göring who had changed his ceremonial uniform; and where the others, the French and the English – who had lunched separately – seemed more relaxed in their attitude, overwhelmed by Munich's late-summer heat.

There were lots of them, so many more, how on earth, the President had wondered, fatalistic in the face of the crush. In fact a good twenty dignitaries had joined the morning's nine participants. The company had now thrown etiquette to the winds. In the hall, people of every nationality mingled in complete chaos: the Italians joked with everyone, the French discovered sudden and unexpected affinities with the Germans, over a battlefield or perhaps a good wine; even the English, so serious and awkward in the morning, began to relax, saying to themselves that the conference was underway, and the final agreement in sight.

Everyone was cordial. They had rediscovered the joyful mood that had prevailed before 1914. They began dreaming of a new four-nation pact, they started conjecturing; imagining, as though peace had triumph, the many alliances that could be forged the following day. The English, with the

Germans, and the French. Even the Italians, if they were reasonable, if they took Corsica, Savoie and Nice out of their sights. Four powers; twelve treaties, as many possibilities for the strategists, an infinity of threads from which to weave the fabric of peace . . .

At the door to the conference hall, the master of ceremonies, the redhead who had been so efficient throughout the morning, was no longer officiating. He was standing in a corner. He had swapped his close-fitting usher's suit for an impeccable black SS officer's uniform, and he was watching. Curiously, he hadn't been replaced. No other maître d', no filter had been put in place for this second session. The experts with their maps, the officers with their whips, the diplomats with their protocol, everyone was in a hurry, everyone was jostling everyone else.

Göring passed and this time his momentum wasn't hampered by the strange maître d'.

François-Poncet, who wanted to repair the humiliation of the previous session, stuck by Daladier.

Everyone surged forward. In the adjacent drawing-rooms, there was no one left but shorthand typists and bored translators.

The conference had become a forum.

It had also become a matter for subordinates. The secretaries and the experts went about their business. The diplomats chattered. The officers busied themselves. The heads of state had come and sat around the sofas. Not far away, the map of Czechoslovakia and her neighbours had been laid out on a table. Too large for the table, it hung off the sides. And it looked exactly like the skin of an animal that was about to be carved into little pieces.

The English were constantly retouching a motion of their own devising concerning the financial and banking aspects of the agreement; the coming and going was ceaseless, and

Chamberlain was forever adding his own modifications. The Italians and the French tried to find a solution for a border to which the Germans had just objected. The tone was civilised: polite exchanges, serious accounting. From time to time a joke relaxed the atmosphere. It was as if all these adults were enjoying themselves at a party game. Whole villages passed, in the course of a few seconds, under the sovereignty of the Reich, only to fall almost immediately back into the lap of Czechoslovakia, within, of course, reserved criteria. Thus tens of thousands of poor Czechs and Sudeten democrats were transported from one country to another, from a future to a hell, and they were blissfully unaware of it.

Private conversations formed in little groups. Hitler wearily observed all the hustle and bustle.

Chamberlain begged Mussolini, and Count Ciano by his side, to delay their departure so that they could talk about this broader agreement with Italy. Mussolini refused in such a way that the British 'ambiguities' were not dispelled. Chamberlain began to sulk.

Mussolini was actually getting bored, and couldn't stand still. He paced round and round the room, rolled his eyes, corrected a motion, fiddled with a bit of map, fidgeted all over the place, as if trying to discharge the tension that had built up during the conversation with Chamberlain. He encouraged the quibbling bureaucrats. His train, his train . . .

The conference began to fray at the edges.

There came the question of the Czechoslovak fortifications.

It was the turn of the French. Now or never. But when the President was supposed to intervene, he lost his nerve. He felt ill-prepared, a little too approximate. He turned towards the indispensable Léger, so much more at ease than himself in diplomatic matters:

'Come on, Léger, old chap, it's our turn to speak. Off you go.'

Léger was surprised by the invitation and the President's tone. He had no precise instructions on this clause. He had his little idea, certainly, but also lots of bad memories. He didn't need to be rebuked once again for governing in the place of the government. His ordeal had already been quite enough.

Again, Daladier whispered to him, 'Go on, it's our turn,' pushing him slightly with his arm, as a trainer might push his boxer.

Léger hesitated, consulted his index cards, and finally launched in: having decided at least to defend the 'Gamelin note' outlined by Daladier an hour earlier.

Léger's intervention was clear and precise.

The Secretary General of the Quai d'Orsay methodically defended the Czech fortifications, their origin, the principle behind them. Everyone's attention was fixed on him, Mussolini serious as a mediator, Daladier proud as a trainer, proud of such clarity, such geographical precision and elegance in his statements. The German delegation jotted down the translation. Göring, who had come progressively closer to the Führer, was attentive, calm and vaguely drowsy.

Only Hitler seemed agitated. He didn't listen to Léger. He had turned right round towards Ribbentrop to chat with him. Little cries could be heard, and barely suppressed laughter.

It was only when Léger had finished his outline that Hitler finally turned round. His lock of black hair hid his face. He was paler than ever. A fleck of white saliva had dried on his bottom lip. In a peasant voice, unexpected at that moment, he said, 'Who's that nigger who's just been talking?'

The Germans, with the exception of von Weizsäcker, exploded with laughter.

Hitler repeated the phrase in the direction of the placid Paul Schmidt; he asked him to translate it.

Alexis Léger had understood. Because in almost every language the word has the same hateful, obscene vibration. It stands out with its guttural vibrations, two dry syllables that contract like spittle, and the electrical rictus that runs across the face of the person who utters it. Alexis Léger, a white Guadeloupian, had had since childhood, like black people and people of mixed race, a highly developed ear for the word.

The Secretary General of the Quai d'Orsay wanted to sink into the ground. He decided to go for confrontation.

He stared fixedly at Hitler, who couldn't withstand his gaze. The President, not having heard the Führer's remark, questioned Léger who, stiff and steady-eyed, did not reply.

Then he turned towards François-Poncet. The ambassador, who had missed nothing of the scene, quickly sought the most suitable way of telling him of the incident. It was all so unusual, so undiplomatic, so violent, that establishing the unadorned truth was a delicate matter; furthermore, according to the way in which it was reported, it risked reinforcing in Daladier's eyes the already considerable prestige of Léger, his rival.

François-Poncet made up his mind, he mumbled in Daladier's ear:

'Oh, nothing of any importance, Mr President. Chancellor Hitler has been . . . let's say a little coarse . . . with the Secretary General.'

Daladier, impatient and suddenly aware of having missed something, frustrated, exasperated as people always are when they don't understand the local language, snapped, 'What was it, though? What did he say, for heaven's sake?'

'I think, Mr President, that Chancellor Hitler spoke of Monsieur Léger in discourteous terms.'

'Discourteous? Say what you mean. And stop hedging.'

'That is ... Chancellor Hitler said, "Who's that ... Martinican ..." or maybe it was "that nigger" ... I can't remember ... who spoke last ... ?'

That Martinican, that nigger ...

The expression froze the President's blood.

By associating for so long with Alexis Léger, he had finally forgotten that the Secretary General was Guadeloupian, a Frenchman from the overseas territory, a Creole, a white from 'over there'.

The President had always seen him as the boss of the Quai d'Orsay, a senior official, elegant and devoted, a figure both Parisian and French. Besides, he had never – as far as he could remember – differentiated between black people and anyone else. Not in the Colonial Ministry in his early days, when he had associated with, helped and protected capitalist colonials. Nor when he was a teacher, fraternally welcoming into his class in Lyon some French pupils who were not, as people said, 'of French extraction': a Kabyle, the son of a senior Algerian official; two twins from Réunion, very good students, incidentally, in spite of their origins; and even some Jews, although he had never really known which category to place them in.

Never, never ever, had the history and geography teacher, the republican who loved the Empire and all the peoples who made it up, never had he been a racist.

So Hitler had said 'nigger', or possibly 'Martinican'.

The President was seething internally.

He was no longer there. He had stopped listening. He didn't care what Mussolini might say now about this clause.

He knew himself. He was sanguine, perhaps a bit too sanguine. What he dreaded most was a sudden burst of fury, an irrevocable exclamation, an act of stupidity, an ill-considered gesture towards the insulting Mr Hitler.

The President turned towards Hitler's victim. He wanted to give himself some momentum, and found in Léger's eye, who knows, inspiration. Léger remained unperturbed, stiff in his armchair. Daladier just held his arm, for a long time, with an air of condolence in his painful gaze. But Léger didn't respond to his boss's appeals, he just stood at outraged attention. Daladier didn't press the point.

You don't treat a representative of France like that. This was a serious matter . . . it was wounding . . . it was unacceptable. The President tried to find an immediate, firm and civilised response. A word, a gesture, a phrase, something that would allow him to show a reaction.

Yes, that was it: show a reaction.

The President at first imagined rising to his feet to make a solemn protest. He quickly abandoned the idea, it would be too much like that morning's intervention. He couldn't start that again.

Then he came up with the idea of going away, leaving without delay, vigorously dragging poor Léger along with him. France would not be humiliated like that, not with impunity. Very quickly he convinced himself that when all was said and done such a remedy would be absolutely dreadful. Once again, he shivered as he imagined the conference without him.

Then, in desperation, he thought that the easiest thing would be to demand an apology from Hitler. But then he began to worry. What if Hitler refused? The humiliation would be even greater for poor Léger, and also for France.

Despairing of ever hitting upon the ideal response, realising that it had already been too long in coming, the President conjectured further. He contemplated, imagined, plotted, surmised. He constructed so many plans that when Mussolini had finished his intervention, the President wondered if the game was still worth the candle. He weighed up the game and the candle. Before being assailed by a doubt that struck him as definitive:

'What if François-Poncet was mistaken? After all, he didn't even know if Hitler had said "nigger" or "Martinican".'

Then the President fabricated a conviction that was stronger than the others:

'If in doubt over a controversial word . . . everything were to be destroyed! Where would we go from there?'

He had very little trouble persuading himself it was not, here and now, and barely a few cables' lengths away from peace, worth provoking Hitler's wrath over a single word.

Of course, if Hitler had said something so uncouth on other occasions, Daladier would have sorted him out, straight away.

The President turned once more towards Léger.

He was relieved to observe that the Secretary General was less pale, that he even seemed to have reacquired an interest in the discussion that was under way. He then calmed himself by reflecting that Alexis Léger must often have encountered such things in his career. He must have developed a thick skin over the years. He would recover from this dent in his self-esteem.

The President tightly gripped his colleague's forearm. He was about to say something to him, and started leaning forward, but half-way he gave up the idea.

2

CHANCELLOR HITLER'S SENSE OF
FAIR PLAY

The conference was buzzing.

The President decided to intervene, firmly, on the question
that was troubling him: the Czechoslovak fortifications.

Even if Léger had been insulted, the fortifications still
couldn't be abandoned . . .

Alas, one might be forced to amputate Czechoslovakia;
murder had never been on the cards! And without her fortifications, Czechoslovakia was finished.

For several days, Zamberk-Fridaldov-Opawa, those places
with their impossible names had become the President's
obsession. The heroism of the French seemed to measure itself
against this yardstick: the fortifications of the Moravian
corridor. The President had no idea of the colours of the
land, the faces, the religion or the customs of those Mora-
vians. He had never heard of the wines of Moravia or the
beauty of the Czech language, but the Moravian corridor
had become his 'blue line of the Vosges'.

France couldn't give in on the fortifications, Daladier
couldn't do it.

He had his vade mecum in his pocket; he still had his last
conversation with Gamelin in his mind.

'At least Czechoslovakia's fortified systems should be maintained,' the general had advised him, 'so that she remains a
viable "state".'

He remembered replying to Gamelin: 'However, I hope we won't be reduced to that . . .'

He intervened with that phrase in mind:

'Gentlemen . . . To remain true to the spirit of this conference, by which I mean respect for the integrity of Czechoslovakia, I propose an exemption to German majority rule: exchanging Czech fortifications in predominantly German territories for a corresponding strip of Czech territory, in the *Böhmerwald*.'

Hitler immediately intervened: 'I reject that proposition, given the purely German character of the region in question.'

The President replied: 'I should point out to the Reich Chancellor that the existence of these fortifications is vital for the Czechoslovaks.'

'I have told you already, Mr President! I don't want any Czechs. I want my Germans and these areas have a German majority.'

The President replied to Hitler, who stuck to his position. The conference was at an impasse.

The arm-wrestling match moved to the map of the region.

The Italians adopted a strong line.

A German adviser proposed the construction of new Czech fortresses, but in the interior of the country.

The English started quibbling.

Both Hitler and the President remained inflexible.

The conference was plunged into a long silence.

After a moment, it was Hitler who seemed to want to make a move. In a resigned, almost generous voice, he said, 'All right . . . If you insist, Mr President . . . In the text of the final agreement, I would like us to be able to ask the international Commission to study a number of exceptions. If you insist, Mr President . . .'

The President couldn't get over it. Hitler's promise was

like a triumph. He didn't want to shatter the lovely harmony of the moment, by worrying pettily about the Commission that would give a ruling on the details or modalities of those exceptions. He was grateful, he was in raptures. He trusted Hitler's word.

The Commission would give a ruling. He had *so to speak* saved Czechoslovakia. He had seen off the worst, the Bad Godesberg *diktat*. He had just preserved their *blue line*. In Paris, he would be able to show them that. In Paris, he would be able to announce the victory that he had stolen from Hitler after tough negotiations. In Paris, Gamelin would be pleased.

The President walked over to Hitler. Beside himself, he showered the Führer with thanks: 'The acceptance of this formula will make my position in France a great deal easier. Thank you, Mr Chancellor. I consider that you have made a personal gesture towards me in this affair.'

His opinion was settled. Chamberlain had understood nothing about the Führer. And neither had the others.

Hitler was for fair play.

3

CHAMBERLAIN IS OBSTRUCTIVE

The discussion had resumed its quiet course, and they were about to pass on to point number three. It was then that Sir Neville Chamberlain intervened. They had forgotten all about him in his corner, silent, far away, hurt by the indifference shown him by Hitler. He had been neglected since his remarks on the presence of the Czechs and the need to talk about financial indemnities, because basically they were satisfied that he was willing to sign the agreement, quickly and at any price.

The British Prime Minister surprised everyone. He launched into a knowledgeable and unexpected lecture on international law. He foresaw difficulties. He was worried about the legal weaknesses of point number two, and the 'guarantee' that Great Britain, France and Italy were to give to Germany, concerning the 10th October, the date on which *evacuation* was to be completed *without destruction*.

This unexpected delay in a programme that was going at top speed bothered the three others. Mussolini rebuffed the British Prime Minister with a coarse turn of phrase. Hitler smiled affectionately at the Italian's expression. Daladier looked at the dictators and shrugged his shoulders. He was embarrassed, as one might be with a dubious cousin that one is obliged to introduce to society.

But the Englishman continued imperturbably, sure of his case, barely unsettled by the jeers, indifferent to the dunces. He had lost none of his rigour, which was well known in

Manchester. He was didactic, he was precise, he was interminable. His demonstration was lost from time to time in the shifting sands of multiple translation; he pursued it, calmly and obstinately.

And yet, the British Prime Minister had just raised a major objection. The three others realised as much.

Great Britain could not, in fact, provide a guarantee without a 'prior agreement' from the Czechoslovaks, even if they were not present. Without which the agreement was non-invocable.

In fact, Chamberlain's logic was implacable.

Mussolini turned crimson. Daladier and Hitler, who were also stunned by this last-minute nuisance, exchanged the same weary and exasperated glance. The President was not impervious to it.

Hitler decided to reply to Chamberlain. He was as disdainful as ever towards the person he had for a month seen as his loyal diplomatic valet. He was calm. Without looking at him, he announced:

'The question of modalities causes no problems . . .'

Then he turned round with a circular movement to seek the approval of Daladier and Mussolini. He found it. It was clear on the part of the Duce, who gestured casually from his sofa. It was resolute on the part of Daladier, who said 'yes' twice with a jerk of his chin. But Chamberlain would hear none of it. He didn't give in. Non-invocable . . . Non-invocable . . . A heresy in international law.

A long silence fell. The assembly dreaded a clash, a new explosion on the Führer's part, or even the departure of Mussolini. It was a fateful moment. Daladier made his mind up, or rather he put himself out. He had been silent since the fortifications, and suddenly grew furious with his ally.

'This is no time for quibbling, Neville . . .

'Not serious ... Not responsible coming from you ... Not that, not here, not now ... The British guarantee, you had promised the British guarantee ...'

He caused a proper scene. He used the tone, the brutal frankness permitted by those endless working sessions in London. The Englishman was taken aback.

Léger murmured in Daladier's ear. He asked him to calm down. The last thing they needed now was for the President to explode, as he had done with his civilian colleagues at the Hôtel de Brienne. Failures of understanding amongst allies, differences of opinion misconstrued, the frustrations of the long negotiations with Hitler in September from which he had wanted to be excluded, all the small humiliations to which he had been subjected during his two emergency journeys to London, it all came back. The President overflowed with those old suppressed furies. He had had enough of that man Chamberlain.

He resumed, even louder than before.

Daladier would tell him the truth.

It was important to show his true face ...

Great Britain is nit-picking now. Too tortuous for my liking ...

The time for manners is past ...

Before concluding, breathless from his diatribe: 'And besides, you know very well ... The decision has been made in London: the approval of the Czechs is not required.'

Chamberlain, white-faced, dismissed this with a gesture.

Daladier insisted: 'But it's true. In London we said that the approval of the Czechs was in the bag. You can't tell me the opposite now.'

Schmidt's translation spilled out in a flurry. The two dictators were interested, as if listening behind the door to some rowing neighbours.

Panic showed on the faces of the British and the French.

Daladier had disconcerted them. Léger and Wilson, François-Poncet and Henderson feverishly passed notes and gestured to one another. The situation was serious, unprecedented. Those London negotiations that Daladier was talking about were supposed to remain confidential. He had no permission to mention them. They all watched Daladier revealing his game as if at the table of a professional poker player.

Daladier hadn't noticed a thing. He dug his hole deeper: 'But as you are well aware, the principle of the cession of territories by Czechoslovakia is taken for granted by all of us!'

Chamberlain flushed and tried to splutter a protest, before collapsing into his chair.

Daladier – who was completely unaware of having made a monumental gaffe – kept on digging. He concluded his charge by saying peremptorily, 'And besides, promises are made to be kept . . .'

A heavy silence fell upon the room.

The English were dismayed. Léger and François-Poncet looked sheepish. Mussolini pulled a sensual pout.

Hitler observed the scene with a very fresh passion. Until then he had been sure he had them surrounded. He thought he knew them, both the Frenchman and the Englishman. He was convinced he had drawn Chamberlain into his net. He had seen right through his puritan English vanity, his desire to be seen as a saint and his obsession with the interests of the British Crown. He had underestimated the disconcerting Monsieur Daladier.

The President finally noticed the turmoil that his speech had provoked, but he didn't understand it. He wondered why everyone was looking at him strangely. Why there was that embarrassed silence from Léger and Poncet when he turned towards them, when he thought he was collecting their agreement, indeed their admiration. He concluded that everyone must be struck by the firmness of his tone, his frankness as opposed to the hypocritical diplomacy of Chamberlain.

He had *reframed the conference*, that was it. He had regained control over the Englishman. He had let him have his way for too long. In this Munich affair there had been – necessarily, because France couldn't appear – too much contact between the Germans and the British, too many ulterior motives, too much coming and going between London and Germany. He had put the Englishman in his place, with his airs and his little secrets. And it was better that way. With Chamberlain's method and pace, one risked the worst. The derailment of the conference. The unexpected accident. War when trying to make peace. It was too much! War, yes war, if one made the slightest false move. And that was something that this confounded man Chamberlain, suddenly so concerned about the Czechs, didn't give two hoots about. Chamberlain wasn't part of the 'war generation'. He didn't know what war was. He was obsessed only with the repayment of interest charges to his banks.

Hitler had observed the clash between the allies. He sensed that he could press his advantage. He addressed Daladier and asked him, with courteous candour, 'And if the Czechs do not accept this hypothesis of ceding the Sudetenland as we define it here?'

Chamberlain prepared to reply. He set great store by his legal demonstration. Daladier pounced. Tapping his chest, he said, 'Then we will force them to.'

4

'BENEŠ'S FAULT!'

Then we will force them to . . .

I was dumbstruck by this discovery, and this time I wasn't shy about talking to him about it.

'How could you have said that: "We will force them to"? How could you have treated a brother country like that? How could such harshness towards the Czechs and their president have been possible?'

Old Daladier's face assumed a look of astonishment as he replied:

'Oh, it was only a phrase, Mademoiselle! No reason to take offence. We were already far into the afternoon. Time was passing. The agreement was in sight, and Mr Chamberlain's sudden faintheartedness risked wrecking everything. I had merely wished to suggest that France was responsible for the execution of the agreement by the Czechoslovak Republic, given our connections with that nation . . .'

And he broke off. He got to his feet and set off more heavily than usual, resting on his cane, muttering. But when he reached the door of the little hangar, he turned back towards me, suddenly brighter.

'And damn it, Mademoiselle, I shall tell you what underlay my thoughts . . . I will tell you truly, without the customary hypocrisies . . . We would not have reached that point, had it not been for the stubbornness of President Beneš. Do not imagine that Beneš has always been the virtuous anti-Hitlerian of legend. Let me tell you a story that will enlighten you. During the summer of 1933 I had met Mr Beneš, who was then the Minister of Foreign Affairs, on the ship taking us to the World Economic Conference in London. We spoke notably of Austria, where Chancellor Dollfuss was coming under serious threat from the Austrian Nazis. On this subject Mr Beneš had said to me: "Sooner the Anschluss than the Habsburgs!" I had been very surprised by these words. The phantom of the Habsburgs was a long way away. But if Austria was ever annexed by the Reich, Czechoslovakia would be surrounded by Nazi Germany on three of her borders.

'And later, in fact, in 1938, at the time of the Anschluss, Beneš was far from exemplary. He didn't want to show solidarity with the Austrians when they were attacked by Hitler. Then, Mademoiselle, if you will forgive me for putting it like this, I wasn't going to be more anti-German in Munich than he was!'

'You're forgetting the context. Czechoslovakia had been under the domination of the Habsburgs for a long time, and perhaps that explains his outburst in 1933.'

'But it wasn't an outburst! Let me tell you, your Beneš was a stubborn man. He had been, along with Masaryk, his mentor, the spoilt child of the Versailles Treaty. All the irresponsible fairy godmothers had leaned over the cradle of Czechoslovakia: Clemenceau, Briand, Tardieu, Berthelot, Léger's predecessor . . .

'It wouldn't have come to that if he had, in 1919, listened to the people who wanted to make Czechoslovakia a federal state. But until 1938, right up until the very last moment, he refused to grant autonomy to the Sudeten Germans. Let me tell you, you can't imagine the obstinacy of President Beneš. He was leading us straight into global war.'

'So, by your account, it's all the fault of Beneš. He's the only guilty party. Hitler doesn't exist in your analysis. You're going a bit far, aren't you?'

'Yes, of course there's Hitler . . . But he's only a conse-
quence. Perhaps if Beneš had been more clear-sighted before;
if he had suitably respected all his minorities; if he had agreed
to a form of decentralisation . . . But he was stubborn, and
more Jacobin than any Frenchman!'

'You aren't giving me an answer. For you, the victim is
worse than the hangman!'

'Basically, Munich was to some extent the brainchild of
your blessed Beneš. It was he who gave his consent to the
cessions of territory. On 19th September, and then again
afterwards. Then he sent me secret messages, through Blum's
entourage, involving cessions that Beneš himself had
accepted. But secretly, without our knowledge. He was
already part of the mechanism of Munich. He isn't as white
as snow.'

'Are you seriously suggesting that he made those first
concessions with joy in his heart? Without being pressured
by you, by the English? Without you threatening to lose
interest in Czechoslovakia if she decided to defend herself?
You did everything to ensure that she didn't defend herself,
which would have forced you to go to war. Everything . . .'

The President didn't reply. He was bent double now. He
was angry with me. He seemed almost humiliated by the
shadow that Beneš had cast over this business. He started
up his indictment again:

'History has made your Beneš into a saint, a democratic
martyr, the wisest man in Europe. Not a bit of it! Beneš was
a politician. Like me. He wasn't the saint he was later turned
into; he too had his tricks, his electoral motives, his errors
of judgement, even his propaganda. I've just received an
article from one of the heads of contemporary Czechoslovakia, Mr Gustáv Husák. Husák isn't just anybody, he's
a big Communist boss. His testimony wasn't written on the
spur of the moment. Here's what Mr Husák says about

Beneš: ". . . A remarkable tactician and strategist. The Machiavelli of our times . . . He's a thinking and working machine without a fibre of humanity." That's what Mr Husák has to say. You hear that: "Beneš the Machiavelli of our times!"'

He had the nit-picking bad faith of the guilty man. He pleaded, he assembled a collection of quibbles; he still believed so firmly in what he said. At that moment I understood that, in spite of himself, he had ended up hating the victim Beneš even more than he did the hangman Hitler.

5

STORMS OF STEEL

Hitler and Daladier were talking a little apart from the others, near the huge fireplace. It was the first time really. Until then the two men had gauged, sniffed, confronted one another. Now it looked as if they were actually getting on quite well. Hitler was speaking bad French that he had learned in the war. No one dared approach him.

The German was polite, astonishingly enough. As he knew how to be when he was far from the propaganda photographers. He had emerged from the state of prostration in which he had been plunged throughout the debates, apart from his two roaring outbursts. He rediscovered his 'Viennese manners', that delightful way of telling stories. With Daladier he was at his best. As he was so skilled at being with those mothering women who decided to support him at the beginning of his political career, in Munich in the early 1920s. Frau Bechstein, amongst others, who had believed in him. She had taught him everything, had slimmed him down, made him lose – so she thought – his beer-hall habits, made him wear tails to go to the opera, she had organised society lotteries to help him develop his little party. Hitler quickly reacquired his social ease:

'I've been told that you had a good war, Mr President. You began as a sergeant and ended up a captain. Yes, that's what one can call a good war!'

Hitler didn't wait for an answer. He gave a chuckle, both bitter and amused: 'I can't say the same. I began it as a corporal and I ended it a corporal!'

Faced with the Führer, Daladier had quickly imposed a rule of caution upon himself. He would not speak much. 'Faced with a foreign official who is a stranger to you – or a French enemy, which comes to the same thing! – you hold your tongue! The more you speak, the more risks you take.' He remembered the lesson taught him by his teacher Herriot. It had always worked for him. He replied soberly, using a formula that he considered diplomatic:

'Yes, but you did so with the Iron Cross, First Class, Mr Chancellor!'

At the mention of this prestigious decoration, so seldom awarded to ordinary soldiers, Hitler appeared for a moment disarmed by childlike vanity. Ah, the Iron Cross, First Class! That moment of weakness did not escape the President.

Of course, the two men went on talking like old soldiers.

Beneš, his Czechs, the Bohemian fortifications, the Moravian corridor, the British guarantee, and even the memory of the Versailles Treaty had retreated into the background. They had become veterans of the trenches once again; hardly anything else was of the slightest importance.

They discovered shared memories, shared trajectories. One had been an intelligence officer, the other a staff emissary. At such moments, big beasts of prey seek their similarities. They might have fought and hated one another, insulted one another at the League of Nations; but they still like to meet up, far from everyone else, and throw the others off the scent with the spectacle of an unexpected harmony. These two men agreed with one another contrary to all expectations. One had only to see them, nostalgic and moist-eyed, freed from the pressure of the conference. Daladier forgot his caution and loosened his tongue.

One man said Verdun; the other replied the Somme, as

though they were returning compliments. They were almost speaking another language: shrapnel, 75 mm field gun, 'kite' for plane, kitbag, prang, kaput: about a world known to them alone; unimaginable to the others, the pen-pushers whom they still despised, as they admitted. About the 'generation of fire' as they termed themselves. About the world of the trenches, about mud and death, the rat-like lives they led for four years in those shelters, about running along the passageways which snaked for miles as far as the first and second lines, and also that special shape that trenches had been given since the days of Vauban, diagonally to avoid bursts of gunfire.

They remembered, together and alike, the days and nights in the trenches. The squeaks of the rats that lived alongside them; the coughing fits in the opposite trenches during wakeful nights; the simple, sweet, sly sound of the bullet piercing the darkness; the more distinctive, crisper sound of the impact it made with a comrade's skull; and the hateful sound of the landmine, the abrupt report of rifle grenades, with blades of steel that took you by surprise, particularly in the back of the neck . . .

The President was touched. He was transported. In spite of that roar that returned when the bombs were mentioned – his 'trench headache', no question.

So this man wasn't a monster . . .

Of course Daladier wasn't naïve. He knew *perfectly well* that Hitler was the adversary; tough, violent, wily, possibly dangerous, particularly if you didn't know how to deal with him; and that his Germany was formidable, particularly in the air. But he also reflected that the man was pure. While he might have been the master of Germany, he spoke like no one else about the war, and about its 'storms of steel' – the President had been struck by Hitler's expression. Moreover, he had remained simple, like an old veteran. Twenty years on, he still knew the significance of the Iron Cross, First Class, that decoration for which coterie, age and rank counted for nothing.

Unmistakably, a man like him, a member of the 'generation of fire', could not be fundamentally bad. You had only to listen to his warm voice, which was so distorted by the radio, to pay attention to his bourgeois manners, which were so far removed from what he had been told; to sort all those prejudices he had imported from Paris about his character – because the man had character, a bit like me, the President thought to himself – to understand that that Hitler was superior to his reputation as a political fairground barker. You had only to look at him, to listen to him to understand. There was a man behind the scarecrow.

The President smiled inwardly at the idea of the scarecrow that had risen up from the depths of his memory. Hitler spoke, and the President remembered that at the age of seven, in the wintry solitude of Carpentras, he had made the acquaintance of a scarecrow.

His cousins prattled as they pointed at something at the bottom of the garden, some poor animal he thought, but really a scarecrow, from which they fled in terror with cries of 'Be off, misfortune.' Most often, his cousins imitated their governess, who never set foot in that corner of the kitchen garden. Édouard didn't want to risk going there either. The scarecrow, with Mont Ventoux behind it, looked menacing. One day, though, little Édouard took his courage in both hands. He wanted to see the monster from close up, to defy it, know more about it. He was alone that day, and he began watching it for an hour at least, in the distance. He spied on it and saw nothing, understood nothing. Until the monster of the countryside violently waved its arms about, just as its cap fell off. He had made a discovery. It was the wind, the rough mistral of his northern Provence, that was the scarecrow's accomplice. The scarecrow was not a monster, but a kind of still life. He liked that story, his little-boy courage. He had laid bare the workings of the devil.

He would do the same with this man Hitler.

While the Chancellor went on praising the courage and self-denial of the soldiers at Verdun, both German and French, the President remembered.

He had always wanted to see Hitler in a different light. Not as a scarecrow. Since 1933 he had tried with Brinon and Ribbentrop. Alas, the Great Reconciliation had not taken place. It was their secret; they had never spoken of it.

The President thought to himself that this was the opportunity. He could not help mentioning the affair. Not to refer to it would be a source of vexation to Hitler, an error of taste, offhand at the very least. He wondered how – in very few words! – he could introduce the subject to the conversation.

Finally he said enigmatically:

'Ah . . . Mr Chancellor, we wouldn't be here if we hadn't met on the Kehl Bridge five years ago.'

Hitler nodded heavily several times.

He had no idea what the Frenchman was talking about.

He tried to find a meaning in the phrase, to think where that bridge might be and what its significance was. Five years ago? He thought it might be a Parisian ruse that Abetz hadn't mentioned to him; or the formulation of an apology after Abetz was expelled from France by Daladier in 1936. He wondered whether this mightn't be another harebrained notion of Göring's – the man was forever wanting to be loved by the French and the English. Five years? The Kehl Bridge? So it was before Austria, before the remilitarisation of the Rhineland. Five years?

193 . . . ? Before Germany left the League of Nations . . . ?

Finally Hitler remembered. An obscure operation by Ribbentrop. A meeting with a Frenchman, a fat, chatty, obsequious little man. Perhaps Brinon. A visit to the Berghof. An attempt at a secret agreement with France . . . France, the hereditary enemy . . . Ribbentrop's pipe-dreams!

Daladier looked like a neglected lover finally voicing what was on his mind.

'You know, Mr Chancellor, I sometimes say to myself that the true boundary is not where one imagines it to be . . . Not between the democracies and – what we call – the dictatorships. The real gulf lies between the members of the generation of fire and the others.'

'How strange it is, Mr President. That's exactly what we were saying the other evening, Field Marshal Göring and I . . . We had reached that conclusion about Mr Chamberlain . . .'

'Oh, really . . .'

'It's very simple, Mr President, Chamberlain and I can't understand one another.'

'Why is that, Mr Chancellor?'

'Well, Mr Chamberlain isn't like us. He wasn't in the war. Now do you understand why?'

'So he isn't part of the "war generation", not like us.'

'Not to mention, Mr President, the boundless selfishness of the English! Fundamentally they are thoroughly uninterested in what happens on the continent. As soon as their ships set sail and the East India Company brings in the profits, they couldn't care less about Europe.'

Daladier pretended to protest:

'Ah, Mr Chancellor, don't force me to defend my English friends. It would grieve me terribly!'

And they laughed together.

* * *

When they had grown serious again, Hitler said confidentially, 'Ah, Mr President ... So many misunderstandings between our two nations! You see, as an art lover, I am unhappy ... I know Paris, such a beautiful city, only from photographs. I would love to see your capital, to study it, understand it ...'

The President couldn't work out whether he was supposed to be flattered on France's behalf; or astonished by all these Germans suddenly dreaming of discovering Paris. Göring a few hours ago, and now Hitler. He just mumbled something, to give himself time to think.

He had understood. There was a message in this idea of visiting Paris, a line being thrown, a desire for entente with France – *understandable enough because after all Hitler's only real enemy was Soviet Russia.* The President glimpsed the political profit that he might be able to draw from so daring a project. A *rapprochement* with the Reich. What did he have to lose? Nothing. What did he have to win? Everything. The chance finally to become the head of this dying Republic.

It was in the same confidential tone, taking care that no one heard them, that he replied to Hitler:

'Oh, that's not the only issue, there's nothing simpler, Mr Chancellor. We could organise something in Paris quite quickly.'

'Do you think that's possible, Mr President?'

'Your Minister of Foreign Affairs, Mr von Ribbentrop, could go to Paris first. Just to prepare the ground ... And also ... my opinion.'

'Why not. What a good idea, Mr President! I dream of visiting your famous Opéra, built by Garnier; your magnificent Arc de Triomphe; and to find out the appeal of that Eiffel Tower which, if you will permit me to say so, is not in the best of taste. Yes, Paris ... Paris ... And Versailles, too.'

For a moment the President had the rather mad idea of suggesting that he take Hitler to Paris, in his plane, that very day.

He didn't dare.

6

THE CZECHS UNDER LOCK AND KEY

Ambassador Mastný was slumped on a chair, arms dangling, eyes vacant. He hadn't replied to Masařík for over an hour. Masařík couldn't stand still, shouted at him from time to time and waited for a comment that never came. He pursued a feverish monologue about war and peace, the strength of the Czech army and its twenty-one divisions – which would resist, there could be no doubt of that – about the exceptional qualities of the national fortifications compared to the Siegfried Line, a real Gruyère cheese, and about Daladier who would not give in, that much was clear.

Mastný remained silent. He had taken off his frock coat, loosened his tie, removed his detachable collar. Little remained of the elegant diplomat who had, for twenty years, been received everywhere, consulted and fêted and who had, just a few weeks before, seemed to inspire respect in Berlin. Mastný waited. There was nothing else he could do. It felt like a nightmare in which they would end up coming to shoot him. Besides, it could only be a misunderstanding, a problem of protocol that was undoubtedly being sorted out, the zeal of Himmler's Gestapo ... Göring was probably unaware of the situation ... Or perhaps his country's French ally had been held up, there were so many things to be done before the conference. How could it be otherwise? You didn't start a conference like this without the main interested party!

The ambassador remembered his meetings with the Reich second-in-command, he could call him his 'friend' Göring.

Their complicity had strengthened over the past few years. In the affair surrounding the Anschluss, hadn't he been the first to be informed of Germany's true intentions? Hadn't he even been consulted about Czechoslovakia's attitude in the event of an annexation? Hadn't he and his country been treated, not as allies, perhaps, but as a true partner who was not unhappy, it was true, to see the old Austrian overlord – the rump of the Habsburgs – becoming a vassal in its turn? Then, after the Anschluss had gone smoothly, without the slightest hostility from Prague towards Berlin, hadn't things resumed their course? There had, of course, been threats from Hitler and that electoral upsurge by the Sudeten Germans, but each time the charming Göring had reassured him. He was under no obligation. 'On no account do the Germans want to see Czechoslovakia dismembered,' he had repeated at the reception he had given on 11th March 1938, at the Berlin Aero Club.

Masařík paced around the little table at which Mastný was sitting. He repeated: 'It isn't possible . . . It isn't possible . . . They won't dare . . . They won't dare.' He no longer paid him any more attention than he would have done to a piece of furniture that he had repeatedly to avoid. He wasn't like Mastný, resigned, defeated, cynical; he was not a professional diplomat.

Whenever an idea or a new hope came to him, Masařík froze in his tracks to articulate, out loud but more calmly, his hypothesis: 'The British may abandon us. They have no treaty with us. Chamberlain doesn't like us. His policy of appeasement favours Hitler over us. But the French can't abandon us. We have France's word. There's the pact signed in 1924. There's the army that they helped us set up. There's Skoda that belongs to them, so to speak . . . No, it would be madness . . .'

He repeated 'It would be madness' several times for

Mastný's benefit, hoping thus to draw him from his vege-
tative state.

'Isn't that so? It would be madness on a moral level. And
also madness on the strategic level ... No, they can't leave
our army, our fortifications, Skoda and our weapons factories
in the hands of the Reich ... No, it isn't possible ... It would
be madness and the French are not mad.'

There was a knock at the door.

The two Czechs sat down. Mastný buttoned his shirt back
up and straightened himself on his chair. Masařík remained
frozen in place. For a moment, a very brief moment, their
faces brightened.

Mr Ashton-Gwatkin entered without waiting for a reply.
The Englishman was breathless. He was in a hurry, and
immediately complained of the fact, not deigning to turn his
pink and pompous face towards Dr Mastný, the elder of the
two men. He stood strangely, distantly to attention; he
wanted to get it all over with. He began in a rapid, detached,
mechanical voice: 'I have been given the task of informing
you that a general agreement is about to be entered into. A
few points still remain to be resolved. I am unable to give
you any details.'

He paused before continuing, in a single breath and in a
voice that left no room for debate: 'But you will have to
brace yourselves for conditions harsher than those of the
Franco-British plan.'

He finally darted a glance at the two Czechs. A reproachful
look. He considered himself authorised to do so by the situation, by Chamberlain, Wilson, Lord Halifax, by the majority
of the Conservative Party in London, by this good chap
Daladier, by the festive atmosphere of Munich and also by
the wretched room in which the two Czechs had been locked
away. An expression of pinched irony ran across his face.

Resting his hands on the table, he leant towards Mastný and said to him curtly: 'It's what you must have wanted. You should have accepted the Franco-British plan when the time was right.'

Mastný didn't have the strength to protest. He sagged, holding on to the arm of the spirited Masařík: 'No, don't do that . . .'

He had worked out that in the eyes of the underling delegated to them he was nothing now. He and Czechoslovakia had just been pulverised, reduced to nothing in this prison, expelled from the nations, from the world of the living who, only a few short yards away, had devised and decided everything.

They were defeated.

Ashton-Gwatkin prepared to turn on his heels. Mastný finally rose to his feet. He walked towards him to take his arm, and held it as tightly as if to squeeze out his last drops of humanity. He asked in the tone of a terminal patient clinging to one last hope: 'Can we not at least be heard before being judged . . . ?'

Masařík approached in turn. He had nothing to add. He simply wanted to see the eyes of the bowler-hatted traitor from close to. The Englishman was startled. As he quickly pulled away, his head struck the cheap lampshade that hung from the ceiling. The room seemed to sway in the play of the light. All of a sudden in that look, that start, that shrinking gesture there was the horror of a tourist who had been touched by a leper. Ashton-Gwatkin drew aside and got his breath back before saying, almost over his shoulder, with his hand on the door-handle, 'One would really think you are forgetting . . . how difficult our position is . . . ! If you had any idea how very . . . how very . . .'

He hesitated: 'how very . . . *awkward* these discussions with Hitler are.' And the door slammed shut.

Masařík, dazed, stood by the door, muttering incoherent phrases.

Mastný slumped once more on to his chair, closed his eyes and tore off the rest of his detachable collar.

PART SIX

1

THE BANQUET

It was 7.30 p.m.

In the banqueting hall of the Führerbau, that morning's maître d' was delivering instructions to waiters standing at attention, and a slew of more indolent lackeys, in the *grand-siècle* black and silver uniforms, with patent-leather shoes and stockings as required by the Wilhelmstrasse protocol. Everyone was busy noting down, meticulously and for the third time, the orders of the Berlin envoy, who had abandoned his black SS-officer's uniform to issue instructions to them:

'The Reich is duty-bound to celebrate the signature of a historical agreement with fitting pomp.

'Here is the seating plan for table one, the seating plan for table two . . .

'As regards the table of honour . . . The service will have to be organised in such a way that . . . Reich protocol decrees that . . .

'A pause of fifteen minutes must be respected between the courses . . .

'For this to be achieved, the synchronisation between kitchen and front of house must be impeccable . . . We must bring out the dishes as efficiently as we bring out planes from our factories . . .

'Where's the vegetarian brigade . . . ?

'Any questions . . . ?'

In Rome, too, it was 7.30 p.m.

Pope Pius XI began to speak. He was sending a radio

message to the world. His voice was choked and barely audible. He spoke of the 'millions of men who live in anxiety about the imminent danger of war and the threat of unprecedented ruins and massacres'. He called the faithful to pray 'that God, in whose hands rests the fate of the world, may help the governing parties to trust in the peaceful paths of fair negotiation and enduring agreements'. And he concluded his intervention with this surprising proposition: he wished to give his life in exchange for peace – in fact, the Pope had just been informed that the agreement was at hand.

'For the salvation and the peace of the world we offer the inestimable gift of a life that is already long, whether the master of life and death wishes to take it from us, or whether, on the contrary, he wishes to prolong still further the days of toil of the weary and afflicted labourer.'

It was 7.30 p.m. in Paris, and an uneasy crowd was beginning to assemble in front of the Quai d'Orsay, beneath the windows of the Foreign Ministry, where M. Bonnet, not having been invited to Munich, had mobilised his administration. The Parisian press was informed, dignitaries were received, reassurances were given to the general staff and President Lebrun. Everyone hung on the information delivered, hour by hour, by Secretary General Alexis Léger. They were in communication with all the capitals of Europe, avoiding Prague, of course. The gathered onlookers were calm. Late-comers, in hushed tones, asked those already waiting for any news. They seemed sad. Both rich and poor. People stopped on their way to dine at Chez Maxim's or Lucas Carton, and Bugattis were seen side by side with the bicycles of the Renault factory workers and the police from the Préfecture. The men and women in the Bugattis set off again. The blokes in caps preferred to wait.

* * *

It was 7.30 and in Munich it was the first day of the Oktoberfest. The cathedral, the Rathaus, the monuments, the façades of the public buildings and the shops were all lit up. But the Führerbau remained in darkness in spite of the waiting crowd. Curious people walked by in silence. In the growing gloom their silhouettes resembled shadows bent double by the wind. They didn't want to go home; they took advantage of a respite, a kind of uneasy parenthesis, to taste a little of this confusion, this gaiety, perhaps, before returning to their night. On Königsplatz their numbers were steadily growing.

Children taken out of school specially, and war veterans who had arrived by bus from the countryside, had made way for late office workers, unemployed bachelors, groups of young people. They were anxious, lifeless, like the faded flags of the four nations that hung stupidly from all the city's flagpoles. On the monumental façade of the Führer's building, the flags were hung in pairs: democrats on one side, dictators on the other. Everywhere else in the city, that rule had been carefully respected; people wondered whether that clear separation was the ingenious idea of a Bavarian bureaucrat, or whether it was a new rule imposed by one of the many administrative offices that proliferated and competed in the Third Reich.

In the square, all heads were raised towards those three second-floor windows, the only ones still illuminated in the spotlit façade.

Time passed.

The crowd of Bavarians thinned out. As night fell, some people were afraid of being spotted by the police, the Gestapo or the SS for assiduously attending what might have been considered a pacifist meeting. The ones who stayed on were devotees. They joined in common worship; Lutherans joined in with the Catholic mass; they prayed together. It was their way of begging for peace, of pleading for it from those windows and the world leaders still shut away up there. A fervent hum ran through the crowd. A man with a loud voice repeated an 'amen' that murmured its way slowly around the crowd.

Suddenly, a movement was seen at the window. Shadows stirred. The Führer's silhouette could be seen, martial and agitated; beside him, Daladier's, short and stocky, slightly bowed. 'And there's the Duce, too, and the Englishman with his umbrella,' a bold student exclaimed. The crowd couldn't help purring quietly.

Not far from there, in the hall of the Führerbau, Herr Ammann, a pot-bellied little man with round, silver-rimmed glasses, knew everything. Herr Ammann was a considerable figure in the Reich. An old companion-at-arms of Hitler's, he had been put at the head of the Party's powerful press group as a kind of rival to Goebbels. He was surrounded by about twenty journalists, all vying for his attention. He happily posed for the photographers of *Paris Match* and *Signal*; affectionately taking the arm of the American NBC reporter, Max Jordan, to whom he had promised to lend the Reich radio studios, he bade him to wait; he sidestepped the excessively precise questions of the special envoy from the *Petit Parisien*; he reassured an English girl reporter, who was on the brink of tears and who wanted to know if the peace was saved.

An SS officer brought him a sealed message.

Herr Ammann apologised with infinite politeness, turning particularly towards Jordan, then tore open the envelope. He read the note ostentatiously, before raising his head. He smiled, apparently in seventh heaven. That sharpened the curiosity of the journalists. They had been getting so bored. There was nothing to do in Munich – the Führerbau was too far from the good pubs and the red-light districts that reporters like to lose themselves in. There was nothing to report on the conference, barely a few details, a break for lunch, an altercation at the first session, the number of Daladier's suite, Herr Göring's lunch menu, and the description of the Prinz Carl Palais, a mansion in the Florentine style from the time of Ludwig II, where Mussolini was staying ... That wasn't going to make the front page. Barely a column or two, on the inside pages, with, for the lucky ones, the *touching* photograph of the hats of the Four side by side in the cloakroom. The special envoys were short of material, and they would have to deliver very soon. The rotary presses wouldn't wait, and neither would Mussolini's train. They were getting ready; they would dash forward; they would claim their sustenance for the morning's edition.

That was why Ammann's smile had been so welcome. A blessing. The German could tell by the way the journalists were licking their pencils.

He chose to say only, 'Congratulations.'

He waved around the little piece of paper holding the big secrets. The twenty reporters didn't ask any further questions when Ammann announced, 'The agreement is, so to speak, signed . . . Only a few details remain. Yes, so to speak – signed.' They could have kissed him, aside from a few big-mouths who stayed apart from the rest. They warmly thanked their fellow pressman. They congratulated him in their turn, and then they dashed off, some to the telephone, the others towards a broadcast studio to dictate their front pages, their headlines, their sensational pieces.

They would get their headlines in on time.

In fact Herr Ammann was bluffing.

By 7.30 nothing had been concluded. Worse than that, the conference was at a very low ebb.

Mussolini left the conference hall dramatically. He was furious, he was seething, he gesticulated for the sheepish Ciano, who tried to follow him. He was no longer strutting about, no longer pretending to be conciliatory. He pushed aside the irksome characters in his way before plunging into his limousine.

Then it was Ribbentrop's turn. He too left the session. The few reporters who were still there and better informed than the others immediately encircled him. The head of the Reich diplomatic service struggled to conceal a haughty rage, in spite of his supposedly phlegmatic nature. He swore as he put his gloves back on. A French journalist asked him *if the peace was finally saved*. He looked him up and down, continued on his way with a snigger, then turned abruptly round to spit at him in impeccably scornful French: 'If the peace, as you say, were to be saved, it certainly wouldn't be saved by you Frenchmen. It is by your pettiness that you are putting it in danger . . .'

'*Rien ne va plus*,' joked one fellow, the American William Shirer, a correspondent with CBS radio. Some of his colleagues took offence at his insolence. They took Ammann as a witness. Ammann was on the point of threatening Shirer, but changed his mind. He would find another way to take his revenge.

Göring left, too. He waited behind a pillar at the top of the large staircase for his rival Ribbentrop to leave, before making his appearance. Göring, who loved to nurture his international image, prepared for the game of questions and answers. Behind the Field Marshal's florid and over-detailed explanations everyone understood that the agreement was running into minor difficulties at the last minute.

Shirer was right: all games really were off.

While the whole world waited for the agreement, while the red-haired maître d' stood at attention in the banqueting hall, while the celebration supper waited, while the newspapers, the radios and the agencies prepared their headlines, the Four had suddenly decided to part.

Rather than heading towards an argument, so great was Hitler's exasperation, he had agreed to assign to a commission of lawyers and diplomats the writing of the final agreement and the suggestion of suitable formulae for the points of disagreement. So they would meet up again in two hours, once the agreement had been translated into the four languages.

The banquet was cancelled; the two dictators would dine alone.

2

FINAL HESITATIONS

Suite 42–44 of the Vier Jahreszeiten Hotel was under siege. The corridor swarmed with agitated journalists, photographers with their big flashes and a few curious guests. The President's suite was guarded, but the special envoy of the *Petit Parisien* had managed to see Daladier in the antechamber. He was surprised by the agitation, and by the journalist's panic.

British radio had just announced the signing of the agreement.

Could they confirm the French side?

The President suspected a journalistic trick. But the other man insisted. Daladier had it checked. The false news had actually been announced on British radio; other radio stations, such as Radio-Cité or Jean Prouvost's Radio 37, and the press agencies had picked it up, dozens of newspapers across the world were also asking for confirmation of the news. There was mass confusion. In Western Europe, the daily newspapers were starting to go to bed; front-page headlines had to be dispatched by ten o'clock; the presses would be turning.

The President denied it. The agreement had not been concluded. But seeing the journalist's alarmed expression he wanted to appear reassuring: 'No, everything's fine. I'm pleased . . . I'm pleased . . .' Before going back to have dinner in his room.

The premature announcement of the signature of the

agreement left the President and his colleagues, assembled around two pedestal tables, in even greater despair.

The brazenness of the press! Announcing the agreement signed when so many things still lay in the balance: the definitive fate of the fortifications, the indemnities claimed by the British. And also that guarantee of new Czechoslovak borders that Hitler insisted on rejecting.

Prostrate before their cold meats, the four Frenchmen said not a word. Clapier was there, an aide-de-camp and Captain Stehlin, who held a post at the Berlin embassy, and was in charge of the air force. Léger, Rochat and François-Poncet had stayed behind at the Führerbau to finalise the planned agreement.

Daladier seemed relieved to be away from the pressure of the Führerbau. He looked sad, exhausted. He murmured from time to time, he talked to himself, muttered crisp, bitter remarks, about what he had just been through. The others barely listened, they didn't want to disturb him.

Suddenly he abandoned his meditations to question Captain Stehlin:

'Captain, you are an airman ... I have seen your boss, General Vuillemin. He's terribly worried. What was your opinion?'

Stehlin spoke, quite willingly. He was well acquainted with the German air force. Indeed, that was why he held his post in Berlin. To spy on the Luftwaffe:

'Mr President, my informers tell me that the Luftwaffe would attack on the same day of the invasion, and suddenly. Two thousand aeroplanes are assembled around the Czech border.

'Each bombing unit, dive-bombing or otherwise, knows its goals most precisely. For many weeks, the units have been rehearsing the execution of their mission on large-scale maps, on photographs and with the help of relief images.

'The sudden attack planned for the first day would be low level, with Heinkel 111s and Dornier 17s. For several days now, five-hundred kilo bombs have been fixed underneath the fuselage of the Junker 87s, with a view to destroying those targets.'

And so, for fifteen long minutes, under the panic-stricken gaze of Daladier and the two others, Captain Stehlin warmed to his theme.

Every now and again the President repeated: 'Junker 87s ... Low-flying Heinkel 111s ...' The rest of the time he listened to Stehlin, he twitched, he grew increasingly alarmed.

He had heard enough.

'Captain, do you think, as Vuillemin does, that in a few days of combat we would have no planes left?'

Captain Stehlin seemed embarrassed. He couldn't contradict his superior.

He hesitated, but the phone rang. It was François-Poncet telling them that they could return to the meeting. The agreement document was ready.

Daladier rose heavily to his feet. He turned towards Stehlin and said fatalistically: 'Now the die is cast. Perhaps there was nothing else to be done. It's the future we've got to think about. We have to make up for lost time to rearm ... The air force! The air force!'

3

'DID YOU PANIC?'

'Did you panic at that moment? Captain Stehlin's report had just confirmed your doubts about the France's weak point: the air force. Is that it?'

'I didn't "panic", as you put it! All through the Munich affair I knew that the air force was our weak point. I had been War Minister four times; I had followed Cot's plan during the Popular Front; we were considering the La Chambre plan. But it's true, the French air force wasn't in a state to allow us to throw ourselves into a war to defend Czechoslovakia. Put it this way, if I'd had eight thousand planes, I wouldn't have been in Munich!'

'Undeniably, what Stehlin told you then, and the Vuillemin report before him, were crucial for your decision?'

'Yes, that's right. In a way.'

'Did you know that Stehlin was a close friend of Göring and his sister? He was a welcome guest at their house. He was treated like a prince. He had permission to fly over German territory – one way or another, he could have carried out official espionage. Stehlin wasn't completely neutral.'

'Stehlin . . . Göring, and his sister! Surely you're joking?'

'Besides, Stehlin had his alarming information first-hand from General Bodenschatz. Göring's right-hand man had just passed it on to him. Stehlin was still in a state of shock. Bodenschatz seemed so pleased that the agreement was in sight that he had told him, in detail, of the cataclysm that

Czechoslovakia had escaped. It was, Mr President – perhaps it's easier to say it now – a coarse piece of manipulation.

'I'll go on. More crucial than Stehlin, there was that famous Vuillemin report, following on from his mission to Germany. It's all based on that, isn't it?'

'Yes.'

'Well, we know now, with the benefit of hindsight and documents, that General Vuillemin's trip to Germany in August 1938 marked the grand finale in a massive disinformation operation. It wasn't a simple protocol visit, as they said, or simply a matter of paying Germany back in her own coin, because General Milch, Secretary of State of the Reich Aviation Ministry, had been received in France the previous year.

'The whole scheme started in France with a little scheme by your "appeaser-in-chief", Georges Bonnet, who insisted that General Vuillemin accept Göring's invitation.

'So General Vuillemin goes to Germany, on 17th August 1938, and spends a week there. A fortnight before the crisis! And while he's in Germany he's seriously taken in hand by the Nazis. The General is received like a head of state; an imposing military parade is organised when he arrives in Berlin. Then they go to the tomb of the Unknown Soldier. A triumphal procession passes through the streets. On the days that follow, he is received by a delightful, peaceful Hitler; he's fêted at solemn banquets all over the country; he's dragged from factories to aerial exhibitions; and Stehlin even gives us to understand that he was very susceptible to the charms of Bavarian girls. After all that, how could you expect General Vuillemin to be able to give you a report that was . . . let's say, honest?

'Once he's back in Paris, the Vuillemin report becomes a political weapon. It's used by the other appeaser in your government, the Aviation Minister, Guy La Chambre. He uses it in the Council of Ministers to impress his colleagues, to get his and Bonnet's point of view across. In fact, there was an axis between Göring-Hitler and Bonnet-La Chambre: the report by General Vuillemin. You doubted it then. You yourself, in London, in the course of your conversations with Chamberlain on his return from Berchtesgaden, told Ambassador Corbin and his adviser Girard de Charbonnières that you were angry with Vuillemin and his defeatism. You even promised to dismiss him when you got back to Paris.'

'Dismiss Vuillemin? I don't remember. But tell me, did they really use Bavarian girls, as you said? This is news to me! I hadn't thought of Vuillemin's mission in such terms. Nevertheless, Vuillemin might have been manipulated, but the fact remains that France wasn't ready. Our air force was too weak. And we thought in those days that the Germans were too strong.'

'The "*rapport des forces*" wasn't in France's advantage, of course, but you greatly overestimated German air power in 1938. Do you know what Field Marshal Keitel said at the Nuremberg Trial?'

'Yes, vaguely.'

'In response to the question from Colonel Eger, the Czech representative: "Would the Reich have attacked Czechoslovakia in 1938 if the Western powers had supported Prague?" the most senior German military officer replied: "Certainly not. Militarily, we weren't strong enough."'

4

LETTER TO IDA

Neville Chamberlain had politely taken his leave from his colleagues, after a final consultation by telephone with his cabinet in London. He was exhausted and had decided to dine alone, in his room in the Regina Hotel. That final contretemps had upset him, and as His Majesty's Prime Minister often said, he didn't need that. He had put on his silk dressing gown, the one that his butler handed him as soon as he returned home to London. This time he wasn't at home, but he needed – even if it was only for an hour before those difficult negotiations resumed – that cocoon, an impression of intimacy regained. For the first time in his life, Sir Neville, who still had a young man's figure even at the age of almost seventy, felt the weight of the years. The model of athletic elegance in his gentleman's club, who had used his slimness when campaigning within the Conservative Party as a contrast to his rival, that fat eccentric Churchill, seemed at a loss. The night was far from over; and the sole manifestation of what he knew to be his true age was a sudden attack of sleepiness.

Aware of this, with great precision and delight Chamberlain therefore set out a little programme for himself for the hour of stolen freedom that lay ahead of him.

First, sleep. A little. The sleep of Napoleon. Fifteen minutes at the most, more would be dangerous. Sleep just to stop this shaking – nerves! – this internal quivering, these recalcitrant jaws that jam in times of tension. This head congested with all the notes I've read, all the speeches and advocacy I have heard, all the hypotheses set out with that good man Henderson. A retreat in search of calm ahead of the big decision.

Then, cancel dinner, have a light snack, some tea, biscuits and a bit of that German cheese from lunchtime. A light dinner, then, to remain *efficient*.

And finally write to Ida; that would clear his thoughts.

At that very moment, what Sir Neville Chamberlain really needed was a cuddle.

Dear Ida,

Today, I had to endure so many things. The furious rages of this man Hitler who clearly has two faces, the charming and romantic one I encountered the first time at the summit in the Alps, in his astonishing residence in Obersalzberg, with whom I had dreamed, out loud and in full sympathy, of a 'new European order' based on two great powers, Germany and Great Britain. And the other, capricious, raging and fanatical, who barely addressed a word to me today, and who tapped his foot like a lunatic when he uttered the name of the Czech President. I also had to endure the humiliation of such a man as Mussolini, who was all sweetness yesterday, but who has now had the gall to refuse me a meeting so that we may dispel our misunderstandings. Not to mention the thick-headed vulgarity of this man Ciano who was plainly spying, and constantly writing everything down in a note-book. To think that I had to remain silent throughout all that, and spend my time listening to pointless nonsense; and that I also had to struggle to keep myself from rebelling against the frivolity of those heads of state who claim to maintain empires, and who couldn't in fact run the board of directors of a City firm. That conference had neither an agenda nor a chairman, it was utter confusion. Not to mention their contempt, their dangerous contempt, in this agreement which we were discussing, for private property and also, one would have to say, for the interests of the British banks in the Czechoslovak Republic – and those, as you know, are far from negligible ... But after all, I did everything I could to keep from 'over-exciting' Hitler. I stuck to that line of conduct in which so far, as you know, I have been rather successful.

I must confess. The most awkward thing throughout this day wasn't Hitler, but Daladier.

I've done everything I can to avoid him, him and his moods. Luckily – and this is an example of Teutonic tact – we weren't staying in the same hotel! In spite of that, I had to avoid Monsieur Daladier all day, both upon my arrival in Munich, when the French were tracking me down to extract from me 'one final point between allies', and during the breaks – which were frequent. Throughout the whole of the conference, Daladier sulked – when he wasn't openly attacking me, and I his ally!

You see, Ida, Daladier perfectly embodies what you and I think of France and the French. They are a weak race, pusillanimous and excessive, whose shortcomings have been exacerbated by their Revolution, their Republic, and also by Napoleon. In fact, the country has been without a stable government for decades; because of that instability, it can turn out to be dangerous in its passion, in its excesses. It was thus, now showing himself as extreme, now passive, that Monsieur Daladier distinguished himself all day. First he clashed so violently with the Führer that I feared for a moment that this conference, in which I had placed all my soul and all our hopes, would capsize before it had even begun. Then he started joking with Göring at the very moment when we were discussing the thorny issue, raised by Britain and thus

by the Allies, of the financial indemnities due to the physical
and moral individuals who would be transferred . . . Nevertheless, writing this makes me feel better. As at the end of a
long climb – even though in fact I do no climbing, even
though the Alpine landscapes enchant me, as you know. I
can glimpse the summit. One more effort. A few details to
sort out tonight, the priority being the problem of financial
indemnities, and I think I might be worthy to present myself
before God, having accomplished this miracle. Peace! Peace,
Ida! Peace for our generation. The peace yearned for and
accepted without any of the torments that seem to have taken
hold of this poor man Daladier. Why doubt when we are
doing good, and when, what is more, there is no other choice?
Were we going to unleash a European war, a World War
even – as I said in the Chamber, thanks to your own excellent phrase – because of a simple quarrel in a far away
country between people of whom we know nothing? Were
we going to sink the British Empire to respond to the whims
of Beneš, cover their tyrannical government, their violent
treatment of the Germans and the Sudetenland? And what
is more, take it all to its conclusion, do we have that choice?
France? Not trustworthy, and a poor air force. The alliance
with the Russians? Allying oneself with the Devil Stalin to
counter a man with whom we can, after all, reach an agreement! The Americans? Roosevelt will never involve the United
States!

Halleluiah, Ida, it's nearly done – barring an act of French
perfidy at the last moment, of course; or unwillingness on
Hitler's part concerning the question of financial compensa-
tion. Halleluiah . . . Gone is the spectre of war, with our
millions of boys, our wives, or children atrociously slaughtered; with our fleet scuppered and our throne in jeopardy;
with even our Empire devastated – for I have no illusions
on the matter, it would only have taken war to break out

for Mr Gandhi to reawaken wicked passions against us in India.

It's strange, Ida, I feel better. Today, in spite of the awkward nature of that encounter, I physically felt that profound harmony with the Lord and his Providence. I saw universal Peace, I felt it, I heard its song. And I told myself that barring some unexpected accident, I was its modest craftsman, and I had been right to choose, along with Hitler in this global affair, the path of 'meekness and moderation' to which the Lord enjoins us.

A kiss, before returning to work.

Your affectionate Neville.

PS: For the meeting that I plan to request from Hitler, tomorrow, in private, pray for me.

5

THE SIGNATURE

On a mahogany table, a monumental inkwell.

It was after midnight, they had been closed away there for two hours now; and that agreement that had been taken as given, trumpeted on the wires of the world's press agencies, was still not signed. Nightfall and exhaustion had brought it to a standstill. It had got stuck on the financial indemnities demanded by Chamberlain, the British draft on the question having gone missing. The discussion had been confused, even more so than in the afternoon, made yet more bitter by Paul Schmidt's translation, by the spelling mistakes in the final version that had appalled Daladier, by Chamberlain's sleepiness, by Mussolini's impatience, and most of all by the intransigence of Hitler, furious at the Allies' final hesitations. The French and the British would not sign while the German guarantee of Czechoslovakia's new borders had not been given. Without it, Daladier went on to say, Czechoslovakia would never be safe in those borders.

All of a sudden Hitler sat up on his chair.

He snapped, calling Göring and Ribbentrop as witnesses: 'I will not reconsider this point which has, it seems to me, been sorted out this afternoon. We will give this guarantee only when the other neighbouring countries concerned, the Hungarians, the Poles and the Romanians, have validated it. Gentlemen, I have nothing to add.'

Chamberlain and Daladier did not dare to insist.

This time Hitler exploded: 'I didn't spend four years in the trenches, twenty years in politics, for people to say that Hitler is a coward! Hitler has the German people behind him, and it is not the people that was defeated in 1918 . . .'

And he had closed himself away again.

The President saw him as he had been in the morning, menace on his lips, tense, pale, frightening.

Chamberlain, crushed and exhausted, had risen to his feet.

How could they quarrel, there, at that time, so close to their goal?

Once more it was Mussolini who found the solution.

Those difficulties would be redirected towards the international Commission charged with fixing borders. Everything: the guarantee by the Germans and the Italians, after the Hungarians, the Poles and the Romanians had expressed their opinion; the promise – which gratified Chamberlain – that the Commission would consider the demand for financial indemnities; and of course, the commitment that the Commission would be interested in the exceptional circumstance of the fortifications as called for by the French.

Daladier consulted Léger.

Chamberlain stepped outside to call London.

The proposed method was miraculous. It had broken the deadlock. Although what it really did was sweep the dust and everything awkward under the carpet.

While the final modifications were just being introduced by the shorthand typists, Mussolini, like a businessman in danger of losing a large sum of money – and Dalmatia, and the Balkans, and the Mediterranean, and his international prestige – moved from one to the other, treading delicately. He

feared some faux pas, some blunder, some last-minute incident. He took infinite precautions, was endlessly attentive.

To Hitler he spoke gently, as one does to the seriously ill.

To Chamberlain, whom he had insulted by refusing him
an explanatory meeting, he promised a major official reunion
'soon, yes, soon'.

Daladier was pacing up and down by the fireplace, his
eye vacant, his fingers hooked to his waistcoat like a restau-
rateur, and Mussolini slapped him on the back, saying, 'Come
along, Mr President, make an effort. On your return you
will be carried in triumph . . .' Hearing these words, the
Frenchman brightened. He emerged from his sulk, stood up
straight and pouted suspiciously at the Italian. He was
perplexed, he would have liked to believe it. The remark
had brought an expression of blurry tenderness to his face,
the frantic anxiety of someone seeking comfort at any price.

With vague concern Daladier asked Mussolini. 'Do you
think so?' The Duce reassured him in a resolute bellow: 'I
am convinced of it, Mr President.' Daladier wanted to pass
on the Duce's sympathetic remark to Alexis Léger – that
might put the smile back on his face. But Léger didn't even
seem to be listening.

This time calm had returned, it was only a matter of minutes.
The shorthand typists got busy with fervent enthusiasm.

Hitler was the first to sit down and sign the document. He
solemnly dipped his pen in the inkwell. A rictus passed across
his face. He dipped it a second time: the inkwell was empty.
A pale Ribbentrop ordered Schmidt to rectify matters.
Daladier grimaced at this bad omen.

Then Chamberlain, Daladier and Mussolini signed.

It was over.

The two dictators warmly congratulated one another. The

two 'democrats' looked at one another with embarrassment. The German and Italian delegations approached, mingled, exchanged noisy congratulations.

The photographers' flashes exploded. A photograph immortalised the scene.

Hitler was at the centre of the picture. He was triumphant. Mussolini, on Hitler's left, sought a pose. Chamberlain seemed proud of his work, the *edification of Universal Peace*. Of the four, Daladier alone avoided looking at the lens.

6

THE PHOTOGRAPH

What time was it exactly? Who had taken this photograph? An Anglo-Saxon photographic agency or the German propaganda department? What is that little piece of crumpled paper that Chamberlain is holding in his hand? The draft clause, finally rediscovered? Or a final entreaty to Chancellor Hitler? Why, in one of the rare other photographs of the event, probably taken by the same team, is Alexis Léger absent when the delegations are all assembled? Alexis Léger ... Saint-John Perse ... How could he have been at once that illustrious poet and the hostage of Munich? Absent from the photograph, he had contrived to be absent from History. He managed better than Daladier.

I return, for the hundredth time, to that moment. My eyes were blurred from studying the tiniest details. Each second of that moment, the moment of the signature, was like an abyss. I searched it for an answer. Not that a hundredth of a second could explain everything, European geopolitics, the problems of France, England's appeasement policy or the fateful French ideas between the wars. But by fitting myself into that brief instant when Daladier passes before the lens, I thought I could read annihilation. What fascinated me above all was the expression on Daladier's face at that precise moment. A defeated expression. *A strange defeat.*

Suddenly I understood.

That moving, sombre, abandoned face embodied, in anticipation, the famous thesis of the historian Marc Bloch. During the crisis, the founder of the Annales School had reported, from his vantage point as an officer engaged in the war, on the hidden undercurrents of the French debacle. He had died as a Resistance hero, shot by firing squad on 16th June 1944, at the age of fifty-eight. His book, *The Strange Defeat*, had been published after the war. Martha had made me read it. Bloch's book had become precious to me. So the 'strange defeat' had pre-existed the crushing rout of May–June 1940, which Bloch describes in minute detail. The planes that don't take off, or don't come out of the factories. Collapsing governments. Wilfully blind trade union leaders. The second world power becoming unstable. Byzantine international alliances. Senior military officers arguing and orders not coming through. The Maginot Line being skirted. A major ambition gone rusty. The triumph of conformity. The ideology of defensiveness. The exhaustion of Liberty. And what followed . . .

I studied that fleeting, guilty expression, and said to myself that Vichy had existed before Vichy. It was Munich. The Collaboration had existed before Montoire, that was the strongest idea that Daladier brought back from Munich; he borrowed it from a French diplomat who had advocated the reversal of alliances as early as 1924. He even used the term in his speech on his return. In Munich, the exclusion of the Jews from the national community was also apparent, albeit in its early stages. Two months after the Agreement, on 8th December 1938, at the big reception in the Quai d'Orsay where Ribbentrop had come to reinforce bonds between France and Germany, the Jewish ministers Georges Mandel and Jean Zay were absent. It had all started there. Daladier had, in his republican manner, outstripped Pétain, Laval, Flandin and his other colleagues. He had wanted, with the Czechs, to *do the work himself.* By exclaiming, 'Well, we will force them to do it,' he had acted just as Laval

had done, when he demanded at the Vel d'Hiv and elsewhere that the round-ups of Jews and members of the Resistance be organised by the French police and not the Gestapo.

On the little island, the mistral had been blowing for two
days. It set the shack vibrating. I gave a start when he
returned. I was still clutching the photograph of the Agreement, and felt suddenly guilty for my thoughts.

As regards the Munich signature, there was something he
had forgotten to tell me, he said.

Old Daladier began a phrase, but his voice choked.

The words wouldn't come out. His eyes misted up. I had
never seen him like that before.

He began by articulating, 'And the worst moment, History
has not recorded ...'

He paused before continuing.

'Because there is something worse than anything I have
told you.'

'It was two o'clock in the morning, it was already 30th
September.

'The agreement had just been signed.

'The room had suddenly emptied of photographers, second-
ranking diplomats, experts and military officers, noise and
smoke. Field Marshal Keitel had headed off to Berlin, carrying
under his arm the roll of maps of the new Czechoslovakia, the
booty of the Germans. Hitler and Mussolini had just emerged
triumphant. I could still hear their voices ringing out in that
desert of marble. In the distance I saw Mussolini slipping along
the floor. He was listening to Hitler, who must have been
telling him a funny story. Hitler had stopped to laugh. He had
tapped his hand on his right thigh, twice, strangely, and made
me think of a wading bird. A drum roll from Königsplatz
announced their departure. Then silence fell in the big empty

building. Footsteps echoed. From time to time one could make out, in the twilight, the silhouette of an SS guard.

'We were there, alone, exhausted, stunned by that tough day in the big office where the conference had been held. When I say "we" I mean Chamberlain, Léger, Nevile Henderson, Rochat, still with his ludicrous red pansy in his buttonhole, and another Englishman, Ashton-Gwatkin.

'Our work wasn't done . . .'

'Two black-clad SS-men appeared. They greeted us with a nod and a loud click of the heels. They had with them two men, whom they pushed forward.

'They were two Czech diplomats, one of whom I knew: Mastný and Masařík.

'They had been unceremoniously dragged out of their cupboard under the stairs in the Hotel Regina, without the respect to which they were accustomed and without a word of explanation, to be brought here. The poor things had been locked up for about ten hours in the Hotel Regina – although I learned that only later.

'Seeing them, I reflected that they had assumed the appearance, within only a few hours, of truly guilty parties. They already wore the stupefied expressions of people summoned unexpectedly. There was something fearful in their bearing; they looked crushed, shrunken, wizened. Dr Mastný, whom I had known quite well, was the more marked of the two. He bore all the stigmata of the condemned man, including that slight physical sense of self-neglect that prisoners often have. He had removed his jacket. He was sweating, defeated, slovenly. I recalled the heyday of the man we had all known, sometimes loved, the man with whom we had socialised, the man whom we French and English had considered our peer. That man was destroyed.

'Masařík had black rings under his eyes, but he wore an

expression of defiance. Insolence must have been his final freedom. That was only to be expected, he was the younger man. He stood up straight, he was gaunt. He had retied his tie, smoothed down his clothes. He clearly wanted to look impeccable in front of us, like the dandy he had been in Prague – at least that was what Léger had told me. We were there, behind an untidy table-top. The two men stood before us. Imagine a court martial made up entirely of their supposed advocates.

'Masařík murmured in French: "The defendants await their verdict." No one felt much like reacting, given the circumstances. It was Chamberlain who began. He seemed to be in a hurry. He began by stammering, staring at his hands, before declaring: "France and Great Britain have just signed an agreement concerning the German claims regarding the Sudetenland. This agreement, thanks to everyone's good will, may be considered to mark a clear advance on the Godesberg Memorandum."

'Then he coughed. He yawned, and handed Mr Mastný the text of the Agreement and the map of Czechoslovakia with the German territories marked in blue.

'Masařík read the text out loud.

'The moment was interminable, lugubrious, unbearable. Masařík read slowly, returning several times to certain words, leaning from time to time towards Mastný to ask his advice: "The four powers: Germany, the United Kingdom, France, Italy, taking into consideration the agreement, which has been already reached in principle for the cession to Germany of the Sudeten German territory, have agreed on the following . . .

'"First: the evacuation will begin on 1st October.

'"Second: the United Kingdom, France and Italy agree that the evacuation of the territory shall be completed by the 10th October, without destruction of existing installations.

'"Third: the conditions governing the evacuation will be laid down in detail by an international Commission.

'"Fourth: The occupation by stages of the predominantly German territory by German troops."'

'The reading was endless; clarifications were required on certain points.

'Masařík questioned Chamberlain: "I would like to ask a question. What precisely are we to understand by 'Sudeten German territory?'"'

'Chamberlain, who wasn't paying attention, hadn't heard the question. He asked Masařík to repeat it. It was Léger, appalled by the situation, who took it upon himself to reply.

'"It isn't a matter of majority self-interest. You have accepted it in principle!"'

'Masařík immediately asked me straight out if such a measure could protect the vital interests of Czechoslovakia. I didn't know what to reply. He was insistent, saying that "this clause had been promised".

'Léger came to my aid, he referred the question to the International Commission, as an over-experienced diplomat. I let him do it.

'Masařík gave me a nasty look, and then said, "Not even a guarantee?"

'I replied that it was too late, that we had examined the question from all sides, that France had been alone, too alone . . .

'The two Czechs asked the assembled company, with a contempt that I will never forget, "Are you waiting for a response from our government?"

'I was taken aback. Léger took charge once again, too sharply in my view. Irritated, he exclaimed, "This agreement is final and unalterable," and continued, in the same tone: "There is nothing to be done. We are not waiting for any response from you. The Czech government will, by five o'clock in the afternoon at the latest, have to send its representative to Berlin, to a session of the International Commission."

'I didn't want to linger in that gloomy palace, and neither did Chamberlain. He couldn't stop yawning. At about three o'clock in the morning, we left those two poor Czechs in the Führer's house, to walk back to their hotel and tell President Beneš.

'The Czechoslovak Republic of 1918 had ceased to exist, and it was not, Mademoiselle, a pretty sight.'

7

A LITTLE NIGHT MUSIC

Daladier was walking towards the entrance of the Vier Jahreszeiten Hotel, slowly, heavily, mechanically, followed by Alexis Léger and Rochat. The cigarette in his mouth had gone out, and his face was covered with red blotches which had suddenly appeared.

Birds passed in the night, uttering deathly chirrups. German workers, up early, recognised the men. They approached them and acclaimed them, in French. A few night owls applauded. A young man came over for an autograph. But Daladier didn't stop. He walked on without looking.

A little further along, by the hotel entrance, two French journalists rushed over: 'Mr President, so, today? What do you think of Hitler?'

Daladier wanted to reply. He merely grunted. His old 'trench headache' had just caught up with him. He untied his tie, tried to articulate a reply, stammered, but his jaw wouldn't respond, as if he had received an upper-cut. He tried to regain his composure, to laugh.

Finally he replied: 'He's a pretty serious character,' but as he saw them writing it down he changed his mind. You never knew with journalists. He found the strength to correct himself: 'No, say that ... He's a man who knows where he's going.'

Then he entered the revolving door of the hotel.

Daladier crossed the hall with the same mechanical gait. There was the sound of an oompah band at a party: the shrieks of drunk women, glasses clinking. Men intoned the 'Horst Wessel Song'. Field Marshal Göring could just be seen behind the glass door of the room where the noisy party was being held. He had changed his uniform again, and had his arms around his young wife, the famous Emmy Sonnenfeld, with whom he had just had a daughter. He seemed to be introducing her to the guests. The severe Joachim von Ribbentrop was there as well. He was noisily clinking glasses with an Englishman, Lord Londonderry, who had come specially to support his German friends. The red-haired maître d', in his SS uniform, was seated not far from Himmler, a serious, severe, unruffled little man in the midst of all this bedlam. The seating plan had fallen apart; toasts were being drunk; dinner was coming to an end, they were going to push the tables aside and dance to the phonograph installed for the occasion.

When Göring noticed Daladier passing in the hall he got majestically to his feet.

He wanted to raise a toast in his honour. He walked towards him, but before he reached the glass door he seemed to change his mind. He waved to him in the distance. Heads turned towards the Frenchman. The music stopped. The laughter, the oompah music, the shrieks fell silent.

Daladier didn't return Göring's greeting. He went on his way.

When he was in the lift, the music and laughter loudly resumed.

8

MUNICH-LE BOURGET

The wing of the *Poitou* sparkled in the blue. The sky was mild, glorious, calming. The plane began its descent. He would have liked the journey to continue for a while. But there, beneath the clouds, was France and, soon, Paris. The return flight had gone without a hitch, without the turbulence that made him feel sick, and without anyone coming to inform him that Chancellor Hitler had violated the Agreement by entering the Sudetenland earlier than anticipated, or that he himself had been voted out of office by the Chamber of Deputies.

The steward had left him in peace this time, but the man, a Provençal like himself, now lacked the spirit that had struck him – and charmed him – the previous day, on the outward journey. He was no longer the same; he seemed shifty now. Captain Durmon had struck him as odd, too. He had introduced himself before take-off as usual, to tell him of the length of the flight, the speed, the cruising altitude, the probable exterior temperature and even the weather in Paris, and done it all calmly enough. This time, however, he had not lingered on the dramatic state of the French air force compared to the Luftwaffe, or the performance of the Potez, whose capacity had had to be increased to rival the Messerschmitt. Léger and Rochat were also behaving strangely. They hadn't said a word since leaving Munich. Their silence had at least allowed him to sleep a little, but the President had woken feeling under the weather, his face on fire, puffy with those red blotches that he got, and his jaw in pain.

The captain appeared, making him jump. He announced, discreetly in his ear, still seeming strange but more agitated now, that the control tower at Le Bourget had just spoken to him of 'events on the ground'.

The President blanched, although the captain didn't notice. Then he snapped in a muffled voice that he couldn't understand a word the other man was saying. Events! What events? Bad weather on the ground? The Selenites landing on earth?

'What in heaven's name are you talking about, Captain? Be more precise!'

Slightly shaken, the airman struggled to repeat exactly the message from the control tower. Considerable crowds gathering around Le Bourget ... Cars and lorries ... And even inside the airport, where the police were thought to be losing control ... And off he went. It was too much for him.

The President was perplexed for a moment.

Crowds?

Rioters on the airfield runway, the forces of law and order stretched beyond endurance. What on earth was going on?

Traffic jams, and lorries ...

He was burning to know more, and violently loathed the airman for the vagueness of his information. He had, like all powerful men, spoilt children that they are, become accustomed to being told everything, immediately, in short phrases, without flourishes and without ceremony, and particularly without blind spots. He liked the neat, clear, precise reports given to him by loyal Clapier who was, alas, still sleeping at the rear of the aeroplane. At that moment the President felt so distraught by this strange information that he was angry with the good Captain Durmon for not being his Clapier, for not being able to enlighten him; for not telling him whether it was an actual riot or a simple meeting of the Salvation Army; for not telling him whether the morning papers had called this demonstration, and if so, which? Whether there were any members of parliament present? Whether these 'mobs' were spontaneous or whether they'd been organised, and if so by whom? Whether it was a left-wing mob? It could be, after all, the workers of the northern suburbs, whipped up to fever pitch by the trade unions who, revolted by the Agreement and standing side by side with the Czechs, were going to repeat the experience of the Spanish Solidarity campaign. Or might it be fascists, with fighting-sticks and war veterans to the fore? A fresh provocation by the fascist leagues, trying for a repeat of 6th February 1934? That would be just his luck, he thought to himself.

The President wanted to go to the pilot's cabin. He imagined taking hold of the microphone and questioning that bloody control tower himself. Or even, by some miracle of French telecommunications, getting straight through to his Minister of the Interior, who would tell him everything about these 'gatherings'. He gave up on the idea. No. Humiliating, too humiliating . . . Until a new order was installed, the pilot, the real pilot of France, was him, not the airman.

The President rubbed his face. He straightened his jacket, his tie, his hair, his jaw, and thought it would be more customary to ask the steward to call the captain.

He had an idea.

He had to gain some time.

So he ordered the captain to extend the flight. They would circle in the air for another half an hour, until they reached the limit of the fuel supply. The news brought him craven relief. It gave him respite, a few minutes' pause, to think about the behaviour he should adopt – because say what you like, no one's ever seen a head of state besieged in mid-air! – which would allow him to wait for more precise information from the Interior Ministry, and most of all to polish up his weapons.

Weapons! He saw again the battlefield again, that grenade exploding like a bloody bunch of flowers and killing everyone. Everyone except him, merely covered with a fine film of earth . . .

He was lost, thrown once more into a world of chaos. The engine surged. All the hypotheses about what was happening 'on the ground' passed before him.

On the ground. It wasn't complicated.

It was death, either that or glory, which didn't seem at all likely.

Then he imagined the worst. He sank into himself for half an hour. Then he pulled himself together.

His weapons . . . No, he didn't need the police, or the army, he thought excitedly.

His weapons were words, and running through his head he saw the pantheon of the people he had admired as a child, the proud and noble bodies of all those revolutionaries who defended the Fatherland in its time of danger. He recalled Camille Desmoulins, that image of him as a slender young romantic reading a copy of *L'Ami Du Peuple*, Marat's paper, at the foot of the tribune of the Convention. In childhood it had been his favourite vignette in his old history text book. He was stirred by the memory, but he hadn't time to let his thoughts wander. Although he had to admit that he himself was more like Danton. And Danton wasn't so bad! Better at any rate than that lunatic Robespierre he had always been careful not to admire.

Words were the only way to make the crowd *on the ground* retreat. The mysterious gauntlet thrown down by the rioters on the ground had fired him up. He had emerged from his torpor. He was moving into action. Ah, they would see what they would see! Daladier wasn't the kind of man to shirk the facts. A fine speech to the nation. A tough speech, not too long, but resolute, one that Jean and the Marquise would be proud of, a speech that would convince the French, so commonsensical yet so stubborn ... What was needed, even if he hated it, was a big speech. The moment had come.

And he had exactly the right man for that, right to hand. He turned towards Léger, who was scratching away at that little notebook that had always intrigued him. What a good idea. He wrote poetry, after all – when he wasn't reading diplomatic dispatches – and he knew the dossier. So Léger would scribble down a few notes on paper for him, a couple of phrases. Of course, he would revise everything, as he always did. He found the idea judicious, and called to the Secretary General without turning round, which wasn't his usual way. Fearing that he might have annoyed him by behaving so casually, he delivered his invitation to come and join him in an unctuous, clumsy phrase.

Léger came and sat next to him. The President told him what he knew. The gatherings, the cars, the lorries, perhaps weapons, and also the crowd that had, so to speak, taken over the airfield ...

As he spoke, Daladier went on looking through the window. He studied something vague in the distance, turned from time to time to stare after a cloud, spoke without looking round, like a contemptuous boss, even though he wasn't one. He thought he could, by means of that pathetic artifice, regain the famous commanding tone that he felt he had lost in the storm.

In fact he was afraid of Léger, of his eyes, which he had not met since the previous day. Returning to the hotel in the small hours the day before, the Secretary General, usually so affable, hadn't said a word, he hadn't unclenched his teeth, he had avoided all comments and drawn no political lesson from the event. Nothing, not the slightest compliment on his damage limitation exercise. Not even a rebuke. Léger upset him. His silences made him feel ill at ease.

In his mind, darkened by too many faces seen, emotions accumulated and decisions adopted too quickly, Daladier considered that Léger was too calm. Too nicely turned out, not even slightly overwhelmed by the previous day's events and, right now, listening so politely that it seemed almost like a provocation.

But Daladier reassured himself. It wasn't the man's way. In important matters, Léger – whether he agreed or not – spoke his mind; then he obeyed. He had been in favour of intervention on the side of the Spanish Republicans, and against Blom, it was said in Paris, but subsequently he had always obeyed instructions of non-intervention. Much the same for the Rhineland, where he wanted, in the government's absence, to declare war on Hitler all on his own. There too he had carried out government instructions and sometimes even beaten the government to it – things wouldn't have been the same with Massigli, his assistant. No, it wasn't that, it wasn't a political sulk.

Still without looking at him, his neck held stiff and with that commanding tone that he thought he had regained, Daladier asked Léger to 'jot down a few notes and a couple of phrases for the welcoming committee, on the ground. You know the dossier better than anyone else.'

The Secretary General nodded. But rather than returning to his seat to fulfil his mission, he stayed there in silence. He was waiting to learn more. There was a silence, before Léger finally asked in a tone that was intended to be as neutral as possible:

'Mr President, what points should be put forward in this declaration?'

'Well ... I don't know, Léger ... What points? What points? You've followed the negotiations to their conclusion ... You just have to do your job ...'

Léger's question seriously annoyed Daladier.

He hadn't picked on him, so why this attitude right now, this stupid question, and the hostile silence that preceded it? Hadn't picked on him – he'd gone one better than that. He had brought him to the Munich summit where he had become his Minister of Foreign Affairs in the eyes of the world. Daladier had had to plot, to lie like a child, and even to tell some of the powers in Munich about his lie. He had done everything, hatched schemes, come up with all kinds of things to make Bonnet give up on the idea of going to Munich. All that for Monsieur Léger who, let's be frank about this, had seriously disappointed him throughout the day. But he had known him for a long time; he thought his assumption was right. He had turned him into his closest colleague, his most intimate adviser in the diplomatic mysteries whose hair-splitting revolted him, he had confided in him his determination, the slightest of his moods, and he had cruelly missed Léger, elegant Monsieur Léger, in Munich. He had been stammering, ill at ease, incon-sistent in his responses to Hitler, he had been vexed about trivia, too inflexible with Mussolini, who was forever making advances to them – oh, that man, how he must regret the Axis and his alliance with Hitler! In a word, Léger had been disappointing, when he had placed his greatest hopes upon his shoulders.

All the more so since diplomatic matters were his depart-ment; Daladier, as everyone knew, was more on the military side.

The President realised that he had been too harsh with Léger. He needed him too badly right now. He tried to regain some ground, his voice sickly, with an allusion that he considered both subtle and welcome:

'So, my dear friend, the time has come to use – I don't know – your natural talent! Tell them . . . Tell them we've saved the peace . . . Yes, it's true, after all. If we hadn't gone to Munich, Hitler would already have been back in Czechoslovakia . . .'

'So that would mean, Monsieur, in your opinion, that we would have gone to war to bring aid to our Czech ally?'

'It doesn't work, you're right, Léger. Of course, Beneš would enjoy contradicting us; and the two-faced British would love to see us in a pickle. It doesn't work . . . And besides, "saving the peace" sounds a bit over-inflated. It sounds like an advertisement for one of the big department stores. Chamberlain could say that. It's basically sentimental English bullshit!'

Daladier went on breathlessly:

'You're right, Léger . . . You're right . . . The French are no fools. They won't believe us if we tell them we've saved the peace in those priest-like tones. So nothing high-flown, just solid stuff, Léger. Solid, realistic, concrete stuff . . .'

Daladier pulled a thoughtful face and then, like someone undeceived, added:

'Besides, do you really believe, Léger, that we've saved the peace?'

Léger didn't reply. He was startled by the other man's appearance. He seemed to have aged twenty years in a single night.

His expression, behind what looked to him like a very artificial frown, was that of an anxious, pleading child. Those hands, those gestures, that voice were so lacking in assurance that he seemed to be tottering even when he was sitting down. Any intervention, any reply to Daladier's question would have struck him as pointless, a waste of time. The

President would have repeated himself, let his mind wander, remade the world, Europe, the Pact of Four, the government to which he now had to explain himself, at least if the rioters on the ground allowed him to, and even – why not – rewritten in his own favour that Agreement the ink on which was barely dry. Any reply, any switch of direction in the conversation would have brought him out of that contemplation that suddenly occupied his mind more than knowing whether or not Hitler would keep to his commitments.

What occupied his mind to the exclusion of all else was the thought of the President, standing behind the curtain, before stepping on to the stage.

'So this is France,' reflected Léger, although he himself had had nothing to add on the subject of the Agreement: it was for him, as he put it, 'a necessary evil'. So here was the man who, if one was to believe everyone, was supposed to embody the nation. This little man, overwhelmed, stammering, gnawed by doubt, assailed by his spots, this was the eternal France.

It wasn't even France in slippers; he was all too familiar with that, after a quarter of a century close to power.

It was France in rags that was revealed to him today, without a mask, without make-up, without the grandiose trappings of power. With all the simplicity of the parable, which as a poet he loved. Scrutinising the body of France and her stigmata on Daladier's face, he suddenly discovered the extent of the damage. And he remembered the lessons of his teacher Briand, his metaphysical murmurs in his twilight years, on the Breton peninsula to which the 'prophet' had withdrawn.

France had to be returned to its proper rank, which it should basically not have left since the extravagances of Louis XIV.

* * *

The Secretary General very much wanted Daladier to pursue his anxious monologue, the better to study him. He suddenly discovered within himself an entomologist's curiosity. He remembered the cricket-hunters that he had known as a child on Guadeloupe. Not that he had seen Daladier as a contemptible insect; or that he wanted to take revenge for past humiliations (to tell the truth, he had never had any reason to complain about Daladier, his best bulwark against his enemy Paul Reynaud). But he was intrigued, curious, fascinated, as he had been as a child during those strange ceremonies after school when, with the maid's complicity, the crickets were grilled and then eaten. He watched each twitch of the insect caught in the flame, he knew the different stages of its torment, all the crackles, the heavy, dull one of the overheated carcase when it yields, the shorter, crisper one of the legs breaking before charring to embers, and the always surprising one of the head as it opened and exploded. This time it was the President breaking down like that before his eyes.

The plane went on turning in the sky. The captain came to tell Daladier that he would soon have to land – they were running out of fuel. Once again he suggested, if the President wished, diverting the *Poitou* towards Villacoublay aerodrome.

'It will be Le Bourget,' Daladier decided.

There was little time left.

Daladier was still trying to find arguments to present to Léger. He muttered, he seemed – old habit – to be counting on his fingers the better to call up his good ideas; he opened and closed them with each internal refutation. For a moment he exclaimed with an air of triumph.

'Well, Léger, let's tell them that . . . Ah, yes, it's obvious. That we wanted to defer the war. The proof: we've secured from the Reich that there will be no immediate and unconditional seizure of the Sudetenland.

'Tell them that we have gained only ten days, Mr President . . .'

'. . . Yes, that is actually a bit short. Geneviève Tabouis might put it on the front page . . .'

'Mind you, they aren't all as extreme as that, Mr President.'

'Then tell them we've saved . . . Czechoslovakia . . .'

'Are you prepared to say exactly that to the French people, Mr President?'

'You may be right, Léger . . . What about the fortifications? Tell them about the fortifications!'

'No, Mr President. That issue is before the international Commission, don't forget . . .'

'But Léger, you told me that was just a formality . . .'

'All the same, Mr President, let's wait for Hitler to put the promise he made to you into effect.'

'Really, are you sure, Léger? You seemed to be saying . . .'

'. . . We will see whether Hitler keeps his word.'

Daladier was startled by Léger's scepticism.

'Léger, do you think he could do that to me?'

Léger didn't reply.

They talked once again about that official invitation made to Ribbentrop, for a 'Paris agreement'; he wasn't terribly taken with the idea. Léger took advantage of the fact to ask for Massigli to be moved to the embassy in Ankara – 'He will become too much of a liability in Paris, with his war-mongering ideas, I'm sure you understand, Mr President.' This was granted. Then he withdrew.

A few minutes later, he handed the President a little note, written in big letters, barely a few lines. Daladier didn't open it immediately, as if out of superstition; but he was reassured by the presence of the paper folded into four in his hand.

* * *

The plane pierced the clouds, Meaux was below them.

Before landing, the captain circled low over Le Bourget one last time, to assess the situation. The President was glued to the window to see what was happening on the ground. The plane nosed up. The crowds on the ground looked like streams flowing to the aerodrome, from the north, from the south, from the main road, from all the neighbouring streets, to hurl themselves into the aerodrome building before spilling out, more numerous, more dense, at greater pressure on to the runway. The building, which looked as if it had been invaded, overflowed with dark shapes. The avenue leading to Le Bourget airfield was blocked with vehicles as far as the eye could see. Lorries, taxis, cars and limousines, two or three police cars seemed to be hemmed in by the crowd, as if unable to escape. No armoured vehicles, but the army, obviously, a few soft and illegible banners, but no red flags; people, lots of people.

The President took a deep breath. He smiled at the sky, which looked like the ones he knew from Provence. He felt the note that Léger had written, as fervently as when he had held Gamelin's vade mecum. He said to himself that it was his turn, his final day had come. It didn't really make him sad. Six years after the tragedy with Madeleine, and twenty-one years after Cheminade, leaving him unfairly alive. In fact, he liked life better than power, but it was too late. This life would doubtless have been different if he had listened more rather than following Herriot, who had spotted him in his youth. At this precise moment he, the confirmed secularist, would be scratching away at old manuscripts rediscovered in the depths of a silent abbey. He would fall, there was no doubt, before the furious people in a moment, or before his peers in a matter of hours.

Yes, his time had come, and in the end it was only fair.

Now, he was walking resolutely towards his execution.

What else could he do? Run away like a coward, by choosing to land on the sly at Villacoublay? At any rate, they would meet again. To confront the situation properly, he started scanning through all his hypothetical endings.

He imagined a death from a thriller. A well-trained commando unit abducting him. In the hubbub, twenty resolute and well-armed men, twenty militant royalists from the 17th Arrondissement. They were quite capable of doing that. Abducting him; dragging him from the crowd; throwing him into a van parked next to the runway. The President saw himself in the cellar of a country house, blindfolded, hands tied behind his back, before a court of military officers who were supposed to judge him. Then his corpse, thrown at the side of the road.

The President imagined a violent death. A death like Barthou's, killed in Marseille, in the carriage of the king of Yugoslavia. That wasn't complicated. A madman, a fanatic hidden in the crowd, with an accomplice waiting for him on a motorbike. There would certainly be no shortage, on the ground, of furious Czechs, Jewish fanatics, Communists trained by the Komintern. A few pistol-shots in the mêlée. And that would be the end of that. It would be the best solution, the quickest, the neatest.

Then he imagined a seemingly gentler death, his political death. There was no doubt about that one. He was condemned; he had known that when he signed the Agreement. It would be long, painful, far from glorious, certainly less liberating, than a death like Barthou's. He saw it as a long descent into hell. There wouldn't just be the vote in the Assembly, his government's revolt, his son Jean's disappointment, his lynching by the newspapers, the hatred of the veterans of the Popular Front along with that of the right, the revenge of Flandin and Laval, of all the most revolting people. He would have them all on his back. The salons of

Paris would be closed to him, Madame de Crussol might leave him, Herriot would take his revenge in the Radical Party, Bonnet and the young Turks would celebrate over his corpse, even the people of the Vaucluse would abandon him.

But first of all, on the ground, there would be the welcoming committee, the French. Before even the Assembly or the Party, there would be the lynching, the real one. The spittle of the growing crowd; the fighting-sticks raining down on him; his coat being torn; his hat trampled; his body toppling, his head striking the ground, his eyes blurred with blood. Once again, he saw the battlefield of Mont Cornillet. He was lying along the edge of the crater left by the shell, among the young corpses. He was not dead; he was barely groggy; but Jean was dead.

Air lashed the cabin of the plane; the descent accelerated. Like twenty years ago, he found himself projected into this world of noise and commotion. That was how he saw that second death. Popular fury overflowing, and the cops and the proprieties. Order collapsing. The Republic tottering. Anarchy and his death. But this time death would come, unlike that day in 1918 when it had spared him, unfairly.

The cabin's vibrations stirred him from his waking night-mare.

The plane had landed. The cabin door was released. He thought again of Jean his son, of Pierre, too, of Madeleine for a long time, of Marie, of the Marquise, less vivid in his mind than he imagined, and the other Jean, Cheminade. Now it was time to face the facts. He was ready for his execution. He didn't stiffen; he didn't want to assume the grotesque appearance of the condemned man going romantically to the gallows, that was all so much nonsense. But the gallows was where he was going.

He had offered himself up. He had sacrificed himself.

The steps shook the *Poitou* as they engaged.

He stepped forward, hat in hand.

And from that moment he understood not a thing. It was as if he was suffering from vertigo. He heard the clamour of the crowd. It was jubilation, not booing. Expecting spittle, he got cheers. The noise of the crowd made him falter slightly. At the bottom of the steps, in the front row, he saw them, arms filled with flowers, Bonnet with his stork-like demeanour, the presidents of the Assemblies, cheering, the most hostile ministers, the most acerbic journalists, all radiant with happiness. The delirious crowd surrounded the plane. The old veterans hailed him; the halt and the lame hurried towards him. The workers threw their caps in the air. They shouted: 'Long live Daladier, long live peace!'

Some people claim the President then murmured, 'The fools . . .'

9

EPILOGUE

'Did you really say, "The fools . . ." when you saw the crowd at Le Bourget?'

'I think it was a writer's idea, Monsieur Jean-Paul Sartre in a novel – it's gone down as a famous quotation. I saw that crowd. I heard that roar of joy. In the front row I recognised all the ministers who wanted to throw me out of office. But I think I was incapable, at that moment, of saying anything at all . . .

'I was staggered, truly. They were cheering, cheering me. So they hadn't understood. They didn't want my sacrifice – and you've grasped that in your story. I had hoped, at least, that the abandonment of Czechoslovakia would come as a shock. I was expecting them to shout me down, to judge me, to finish me off. That would have been the normal reaction of any people, I said to myself.

'But no . . . They fêted me. They treated me like Caesar returning in triumph. They honoured me, and Chamberlain, too. They even wanted to name streets after us. They launched a subscription to give my British colleague a country house in France. We were saints. I wanted to tell them, I tried to explain to them. In Munich I had obtained a temporary reprieve, but the execution would still take place. They didn't want to hear! In the Assembly, in the government, and even in the press, remember, they all voted as one man for Munich – apart from the Communists and that lunatic Kerillis.

'So I went along with it. So as not to vex them, and perhaps also to avoid humiliating France. I had to do my share of boasting at a good few conferences. Everyone believed it. So I went on pretending and so things went for months and months, with everyone determined that I stay as their head.

'I was their hero. We were all complicit in the same lie. We all wove, together, the veil that masks the unbearable truth. France, great France, imperial France, was dead. It was no longer the great nation that made the big decisions about war or peace on the continent of Europe. And it hadn't been, believe me, for a long time. Long before Hitler or Daladier! Since the fiasco of 1871? Since the bloodbath of 1914? Since Napoleon and his follies? Since the great Revolution? Some people even trace that decadence back to the European lunacies of Louis XIV . . .

'After Munich came what they called the "Daladier dictatorship" – the idiots! – when we pretended to rearm and fight against the fifth column and the Communists. In 1939 there was nearly another Munich: the Polish affair. This time England wasn't fooled by Hitler. And we, France, followed them once again. We declared war on Germany, dragging our feet, four hours after London. It was the *drôle de guerre*, a war without war, that I was forced to wage without really wanting it. You know what happened next . . . In truth I was no longer there, since coming back from Munich. I had withdrawn from the world – I realised as much years later. I had been KO'd in the ring of the century.'

ACKNOWLEDGEMENTS

My thanks go to M. Eugène Faucher, the son of the admirable General Faucher, who gave me a great deal of advice, to Mlle. Léa Beuve-Méry for her work on the Prague period of Hubert Beuve-Méry; to François Samuelson, who understood everything immediately; to Vincent Loewy for the films he helped me discover, particularly his university dissertation on Munich on the screen; to Marie-Caroline Boussard for her research; to Dr Pierre Philipp for his advice on shellshock; to Aldo Cardoso for Nizan; to Stéphane Benamou for ever; and to Alice d'Andigné, Danièle Houssaye and Violaine Aurias.

SOURCES

The Ghost of Munich offers a personal vision of that 'particular day'. It is a novel; it has lodged itself in the many
gaping holes of that event; it has sought to fathom souls,
pursue doubts, distinguish the external and internal pres-
sures on the characters, and of course to break down the
'mechanism of cowardice'. Of the course of that day and
its final outcome, other interpretations are possible. Zola
wrote: 'The time has therefore come to put the republic and
literature face to face, to see what one should expect of the
other, to examine whether we analysts, anatomists, collec-
tors of human documents, scholars who admit the authority
of facts alone, we will find in republicans [. . .] friends or
adversaries' (*The Experimental Novel. The Republic and
Literature*), and it was on these words that I based my docu-
mentary research. This novel relies on the work of historians, on the (few) accounts of the Munich Conference by
direct or indirect witnesses, on the Daladier archives stored
in the Archives Nationales; on the indispensable biography
of Édouard Daladier by Élisabeth du Réau; on the major
book by Pierre Miquel, *Le Piège de Munich*; on the
pioneering work by Henri Noguères, *Munich ou la drôle
de paix*; and on a number of memoirs by authors both
known and, more often, unknown, sensible and curious
people, more lucid than the rest, a list of whom will be
found below.

My gratitude first to certain great figures from the past.

To Paul Nizan, whose essential *Chronique de Septembre* Olivier Todd has enabled us to rediscover. Nizan's tireless methodology is a gift to any writer.

To Hubert Beuve-Méry for his articles and attitudes, to William Shirer, to Martha Gellhorn, great and admirable American reporters, lucid observers of the Czechoslovak tragedy. To Yvon Lacaze, the eminent palaeographic archivist who recently passed away, the author of two major works to which I was introduced by Eugène Faucher: *L'Opinion publique française et la crise de Munich* (Berne, New York, P. Lang, 1991) and *La France et Munich: étude d'un processus décisionnel en matière de relations internationales.* (Berne, New York, P. Lang, 1992).

To Marc Bloch for *L'Étrange défaite.*

Where the correspondence between Chamberlain and his sister is concerned, it too is a work of the imagination. None the less, it is based on the extensive epistolary relationship between the British Prime Minister and his two sisters, Ida and Hilda (*The Neville Chamberlain Diary Letters. The Downing Street Years, 1934–40*, Aldershot, Ashgate, 2005).

Archives

Secret archives of Wilhelmstrasse, Vol. 2: *L'Allemagne et la Tchécoslovaquie, 1937–38*, Paris, Plon, 1951.

Édouard Daladier private collection kept at the National Archives, Paris.

French Ministry of Foreign Affairs, *Livre jaune Français: documents diplomatiques, 1938–39*, Imprimerie nationale, 1939.

Trials of the Major War Criminals before the International Military Tribunal, March 1946, Nuremberg, International Military Tribunal, 1947–49.

Rapports faits au nom de la Commission d'enquête chargée d'enquêter sur les événements survenus en France de 1933 à 1945, Paris, Imprimerie AN, 1951.

BIBLIOGRAPHY

Memoirs and Analyses

Anfuso, Filippo. *Du Palais de Venise au lac de Garde*, Paris, Calmann-Lévy, 1949.

Beneš, Edvard, *Munich*, Paris, Stock, 1969.

Bonnet, Georges-Étienne, *Dans la tourmente 38–48*, Paris, Fayard 1970, and *De Munich à la paix*, Paris, Plon, 1967.

Churchill, Winston S., *The Second World War, Vol. 1: The Gathering Storm*, London, Cassell, 1948.

Ciano, Galeazzo, Count, *Diary 1937–48*, London, Methuen, 1952.

Crouy-Chanel, Étienne (de), *Alexis Léger – ou l'autre visage de Saint-John Perse*, Paris, Picollec, 1989.

Dans les coulisses des ministères et de l'état-major, 1932–40, Paris, Les Documents contemporains, 1943.

Daridan, Jean, *Le Chemin de la défaite 38–40*, Paris, Plon, 1980.

Fabre-Luce, Alfred, *Histoire secrète de la conciliation de Munich*, Paris, Grasset, 1938.

François-Poncet, André, *Souvenirs d'une ambassade à Berlin, Septembre 1931–Octobre 1938*, Paris, Flammarion, 1946.

Gamelin, Maurice Gustave, *Servir*, 3 vols, Paris, Plon, 1946.

Genebrier, Roger, *La France entre en guerre: Septembre 1939: quelques revelations sur ce qui s'est passé dans les derniers jours de la paix*, Paris, Éditions Philippine, 1982.

Hitler, Adolf, *Mein Kampf*, London, Hutchinson, 1969.

Jesenská, Milena, *Vivre*, Paris, Lieu commun, 1986.

Jouvenel, Bertrand de, *Un voyageur dans le siècle*, Paris, Robert Laffont, 1980.

Lazareff, Pierre, *De Munich à Vichy*, New York, Brentano's Inc., 1944.

Lebrun, Albert, *Témoignage*, Paris, Plon, 1945.

Montherlant, *L'Équinoxe de Septembre*, Paris, Grasset, 1938.

Nizan, Paul, *Chronique de Septembre*, Paris, Gallimard, 1939.

Pertinax (André Géraud), *Les Fossoyeurs*, 2 vols, New York, Éditions de la Maison Française, 1943.

Ribbentrop, Joachim von, *Mémoires: De Londres à Moscou*, Paris, Grasset, 1954.

Schmidt, Paul, *Hitler's Interpreter*, London, Heinemann, 1951.

Stehlin, Paul, *Témoignage pour l'histoire*, Paris, Robert Laffont, 1964.

Stéphane, Roger, *Chaque homme est lié au monde, carnets (Août 39–Août 44)*, Paris, Éditions du Sagittaire, 1946.

Strasser, Otto, *Hitler*, London, Cape, 1940.

Tabouis, Geneviève, *Vingt ans de suspense diplomatique*, Paris, Albin Michel, 1958.

Ullmann, Bernard, *Lisette de Brinon, ma mère. Une Juive dans la tourmente de la collaboration*, Bruxelles, Complexe, 2004.

Novels

Aragon, Louis, *Les Communistes*, 1949–51.

Daudet, Alphonse, *Tartarin de Tarascon*, Paris, Gallimard-Jeunesse, 1997.

Jünger, Ernst, *Storm of Steel*, London, Penguin Classics, 2004.

Sartre, Jean-Paul, *Le Sursis*, Paris, Gallimard, 1976.

Studies

Azéma, Jean-Pierre and Bédarida, François, *Munich 1938–1948. Les années de tourmente*, Paris, Flammarion, 1995.

Belperron, Pierre, *Neville Chamberlain*, Paris, Plon, 1938.

Bertrand, Louis, *Hitler*, Paris, Fayard, 1936.

Bloch, Michael, *Ribbentrop*, Paris, Plon, 1996.

Bouillon, Jacques, Valette, Geneviève, *Munich*, 1938, Paris, Armand Colin, 1964.

Coudurier de Chassaigne, Joseph, *Les trois Chamberlain. Une famille de grands parlementaires anglais*, Paris, Flammarion, 1939.

Crocq, Louis, *Les Traumatismes psychiques de la guerre*, Paris, Odile Jacob, 1999.

Delpla, François, *Les Tentatrices du Diable*, Paris, L'Archipel, 2005.

Duroselle, Jean-Baptiste, *La Décadence, 1932–39*, Paris, le Seuil, 1983.

Édouard Daladier chef de gouvernement, Avril 1938–Septembre 1939, Paris, Presses de la Fondation nationale des sciences politiques, 1977.

Gallo, Max, *L'Italie de Mussolini*, Paris, Perrin, 1964.

Irving, David, *Göring, a Biography*, London, Macmillan, 1989.

Kershaw, Ian, *Hitler, vol. 1: 1889–1936: Hubris*; *vol. 2: 1936–45: Nemesis*, London, Allen Lane, 1998, 2000.

Klemperer, Victor, *The Language of the Third Reich: LTI, a Philologist's Notebook*, trans. Martin Brady, London, Athlone, 2000.

Lacaze, Yvon, *La France et Munich: étude d'un processus décisionnel en matière de relations internationales*, Berne, New York, P. Lang, 1992

Lacaze, Yvon, *L'Opinion publique française et la crise de Munich*, Berne-Paris, P. Lang, 1991.

Lapaquellerie, Yvon, *Édouard Daladier*, Paris, Flammarion, 1939.

Maria, Roger, *De l'Accord de Munich au pacte germano-soviétique du 23 Août 39*, Paris, L'Harmattan, 1995.

Milza, Pierre, *Mussolini*, Paris, Fayard, 1999.

Miquel, Pierre, *Le Piège de Munich*, Paris, Denoël, 1998.

Noguères, Henri, *Munich ou la drôle de paix*, Paris, Robert Laffont, 1963.

Réau, Élisabeth du, *Édouard Daladier, 1884–1970*, Paris, Fayard, 1993.

Shirer, William, *The Rise and Fall of the Third Reich*, London, Secker & Warburg, 1960.

Steinert, Marlis, *Hitler*, Paris, Fayard, 1991.

Winock, Michel, 'Les Intellectuels et l'esprit de Munich', in: *Des années trente. Groupes et ruptures*, Anne Roche and C. Tarting, Paris, Éd. Du CNRS, 1985.

Film

Ophüls, Marcel, *Munich ou la paix pour cent ans*, INA, 1967.